Praise for *New York Times*
and *USA Today* bestselling author
AMELIA GREY
and her acclaimed novels . . .

"Each new Amelia Grey tale is a diamond. . . . a master storyteller." —*Affaire de Coeur*

"Enchanting romance." —*RT Book Reviews*

"Devilishly charming . . . A touching tale of love."
—*Library Journal*

"Sensual . . . witty and clever . . . Another great story of forbidden love." —*Fresh Fiction*

"Grey neatly matched up a sharp-witted heroine with an irresistible

"Delightfu

"A beautifully written tale . . . delicious historical romance."
—*Romance Junkies*

"Such a tantalizing and funny read, you won't be able to put it down." —*Rendezvous*

"Fun, fast-paced, and very sensual." —*A Romance Review*

"Well written and entertaining."
—*Night Owl Romance* Reviewer Top Pick

Also by Amelia Grey

Wedding Night with the Earl

The Duke in My Bed

The Earl Claims a Bride

Last Night
WITH THE Duke

Amelia Grey

St. Martin's Paperbacks

This is a work of fiction. All of the characters, organizations, and events portrayed in this novel are either products of the author's imagination or are used fictitiously.

LAST NIGHT WITH THE DUKE

Copyright © 2017 by Amelia Grey.

All rights reserved.

For information address St. Martin's Press, 175 Fifth Avenue, New York, NY 10010.

ISBN: 978-1-250-10249-2

Our books may be purchased in bulk for promotional, educational, or business use. Please contact your local bookseller or the Macmillan Corporate and Premium Sales Department at 1-800-221-7945, ext. 5442, or by e-mail at MacmillanSpecialMarkets@macmillan.com.

Printed in the United States of America

St. Martin's Paperbacks edition / March 2017

St. Martin's Paperbacks are published by St. Martin's Press, 175 Fifth Avenue, New York, NY 10010.

10 9 8 7 6 5 4 3 2 1

Last Night
WITH THE Duke

My Dear Readers:

It is my hearty belief that most everyone in Society agrees that it's Lady Sara and Lady Vera's misfortune that it's up to their brother, the Duke of Griffin, to see to it they are suitably wed. The duke, who as far as anyone I know can tell, has never sought redemption for his wicked ways as one of the Rakes of St. James. That the duke himself is now the protector of innocent young ladies is dismaying to many, yet may prove to be the punishment that has long escaped him and perhaps force a measure of penitence upon him as well.

MISS HONORA TRUTH'S WEEKLY SCANDAL SHEET

Chapter 1

Benedict Mercer's impatience was beginning to grow, and it didn't appear that the fourth Duke of Griffin's disposition would improve, judging by the fact that there was no one in the front office when he stepped into Miss Mamie Fortescue's Employment Agency. He removed his damp hat while noting the room was sparsely furnished with an old, inexpensive desk and a couple of chairs, but little else.

"Not even a bed of warm coals in the fireplace to take the chill off the wet day," he grumbled to himself, holding his hat under his arm while he took off his leather gloves. Even the walls were bare of adornment, though they were littered with nails and the holes where paintings, mirrors, sconces, or something else had once hung.

That no one was in attendance at the front shouldn't have surprised him, considering the way his luck had been running. It was bad enough hearing yesterday that rumors were swirling there might be retaliation against his sisters because of his past misdeeds, but then this morning he'd received word his aunt had taken to her sick bed and couldn't accompany the twins for the Season. He would keep watch on them as much as possible in the evenings and make certain they didn't fall victim to a prankster or any bachelor seeking to get even with him, but he couldn't go to every afternoon gathering those two would want to attend.

The last thing he wanted to do for the better part of six weeks was follow his sisters around to shopping adventures, card and tea parties, and daily walks in the park. Their constant chattering, high-pitched giggles, and occasional arguments would drive him insane. He needed a chaperone for them. Preferably a strong, commanding one for those duties.

But apparently he wasn't going to find anyone to help him with that today in this establishment.

Griffin started to turn around and walk out when he heard a woman's voice from an inside door that was open. Someone was present after all. *Good,* he thought impatiently. He wanted to get this annoying business settled as quickly as possible and get on with other things he had to do. He walked toward the doorway and listened while he waited for a break in the conversation so he could announce himself.

"Clearly that's not acceptable, Miss Pennywaite. You are a well-trained, fully capable governess and have been for the better part of a year. You should know how to handle ill-behaved children by now. What is the problem?"

Judging by the woman's words and authoritative tone, Griffin would say she wasn't happy with whomever she was speaking to.

"But what am I to do?" This question came from a

woman who sounded on the verge of tears. "I've tried. He won't obey me."

"Then you haven't taken control of your charge."

"I've tried," replied the timorous voice. "He refuses to listen to me and do what I say."

"You must try harder," came the firm answer.

Griffin eased a little closer to the doorway. The woman was not backing down. Showing no mercy to the poor soul on the receiving end of the effective lecture.

"You cannot allow a seven-year-old boy to master you, Miss Pennywaite, even if he is by all accounts the master of the house and will be an earl one day. You must take him in hand; show him you are the adult, you are the teacher. Let him know without hesitancy that he is the pupil and he will behave himself and act as a proper young man should while he is in your care or you will tie him to a chair if you must and then put him to bed without so much as a crumb of bread to eat."

Griffin blinked at that last statement.

He heard the timid voice gasp and then sniffle before asking. "Have you done that?"

"Oh, for the love of heaven, Miss Pennywaite," came the stronger, frustrated voice. "Of course not! Don't look so stricken."

Intrigued, he moved closer to the door again. Now she sounded like just the kind of woman he was looking for. He needed a passionate-talking chaperone with an eagle eye that could spot a mischief-maker a mile away. All the better if she was tall, big-boned, and wore a perpetual scowl that could scorch a man with a glance from twenty feet.

"I've never had to be so unkind and neither will you. You won't actually tie him to a chair or starve him to the point of fainting, but he must believe you will by the stern look in your eyes and the unyielding tone in your voice."

If this woman was Miss Fortescue, Griffin had come to the right place. It would take someone of this fortitude to handle his two spoiled sisters and keep them in line as well as being on the watch for gentlemen who were only out to get even with him for a wager that had left all of Polite Society and the rest of London stunned and in no mood to forgive or, it seemed, to forget.

Griffin eased to the center of the doorway and caught sight of a tall and, from what he could tell, supplely built young woman with finely molded features standing behind a desk. At first he thought she was the one getting dressed down to her unmentionables, but then she spoke and Griffin was surprised to discover she was the confident one.

"Now lift your chin and square your shoulders, Miss Pennywaite. There will be no handwringing or tears from anyone associated with this agency. You will not lose this assignment over an unruly child. You have outstanding credentials and excellent references. You are quite able for this post. I have all faith you can handle this youngster with firm diligence. But you must believe in yourself first."

Unable to take his gaze off her, Griffin studied the woman with determined concentration. Her face was lovely. She would easily be the most beautiful woman he'd ever seen, if not for her appearance. Her golden-blonde hair had been severely swept into a tight chignon at her nape and covered with a square of white lace. She wore a simple, long-sleeved high-waist dress in a dull and unbecoming shade of gray velvet. A brown woolen shawl hung loosely across her slim shoulders. He guessed her age to be near thirty yet she talked with the air and authority of one much older and wiser.

Perhaps he made a movement, a sound, or maybe she simply sensed his intense scrutiny, because he caught her attention. Something warm curled deep inside him when his gaze met hers from across the room. A flicker of shock in the depths of her eyes wasn't lost on him. Though she hid her surprise quickly behind the bold lift of her chin, a flush of pink lightly stained her cheeks, giving proof of guilt. She was unmistakably rattled for an instant to see him standing there watching her, listening to what could only be called a strong motivational speech.

She remained silent for a moment, taking in his un-flinching scrutiny as intensely as he had hers. He knew she was trying to decide if he could have possibly over-heard her conversation with the other woman, and if so, how much of it.

For now he'd let her wonder. He wanted to see how or if she tried to defend her rather hard perspective on what she considered the delicate woman's shortcomings.

Griffin watched as she inhaled a deep breath and drew on that confident strength she'd been displaying since he'd first heard her speak. She cleared her throat and in a qui-eter voice said, "We will continue this discussion at a later time, Miss Pennywaite. I suggest you return to your post now feeling resilient and more committed than when you left. I'm sure you'll do just fine."

The woman then adjusted the shawl higher on her shoul-ders and came around from behind her desk and walked toward him with a slow, assured stroll that allowed him time to peruse her lovely face. Her complexion was delicate and parchment pale. Her wide, golden-brown eyes were framed by fan-shaped brows and long dark lashes. She held a steady, uncensored gaze on him too.

There was a full, sensuous quality to her sweetly shaped lips. Her nose was small and nicely shaped. For the life of him, he didn't know why, but he had a sudden desire to reach down, kiss the tip of it, and say to her, "Well done." The corners of her beautifully formed mouth lifted slightly with a perfunctory smile, letting him know that whatever he may or may not have heard her say was not going to alter her appropriate response to him.

Her quick change in demeanor amused him, but impressed him too. He had a feeling she had no idea how much of herself she'd revealed to him in such a short time. For now, he wanted to keep that bit of information to himself.

As he watched her, he realized he was drawn to her in a way he hadn't been attracted to a woman in a long time. A very long time. He couldn't put his finger on what it was yet, but there was something more than just her understated beauty that beckoned him.

Griffin didn't know who she was, but she couldn't be Miss Mamie Fortescue. She was much too young. The employment agency had been a mainstay on the street for as long as he could remember. Perhaps she was a relative of the owner. One other thing he was certain of as she stopped a respectable distance from him and stared directly into his eyes as boldly as any man ever had—Griffin was already more than a little intrigued by her.

"May I help you, sir?" she asked as the other young woman hurried past with her head bent low and rushed out the main door without so much as a backward glance.

Oh, yes, he thought. But he said, "Possibly. I was looking for Miss Mamie Fortescue."

She clasped her hands together in front of her and answered, "I regret having to tell you she is no longer with this agency though it still bears her name. I'm Miss Esmeralda Swift, the administrator. Perhaps I can help you, Mr.—?"

He was silent for a moment as he pushed his cloak aside and stuffed his leather gloves into the pocket of his coat. Then he answered softly, "I am Griffin."

A flash of knowledge sparkled in her eyes and she

quickly curtsied. "Your Grace, pardon me for not recognizing you. It's not every day a duke walks into the agency."

He'd wager on that statement.

He wouldn't have come inside today either, had he not noticed the sign as he was passing by and acted without forethought. All things concerning staff were usually left to his more-than-confident butler and housekeeper. However, on a rare streak of impulse, he decided he had to take matters into his own hands and exert a personal interest in who would be watching out for his sisters' best interest during the Season.

Ever since the ill-fated wager was made known years ago, Griffin seldom attended the large balls and parties where most of the *ton* assembled, preferring the smaller, quieter dinners during the Season. Now, he was forced to begin attending them again. He knew his sisters, and they wouldn't be easy to keep up with. It was up to him to escort them in the evening and keep an eye on them. It wasn't a responsibility he'd ever expected to have, and while he wouldn't look forward to it, perhaps it was the best he deserved for his past misdeeds.

"No need to concern yourself with that, Miss Swift. You may not have recognized me," he said ruefully, "but I can see there's no doubt you've heard of me."

Miss Swift opened her mouth to speak, but then as if thinking better of it, pressed her lips together and refrained from making a comment. He could only imagine what she must be thinking.

None of it good, he was sure.

Though he gave up worrying about what was thought or said about him long ago, Griffin's awareness of her as a woman who was not shy of courage continued to grow.

He wanted to know what she'd started to say, so he added, "Please don't be bashful with me, Miss Swift, or let my title keep you from speaking your mind. I assure you it won't upset me or alter the reason I'm here."

"Truly?" she asked with the first real sign of trepidation he'd seen her show.

He liked the fact she was inquisitive enough to want to test him yet wary enough to be cautious. "You have my word."

"In that case, aside from the fact that it's in my best interest to know the names of as many people as possible in Polite Society, I would venture to say every female between the ages of eight and eighty in all of England, Scotland, and Wales has heard your name, Your Grace, and knows what you and your friends did a few years ago."

That many?

So she had a sense of humor.

Her observance was cleverly stated. He smiled and relaxed his stance. It was refreshing that his being a duke hadn't intimidated her once he gave her permission to speak freely. All too often his title seemed to petrify young ladies. Most had no idea what to say to him or how to answer him with a direct response.

With a casual shrug, he said, "You forgot France, Portugal, Spain, and probably most of the Americas too."

A hint of good humor twitched at the corners of her mouth at the embellishment of what he stated. That pleased him too. Though in truth, he hadn't been many places that didn't know of him as one of the "Rakes of St. James."

"I stand corrected, Your Grace, but not surprised that *Miss Honora Truth's Weekly Scandal Sheet* is that widely known."

Her tone of voice lent veracity to her words, and his interest in her heightened. There was something about her self-confidence, and about how easy she was with it, that drew him.

"I have little doubt that writing about the Rakes of

St. James these past weeks has made Miss Truth a wealthy woman by now, though the three of us have stayed out of Society the past few years except for an attending an occasional dinner party or ball."

"So I've heard."

Heard?

He smiled again at that softly spoken comment. She wasn't fooling him for a moment. He felt certain that she read, no *devoured,* every salacious word the gossip columnist wrote—and all the other tittle-tattle sheets too. From what he'd been told by his aunt, most all of London did too.

"Miss Truth is obviously very good at what she does," Miss Swift added confidently.

"No doubt. Since she revived the old story weeks ago, she somehow manages to mention one of us at least once and sometimes twice a month in her scandal sheet."

"Perhaps that means there are times that neither position nor fortune can shield a man from his guilt no matter the lapse of time."

Miss Swift had pluck in spades. He'd give her that, and his affinity for her increased. "Well said, Miss Swift. I found out long ago that there is no use in trying to bury the ghosts of one's past."

"I am quite willing to admit that can't be done. The best to hope for is to hide them in the closet."

He gave her only the slightest of nods. "And then one can only do that for a time."

"That is probably everyone's greatest fear."

Her response caught him off guard and stirred emotions in him he hadn't felt in a long time. Griffin digested what she'd said, as compassion for her rippled through him with disquieting speed. So were there regrets in her past that she was hiding too? If so, what? he wondered. Emotional hurts or something else?

Silently, he wished she'd said more.

Griffin looked deeper into the depths of her golden-brown eyes and saw clearly that there were unburied ghosts lingering around her. He couldn't help but wonder if she'd worked as hard to put her demons to rest as he had his.

Instinct and a fair amount of curiosity bid him to question her at length. He wanted to delve into her feelings, explore her past, and determine what haunted her, but he didn't. The sudden fragile expression on her lovely face caused him to resist the urge. This was not the time for such talk. Perhaps another time would be, but for this day he would repress his acute interest in her past and not rummage into such affairs no matter if she would be willing. He wasn't looking to become enamored of this young woman, yet one thing was certain—she had evoked more than mere curiosity.

"So that brings us back to my reason for being here in this establishment. I find that I have need of your services."

"Yes, of course," she said suddenly returning to her more-detached tone of voice, all vulnerability instantly gone from her face and her deportment. She retreated to the competent woman and glanced around the room before motioning to one of the well-worn chairs. "Please take a seat and tell me how I can help you."

Griffin didn't bother to sit down and neither did she. "Though I would rather spare the *ton* my presence at all the usual gatherings of the Season, I'm afraid that won't be possible this year. My twin sisters, Lady Vera and Lady Sara, will be making their debut when the Season starts."

"Twins. How fortunate."

"I consider it a misfortune, Miss Swift," he said sardonically.

"Because they are your responsibility?"

"Yes. No doubt you and all of Society would agree that I'm the last person who should be in charge of young ladies making their debut, but the fate of their future fell to me when I became the duke. And to add to that obligation, I received word just today that my aunt, who was to accompany my sisters to all the events for the Season, is ill and can't make any of the outings, parties, or balls."

"That is unfortunate, Your Grace," she said with quiet resolution.

"And that is why I'm looking to employ a chaperone for them."

"I don't mean to sound trite, but while we can't replace the love and attention your aunt would give your sisters, I'm confident we can help you find the right person to take over your aunt's duties. We have three well-qualified women with excellent references and credentials who should be available to start at your convenience. May I set up interviews with them for you?"

Griffin realized that the reason he couldn't figure out exactly what it was about Miss Swift that attracted him was because everything about her did. *Almost everything,* he corrected his thoughts. He didn't like the matronly way she wore her hair with the spit of white lace covering her chignon or the unbecoming shade of gray she was wearing, but other than that, he hadn't discovered one thing about her that wasn't enticing.

It was obvious she was schooled in manners and conviction and was well-trained to handle anyone who walked through the door. Her speech was faultless and her courage dauntless. Her wit was an added bonus. The way she carried herself and the ease with which she traversed the conversation with him made her appear a cut above her station in life. *Well above.* She'd obviously learned a lot from being in service in the homes of Polite Society.

If not for the fact he'd mended his wicked ways, he could have easily succumbed to the wanton feelings she created in him—to touch her satiny-looking cheek, to hear her little gasps of breath while he tasted her enticing lips, and to pull the pins from her golden-brown tresses and watch them tumble deliciously around her softly rounded shoulders.

At the thought of kissing her, a warmth of slowly rising passion settled low in his loins. He was tempted to let the primal heat stirring between his legs build and linger, but enjoyment of those pleasant feelings was not the reason he'd walked through the agency's door today. There were more pressing matters to attend to than his male stirrings for a beautiful young lady. He had to ignore those feelings and change the direction his body was taking him.

Blast it, quite simply, she fascinated him.

Suddenly he knew exactly what he wanted to do.

Grudgingly clearing his head of the wayward thoughts, Griffin moved to stand toe-to-toe with her and said, "No."

"No?"

She didn't back away from his nearness, but he watched the faint stain of an embarrassed flush ease up her slender neck and settle in her pale, soft-looking cheeks.

When he didn't immediately respond, she gave him a long, hard look before her spine stiffened. She obviously thought he wasn't interested.

"All right," she said, quickly regaining her professional composure. "That's not a problem. Perhaps you would like to tell me more about your sisters. I would be happy to make the decision for you and save you the trouble."

"That won't be necessary either, Miss Swift. I've already decided who I want."

"Oh, I see." She paused as if she were weighing what she should say next.

Clearly he'd confused her, and he sensed her retreat from him.

"Perhaps you are already familiar with someone who's currently in our agency."

"Yes."

"Wonderful," she said with the first genuine smile she'd given him, though she was careful not to inflect too much happiness in her tone and appear too eager to hear who had captured his notice.

Pleasing her with such a simple word as "yes" caused Griffin's lower body to tighten again.

"That makes things easier for both of us," she continued. "Unless of course, she's already positioned with another family and not willing to agree to make a move in order to accommodate you. But that would be doubtful, I'm sure."

"I believe she's available."

"In that case, tell me who you're referring to and I'll do my best to obtain her."

Griffin reflected again on the events that brought him to this moment. According to the gossip, his sisters could be in real danger from someone wanting to ruin their chances at making a good match or simply playing them for a fool in hopes of breaking their hearts. Rumors or not, he couldn't take that information lightly and do nothing to protect them. He needed a strong and fearless chaperone to watch over their every move when he wasn't around. Sara and Vera were clever in an innocent way and would not be easy to keep up with.

Even though Miss Swift had shown she had backbone, talked with mettle, and maintained a self-reliance that impressed him, Griffin had also seen what he was sure was a rare moment of vulnerability in her too. He sensed a sweetness, a kindness, and an intangible warmth inside her that couldn't be deliberate or pretend.

He liked those things about her most of all. Griffin let his gaze glide over her lovely features once again. Oh, yes, she would do nicely handling his sisters and keeping them in line.

He stepped still closer to her and, keeping his voice low, said, "You, Miss Swift. I want you."

Chapter 2

Don't turn down employment no matter how
menial or challenging it might appear.
Do make something good come out of it.

❧

MISS MAMIE FORTESCUE'S DO'S AND DON'TS FOR
CHAPERONES, GOVERNESSES, TUTORS, AND NURSES

A breathless surprise washed over Esmeralda Swift.
The words "I want you" reverberated in the silence of
the room, fluttering around her like delicate flakes of snow
seeping into her heated skin, nourishing her. And for the
briefest amount of time she took the comment at face value
and gloried in the purest meaning—*he wanted her!*

Esmeralda stood transfixed in front of the most imposing
man she had ever met and looked into the most intriguing
blue eyes she'd ever seen. She'd been trying to calm her
ragged breathing and quaking stomach since she had looked
up to see him watching her with such deep intensity that it
had startled her. It was a mystery to her why her knees
weren't knocking together from his sheer presence in the
agency. Not only was he a duke, he was tall, powerfully
built, and quite possibly the most handsome man on earth.

He stood straight, commanding, and intimidating in his buff-colored riding breeches and shiny black knee boots. The tiered dark cloak he wore over his wide shoulders was held together at his throat with a large, engraved pewter medallion, giving him a rakish appearance that made her heartbeat whirl like a spinning wheel in her chest.

Thick dark brown hair was cropped short over his ears but fell to the crest of the white collar that showed at his nape. There was an inflexible quality to his strong features—wide, attractive mouth, high-bridged nose, and determined set to his chin.

Yes, he had said *I want you,* and for a moment it had thrilled her to her core. Esmeralda was seldom at a loss for words, but the duke had completely stunned her by his statement. She wasn't a foolish miss. She knew what the duke meant.

Thankfully, so far at least, she'd managed to control the flustered feeling that had assailed her when she first looked up and saw him gazing so keenly at her through the open doorway. She still hadn't been able to ascertain whether he'd overheard her reproachful conversation with Miss Pennywaite, but surely if he had, he wouldn't now be asking that she chaperone his sisters.

Something she couldn't possibly do.

She knew she must be staring at him as if his words weren't making any sense, so taking in a short breath, she backed away from him and moved closer to the desk behind her.

"I'm sorry, Your Grace," she finally said, her voice a mere whisper. "I don't actually chaperone. I am the administrator of this agency. I coordinate and counsel the women who are under my direction. It's also my duty to make sure we place the right person in your household."

He didn't move an inch from his uncompromising

stance, and his gaze didn't leave her face. "But you are trained and fully capable, are you not, Miss Swift?"

Esmeralda wasn't sure if he was giving her a compliment or merely stating what he felt was the obvious, but she responded, "Of course. Quite capable. I couldn't properly supervise the women who work out of this agency if I didn't understand their duties."

"I thought so."

He glanced around the room for the second time. Esmeralda watched his striking blue gaze take in the worn, aged furniture, the unadorned front window, the barren walls, and the unlit fireplace. There was no doubt that just as he had assessed her, he was now assessing the office.

There had been nothing she could do after Mr. Fortescue had stripped the building clean. She had no money for appropriate furnishings. When he'd approached her about leasing the business and the two-story building from him and paying him from the earnings each month, she'd assumed the office decorations would be included. She had wrongly presumed many things, including that the man was honest in his dealings with her.

"I must admit that I've never actually been a chaperone. I was a governess for eight years before taking responsibility for the agency." As Esmeralda said the words a sudden sadness gripped her as it had when the duke had mentioned the ghosts of one's past.

At first, it hadn't been easy for her to go from having a governess when she was a child to becoming one when she turned nineteen, but that was the life she'd been dealt after her mother had become an outcast in her own family. Once Esmeralda had realized there was no other alternative, she'd shouldered the responsibility and determined to be good at it. She hadn't needed much training, already knowing exactly what was expected of a governess.

"Tell me, what happened to Miss Fortescue?" the duke said.

Esmeralda shook off the offending memories and replied, "I'm sorry to say she passed on and left the building and agency to her nephew. Knowing nothing about a business such as this, he asked if I would like to lease the agency, administer it, and keep everyone employed for him. I agreed."

"How long ago was that?"

It seems like forever, she thought, but said, "Just shy of a year."

"And you're doing well?"

"Well enough," she hedged, knowing that was far from the truth. And judging by how high the duke's brows rose—and much to her chagrin—he knew it too.

His gaze scanned the sparsely and poorly decorated room one more time, zeroing in on the unlit fireplace before he settled his attention back on her face. She knew he must be thinking that anyone who had a bit of fuel at their disposal would have a fire lit on such a cold and dreary day. More from a feeling of protection than chill, Esmeralda wrapped her shawl tighter around her shoulders. She may not have much, but she did still have her pride.

To keep from appearing completely foolish by her guarded comment, she added, "It's been a struggle from time to time, but nothing I haven't been able to manage so far."

The duke acknowledged her comment with a slight nod and said, "I'm glad to hear that you are managing."

Barely, she thought.

Because of Mr. Fortescue's false reporting of the agency's income, Esmeralda had agreed to pay him way too much each month for the right to manage the agency and live in the small residence above stairs. At the time, the

steady employment and a place to live was a godsend. By
the time her second payment was due, she was well aware
of the fact the man hadn't been honest with her about how
much money the business brought in each month.

Esmeralda was good with sums and after triple-
checking her arithmetic she realized Mr. Fortescue must
have shown her a false set of books. He had inflated the
income by at least three times what actually came in from
the ladies who worked for the agency. When she took him
to task over the discrepancy, he'd only laughed and told
her he was more than willing to throw her out and obtain
someone else to oversee the business and render payment
to him.

There was no way she could have known she couldn't
trust the man to be fair and honest. She had worked for
Miss Fortescue for more than eight years and considered
the woman's reputation above reproach. Not so for her heir.

It was taking every penny the agency brought in just to
pay him and buy a little food. All her winter debts remained owing, including the coal bill, which was the reason there was no warmth in the large room on such a cold
and wet afternoon. She still had plenty of oil for the lamps
and tallow for candles, but they offered very little warmth.

Esmeralda had to pay Mr. Fortescue first. He was a mer-
ciless man. She had no doubt that if she failed to make one
payment, he would make good on his promise to throw her
out and find some other unsuspecting woman to lease his
agency with his false kindness and fraudulent bookkeep-
ing records. Besides, she had nowhere else to go.

The duke said, "I'd like you to start as chaperone tomorrow morning."

As she should have expected, the duke wasn't used to
taking no for an answer. She knew well that peers were
seldom told *no* by anyone. A small part of her would have
liked to decline the handsome duke with relish, but she

must tread carefully in how she spoke to him. Already she'd been too impertinent and outspoken with him at times. Placing an employee in his household would bring in some desperately needed income. She couldn't possibly do the job for him, but she had someone available who could. So she would keep her disdain for the peerage to herself.

"I apologize, Your Grace," she said, using her placating tone. "I'm afraid I didn't explain myself well. I'm not available to work in homes. My presence is needed here."

He took an easy, confident step toward her and closed the distance she'd put between them. Esmeralda's natural instinct was to back up again, but she forced herself to stay still.

Never taking his gaze off hers, he leaned in and reached around her, placing his hat on the desk behind her. He came so close she caught the clean, enticing scent of shaving soap. She felt warmth from his strong body. It heated her as thoroughly as a blazing fire on a freezing night. The fine fabric of his cloak brushed lightly across her arm. A scintillating sensation tightened her chest and tingled through her breasts. Her lower stomach contracted as she breathed in deeply.

He looked down into her eyes with what could only be called intense interest. "I understood you perfectly. I don't accept your answer. You are the one I want."

You are the one I want.

He said it again, and started her heart spinning out of control—again. She took a calming breath and, much to her consternation, had to remind herself that he wanted her to care for his sisters and for no other reason.

That he was so adamant after she explained she had never been a chaperone didn't surprise her. It only reinforced her feelings that to the titled few it didn't matter what anyone else wanted. Only what they wanted. And they expected to be obeyed.

But once again she tamped down her feelings of resentment and asked, "Did someone perhaps recommend me?"

"Yes, as a matter of fact someone did."

She studied over that assertion. During her time as a governess, she'd held only two posts. Both families had been happy with her performance and had given her excellent references. She wondered which family must have mentioned her to the duke but decided it was best not to ask.

"That was very kind of whoever it was, but I'm sure you must have been told that I was a governess. Not only do I not have any practical experience as a chaperone, I feel sure some members of Society would consider me too young to be a proper companion for ladies starting their first Season."

"How old are you?"

"Twenty-six at the end of next month."

He studied her for a moment and then asked, "Is there a minimum age requirement on being a chaperone?"

"No, not that I'm aware of."

"Good. You are old enough as far as I'm concerned."

"I fear you may be the only one who would think that," she countered as quickly as he'd spoken.

He inched another step closer to her, lowered his head toward her face again, and stared at her with his gorgeous, fathomless blue eyes. "I am the only one who matters when it comes to the care of my sisters, am I not, Miss Swift?"

His nearness caused more new and wonderful sensations to awaken her senses. "To be sure, but what if it causes a scandal for your sisters?"

"I am no stranger to scandal, Miss Swift. It's true there will always be certain people in Society who are unforgiving. Especially when we fail to live up to the expectations they have set for us."

Like the duke, Esmeralda knew that better than most, so she quipped, "I can't argue with that assessment, Your Grace." Her mother was never forgiven for falling in love with the wrong man and having the nerve to marry him after Esmeralda's father died.

"But that is no reason for anyone to back down from what he knows is best, is it?"

"I believe you just made my point for me, Your Grace."

His mouth quirked into an attractive grin. "You are quite clever, Miss Swift. I don't usually find myself in the position of having my own words used against me."

She couldn't keep her own lips from forming a smile. It felt very good to best him at his own game. "What a shame."

"Your sarcasm will not sway me, either. It only encourages me to continue."

"That wasn't my intention."

"I know. Nevertheless, it does. My aunt has already accomplished most of what needs to be done to get Lady Sara and Lady Vera ready for the Season. She will be in the house and available to help with the finer details. What occasions they will attend, which gowns they will wear, and the like, but she won't be able to attend any of the festivities. That will be your obligation. I wouldn't have decided on you if I didn't think you were up to the task. I'll pay handsomely for you to be their chaperone. And I'll give you more time to make arrangements. I'll expect you to arrive day after tomorrow at the latest."

Esmeralda forgot all about her resolve to tread lightly and not miss this opportunity to be of service to the duke and earn the much-needed money for now and the future with a good reference from him. Before she had time to reflect and consider how she should correctly respond to the duke's manipulations, she stated, "I'm sure you will pay well, Your Grace, but I have just told you I can't do this for you. And furthermore, you can't come in here and start ordering me to appear at your house tomorrow, or the day after, or next week and take care of your sisters."

He bent still closer. His lips mere inches from hers, he softly said, "It's not an order, Miss Swift. It's an offer. For employment."

His tone, his words, his nearness swept the breath from her lungs, and compelled her to acquiesce to whatever he wanted. She had no will or desire to shift away from him. Instead, she only wanted to please him. But . . .

"Even if I could do it, which I can't, I would need more time than that to make necessary arrangements here at the agency and get ready for an extended stay in your house. I must decline for myself but insist I have women who can do this position for you."

He lifted his head a little and asked, "Is it my reputation that bothers you and causes you to deny me your services?"

"No," she said without hesitation. "Though in truth I have no idea why. It should give me great pause." Especially since his presence had all her feminine instincts on alert.

His gaze raked slowly down her face and then back up to her eyes once more. Her skin prickled deliciously.

"You sound as if you mean that."

"I do," she answered honestly. She felt no fear whatsoever concerning this man. "I have no uncertainties that I could take care of myself should I feel you were stepping outside the lines of propriety and forgetting that you are a gentleman."

The duke took his time and smiled slowly. A low, attractive chuckle passed his lips.

He was such a handsome and devilishly arrogant man.

She couldn't deny that she found everything about him pleasing, from his powerful good looks to the tone of his mellow voice. It was maddening that she was attracted to him—a peer—considering her dislike for them. And yes, she could ward off any advance from him, but first she would have to want to. That would take reminding herself that it was because of a titled gentleman that her mother's life had changed so dramatically. Esmeralda had no desire to ever become a member of Polite Society again.

"I have no doubt of that either, Miss Swift. You are the one I want watching over my sisters."

What nerve he had to continue up this path, she thought. Even for an arrogant duke!

"I appreciate that you are a duke and—"

"That I'm used to getting my way," he interrupted, finishing her sentence for her.

"Yes." Her voice was a mere whisper. "That's exactly what I was going to say."

"And it's true."

She observed him while she did her best to come up with an answer that would satisfy him. The way he was looking at her, the nearness of his body to hers, was playing havoc with her senses and she felt her resolve weakening.

But placating the duke was beyond her strength to accomplish at the moment, so she huffed aloud and said, "For the love of heaven, Your Grace. You are being obstinate."

He blinked and looked as if he couldn't believe she said that to him and, quite frankly, she couldn't believe she had either.

He was a duke!

Covering for herself, and hoping to minimize the effect of her cutting words, she said, "You did give me permission earlier to speak my mind. I assume you meant always, right? Not just that one time?"

"Always," he answered without hesitating. "I respect

anyone who has the courage to speak their mind whether or not I agree with what they say. But you are the one being obstinate."

He had an aura of authority that was fair and yet intimidating at the same time. She swallowed hard and answered, "I am being truthful."

"If this is to be a battle of wills between us, Miss Swift, I must let you know that I don't like to lose."

Chapter 3

Do find a way to be reasonable. Everyone will
appreciate you for it in the end.

❦

MISS MAMIE FORTESCUE'S DO'S AND DON'TS FOR
CHAPERONES, GOVERNESSES, TUTORS, AND NURSES

It had taken a long time, but Esmeralda had finally
met her match. The duke was not a person she could
easily win over to her way of thinking.

"I don't know of anyone who likes losing."

The duke nodded once. "But I usually don't. Accepting
defeat is not in my nature."

"Obviously it's not in mine either."

"Good. I enjoy a worthy opponent."

And therein was the problem. So did she.

In spite of her obvious need for money, and her very real
attraction to him, she resented his demanding way of not
taking no for an answer. Why did he continue to refuse to
compromise with her and accept another woman for the
post of chaperone?

Her shoulders lifted automatically as her resolve
strengthened. She responded, "So to that end, I can only

continue to state, I'm not available but I have employees who are."

"Something tells me you are one good game player, Miss Swift. You hold your cards close to your chest and drive a hard bargain. I'm willing to double your usual price."

Esmeralda gasped. He thought she was holding out for more money when that couldn't be further from the truth. She would happily accept the standard fee if only she could.

"One full payment the day you start," he said. "And one at the end of the Season. And, I'll give you until the end of the week to arrive."

She took another step back, her legs hitting the desk. It did her no good to put distance between them again because it only made him move forward. He bent his head still closer to hers. She could go no farther.

Placing her hand on the edge of the desk to steady herself, she said, "That would be a lot of money."

Oh, she was tempted.

Sorely tempted.

She needed that money. With that amount she could pay off all her debts, and have a little left over for next winter's coal payment too.

She wanted to say yes.

But how could she?

"Perhaps it is only a fair amount anyway," he continued. "I do have two sisters after all. Their welfare is important to me. Surely you know that some things are worth the price you have to pay."

"Very well, I do know that, Your Grace. And probably more than most. I want to help you. I have capable women available and urge you to at least take an interview. But I can't do it."

His breath glided across her heated cheeks when he said, "There will be a handsome bonus."

"A bonus?" The spinning wheel of her heart made her legs go weak. Her breathing became so choppy she could hardly speak. Her eyes searched his to see if she could fathom the reason for his insistence other than he simply didn't want her to best him in this situation, but she found no answer. "You are not playing fair, Your Grace."

"There is no need to, because I am not playing, Miss Swift. I'm fighting for something I want and will use all that is available to me in order to get it. I aim to win this battle. Aside from the fact I don't like to lose whether it's an argument, a wager, or a card game, this is business to me. I'm serious. If one of my sisters becomes engaged by the end of the Season, you'll have a bonus. I'll double it if both are."

"That sounds unbelievably generous, Your Grace, considering it would be easy money to earn." She paused to weigh his offer again. "Surely, I don't have to tell you that the hand of a duke's sister is always highly sought. If either of your sisters want to marry, there will be an enormous amount of gentlemen eager to offer for her hand."

"You've not met my sisters, Miss Swift. The task will not be as easy as you might think."

There was only one way she could settle this with the duke. She had to make him be the one to back away. "All right," she said before she could talk herself out of the plan that suddenly came to her. "You have made the offer very appealing. Regrettably, it's not only my responsibilities here at the agency that hold me back. I have obligations at home that I cannot neglect."

A frown creased his brow and he grunted suspiciously under his breath. "What are they?"

"Well, there's Josephine."

"Josephine?" he questioned.

"My sister. She's my responsibility and I can't leave her alone all day and at night too. I will come to your house and chaperone your sisters if I can bring my sister with me."

The duke's eyes narrowed as he searched her face so intently she thought she might take back the demand.

"That would be unconventional to say the least."

"I know, but that is the way it will have to be," she said, hoping that now he would agree to letting her provide someone to help him rather than going elsewhere to secure a chaperone.

"Do you have no one to help you with your sister?"

Her cousin who was now Viscount Mayeforth could help them, but since his father had disowned her mother several years ago, Esmeralda had never considered asking him for help with Josephine after Josephine's father died. Esmeralda remembered quite vividly the loud and hurtful row between her mother and her mother's brother, who was the viscount at the time. He'd told her mother if she went against his wishes and married the Irish poet, she would never be welcomed in the family again.

As far as Esmeralda knew, her mother never had contact with her family after she left. And neither had Esmeralda. She had no reason to believe the current viscount felt differently from his father. If they didn't want her mother in the family, surely they wouldn't want her daughter by an Irishman. In any case, Esmeralda had no plans to find out. She would take care of her sister.

"No one," Esmeralda said firmly with a shake of her head, feeling no guilt about not acknowledging her relationship to Viscount Mayeforth or any of her mother's family.

"How old is your sister?"

"Twelve. So you see I couldn't possibly leave her here

for weeks to go and take care of Lady Vera and Lady Sara for you."

His gaze searched her face. Assuming he would reject her requirement, Esmeralda started breathing a little easier and said, "Now may I select a chaperone for you?"

"No. She can come with you."

Esmeralda felt as if her heart jumped up into her throat and she coughed. "You don't mean that?"

"I'm not in the habit of saying things I don't mean."

What could she say? She never expected him to agree to her preposterous demand. Thinking quickly, she added, "There's Napoleon too. I won't leave him either."

A slow grin spread his masculine lips, and her heart tripped again.

"Josephine *and* Napoleon?" He straightened, putting a little more distance between their faces as he rubbed the corner of his mouth with the pad of his thumb. "I suppose he is your brother?"

"No. Napoleon is our dog. He is my sister's responsibility. But I won't leave either one of them behind for anyone."

"I'm curious, Miss Swift. Was the dog named out of admiration or contempt for the emperor?"

"Neither, of course," she told him. "When we found him wet and shivering by our back door, his long hair was so dirty and matted he looked as if he were wearing the kind of hat Napoleon wore in a painting we'd once seen of him. The poor thing was starving, so we brought him inside to nurse him back to health. Josephine fed him and washed and trimmed his long hair. She adored him on sight and thought it would be clever to name him Napoleon."

The duke seemed to study on what she'd said and then asked, "What breed is the dog?"

"Skye Terrier. He must have belonged to someone for a time because he was already trained. After he was well enough, we walked him in the mornings and afternoons hoping to find his owner, but no one stopped us to inquire about him. He's never tried to leave."

"Then he must be home."

"Yes, that's a comforting way to look at it. And I'm glad you can see why I can't be your sisters' chaperone. My responsibilities here are too great to accept more."

The duke stared at her for a long moment before finally saying, "Napoleon is a small dog."

"Reasonably," she said cautiously.

"Fine. They can both come with you."

Esmeralda's stomach clenched so hard her hand jerked to her abdomen. "You jest, Your Grace."

He slowly shook his head as her thoughts whirled.

"I'll need you to be in a room on the floor with my sisters," he continued as if he considered their bargaining done. "Josephine can have the room in the nursery. There are always servants in the house, so she won't be alone when you go out with the twins in the evenings. Napoleon, of course, will continue to be her concern."

It was impossible to calm her ragged breathing, but she managed to say, "My sister and Napoleon can live with me in your house?"

His eyes softened indulgently. "I've already said they can come. You don't have to convince me all over again."

"Oh, yes, I know. I just can't believe it. That's more than I could have wished for."

"However, I don't expect your sister to hinder your duties or to have neighbors complaining about being awakened in the middle of the night by a howling dog."

"No, no. Napoleon seldom barks, but . . ."

What was she thinking? She couldn't do it. The duke was being more than fair and she needed the employment he offered, but she couldn't.

As if sensing her trepidation, he said, "I haven't heard a yes from you yet, Miss Swift."

"I can't," she whispered earnestly. "I'm afraid there is still one thing holding me back, Your Grace."

"Your dog has a sister too?"

In spite of her spinning heart, Esmeralda smiled. And so did the duke. "No." She truly wanted to take this position, knowing there was no easy way to say what must be said.

He cocked his head. "A brother?"

He was teasing her, but not in a mean-spirited way. She suddenly felt shy. If she could think of any way around telling him the truth, she would take it.

There was none, so she swallowed hard and allowed the words to tumble from her mouth before she could think twice. "I don't have the proper clothing needed to chaperone young ladies to balls, parties, and other outings." She looked down at her serviceable dress, which was one of her best, but nowhere near good enough to wear to a ball or an afternoon card party. She lifted her head and chin. Looking directly into his eyes, she swallowed her embarrassment and said, "I have women who do. Though you were kind enough to say I can bring my sister and her dog, I must ask again that you allow me to suggest someone else to chaperone your sisters."

"Lack of appropriate clothing will not keep you from my employment either, Miss Swift." He pushed his cloak aside and reached into the pocket of his coat and pulled out a small drawstring bag. Once more he slowly reached around her, placed it on the desk behind her and picked up his hat.

Again, she sensed the warmth of his strong body. She caught a whiff of shaving soap and felt the brush of his arm against hers. This time, his nearness made her whole body feel as if it were melting.

"Surrender, Miss Swift. I have won this battle."

Had he?

"There should be enough in there for gowns, day dresses, as well as anything else you might need. Go to Madame Donceaux's Shop."

"No, I couldn't possibly take—"

"You will be working for me, Miss Swift," he interrupted. "I provide livery for my driver and footmen. I provide work tools for my gardener, and pots for my cook. I will provide whatever you need in order for you to properly chaperone my sisters."

Why did he have an irrefutable answer for all her arguments?

"I will pay you back every penny," she insisted.

"Must you take me to task over everything I say?"

"I don't mean to sound ungrateful. I am pleased that you want me to chaperone your sisters, but . . ." She stopped and took in another deep breath.

"Why do I get the feeling the final shoe has not yet dropped to the floor?"

"I must admit I'm suddenly feeling fearful that I am inadequate to properly chaperone two young ladies up to your expectations," she admitted, knowing Miss Fortescue schooled her well but aware that she had no practical experience to draw from. Her mother had been ostracized from the family before Esmeralda made her own debut.

"If that is all that is bothering you now, then perhaps you should take your own advice, Miss Swift."

A shiver of unease prickled her nape, causing a slight shiver. "What do you mean?"

"When you tell Lady Sara and Lady Vera what to do and they don't do it, or when you tell them not to do something and they do it anyway, I expect you shall tie them to a chair and send them to bed without a crumb of bread to eat."

Esmeralda's back stiffened again, though from the expression in his eyes she could see he was teasing her. That bothered her all the more. "So you *did* eavesdrop on my conversation with Miss Pennywaite," she accused. "I thought you had."

"I didn't eavesdrop. I overheard."

"They mean the same and you know it," she insisted as she once again tightened her shawl in indignation about her chilled shoulders. "Have you no shame for what you've done?"

"None whatsoever. But unlike Miss Pennywaite, I never considered you had done either to a child. I knew you were just trying to shock her into understanding what she must do."

"Why didn't you just tell me you'd listened to my conversation with her?" she asked crisply.

"And risk the wrath of someone I wanted to employ? That would have been foolish."

"It would have been nice," she countered. "You should have immediately cleared your throat to let me know you were there. Or, you could have said, 'I'm sorry, but I couldn't help but overhear your conversation.' Something!"

He smiled sheepishly and shrugged his shoulders, irritating her even more.

"Neither of your suggestions crossed my mind. I wholeheartedly approved of the way you shook the governess to her core and sent her running from the room."

"But there should not have been a witness to it."

"On that I agree. But that said, you gave her good, sound advice and, like you, I hope she took it as you intended it. I'm sure you can take care of my sisters and if need be have both shaking in their skirts as well as you handled your employee."

"If that was supposed to be a compliment, take my word for it, it wasn't."

One corner of the duke's mouth lifted a touch. "Take it however you wish. It won't change the fact you were stern, sensible, but somehow managed to be quite nice about it at the same time. That let me know while you will be thorough with my sisters and their behavior, you will also be kind and fair. So see, when I said someone recommended you to me, it was you, Miss Swift. You recommended yourself without knowing it."

His words of praise covered her like a warm blanket on a snowy night. She shouldn't be susceptible to his compliments. They were simply a device to get what he wanted from her.

The duke pulled his gloves from his coat pocket and gave her a half smile. "And I've decided to give you until next Monday to be at my house with Napoleon, Josephine, and your new wardrobe in tow. That gives you a week to settle all your affairs. I'll send a carriage for you at eight."

With that he turned and walked out, the tail of his black cloak flaring out behind him.

Chapter 4

Don't back down when you are right, but if you
must, do find a way to back down nicely.

ജ⁓

MISS MAMIE FORTESCUE'S DO'S AND DON'TS FOR
CHAPERONES, GOVERNESSES, TUTORS, AND NURSES

Esmeralda watched the broad-backed man quietly close
the door behind him.

She didn't know how long she stared after him before
relaxing her tense shoulders and letting out a long sigh of
relief. For an instant she wondered if there was any possibility she'd imagined the entire conversation that had just
happened. A quick glance over to the desk behind her assured her it was no flight-of-fancy that the Duke of Griffin
had just walked into her life and talked her into chaperoning his twin sisters. The brown velvet purse was proof the
handsome, determined gentleman had been there.

Squeezing her eyes shut, she shook her head, still in awe
of what had transpired between them. If only she'd spoken up right from the beginning and been truthful with the
duke about her sister, the dog, and the fact she didn't have
sufficient clothing appropriate for the position, she could

have saved herself from a lot of nervous frustration. But then she would have denied herself all the new and wonderful feelings he'd stirred up inside her.

Their exchange had been an absolutely grueling tit for tat, and in the end, she didn't know who had won.

But she must have.

For some reason though, she wasn't feeling much like a winner right now.

A breathy laugh passed her lips. She'd had to say yes to the duke. What else could she have done? She'd desperately tried to say no and he wouldn't let her—even when she made outrageous demands she never expected him to accept.

Her luck had been so bad for so long, she was still reeling from the fact she might actually earn enough money to pay her debts and have a little left over for next winter. Being in service to the duke during the few weeks of the Season, she could possibly make more money than her agency had brought in for an entire year.

That thought was exhilarating and definitely making her begin to feel more like the winner. First, because she would be earning the entire amount of the payment rather than only the small percentage of the money paid by the earnings of the ladies assigned to the agency. Second, because Josephine and Napoleon would go with her. And a new wardrobe, too.

Yet, some apprehension still assailed her. As she'd told His Grace, she knew the duties of a chaperone, but she'd never been one. What if she did something wrong? What if the duke was unhappy with her? What if he turned her off after the first day? What if Society didn't accept her as a chaperone and shunned her? Or the twins because of her? She would have bought the new gowns for no reason and with no possibility to repay the duke.

There were other things she had to consider. The last

she'd heard, Viscount Mayeworth was in poor health. She doubted he'd attend the Season, but what if he did? Would he recognize her as his cousin? If he did, would he do what his father promised her mother, and pretend he didn't know her? Pretend there was no blood between them?

That would suit Esmeralda just fine.

She rubbed her forehead and sighed heavily again. The possibilities of things going wrong were endless. If she kept thinking that way, she'd be ready for the insane asylum. One of Miss Fortescue's rules was "Don't borrow trouble." Esmeralda had to hold to that one right now. She would go back and reread *Miss Mamie Fortescue's Do's and Don'ts for Chaperones, Governesses, Tutors, and Nurses.* Brushing up on the woman's rules would help her feel more confident when she arrived at the duke's house next week.

She would be ready.

Esmeralda would make sure she didn't give the Duke of Griffin reason to be unhappy he chose her. For now, she would simply be grateful for the employment and not think about failing or how attractive the man was.

Now that she had the position, she didn't intend to lose it.

Since her mother's brother had disowned her mother, Esmeralda had had resentment in her heart for all peers. The duke had done nothing to change her feelings and a lot to substantiate them by his firm insistence she must be the one to help him. Most of the titled few got what they wanted. Peers were difficult to please and expected to be obeyed. Their expectations were high and their tolerance low. If a family member could be dismissed on a whim, so could an employee.

A pang of sadness tried to settle over her as was often the case when she thought about how mercilessly her mother was treated by her own brother. And as usual, she managed to brush it away. It didn't matter that she was once destined to have a chaperone and attend the Season as a diamond of the first water. Those dreams were shattered when she was fifteen and her mother went against her family and married the young and handsome but penniless Irishman, Myles Graham. Now, Esmeralda was to be a chaperone instead of having one.

Just as she'd had to do when her mother died, and when Josephine's father had died, she would take on this new task and find a way to be good at it. She would adapt to this new role. She had to. Her sister had no one else to take care of her.

Esmeralda looked at the coin purse again. Though she was reluctant to spend money on clothing she may never wear again, she would swallow her pride, take the duke's money, and purchase new gowns. When the Season was over, if she failed to gain another position as a chaperone, perhaps she could sell them. Or maybe she would save the gowns and have them remade for Josephine. It wouldn't be too many more years before her sister would be old enough to catch the eye of a handsome young man.

"No," she whispered aloud. Thinking about Josephine old enough to marry was a worry she didn't need right now. She would take one day at a time. The duke thought her capable to chaperone his sisters. That was enough to accept right now. She would prove to him and to herself that she was.

Her stomach did a slow tumble when she picked up the velvet purse. It was heavier than she expected. She untied the short drawstring and looked inside. There were more than enough coins inside for a few gowns, capes, gloves, hats, and other necessary items as well as some new clothing for Josephine too. Esmeralda would count it and know exactly how much was in the bag, so she could repay him.

Whether or not the duke wanted her to do it.

Chapter 5

Don't think that past mistakes will stay buried.
There is always someone willing to remind
you of them.

~∞~

Miss Mamie Fortescue's Do's and Don'ts for
Chaperones, Governesses, Tutors, and Nurses

Griffin quietly closed the door of the employment
agency behind him as he stepped out of the two-
story building. He stood under the entrance of the covered
archway for a moment and watched the rain come down
in a heavy, chilling stream.

He didn't know how long it'd been since he'd had such
an invigorating conversation with a woman—if ever he
had. For far too long he was used to the fairer sex only saying things they assumed he wanted to hear rather than
actually being brave enough to speak their minds. Even
when he gave them permission to do so. Too, there was a
freshness about Miss Swift that piqued his interest. He was
used to women who knew how to make their lips rosy and
cheeks pink with creams, ointments, and dyes. On Miss
Swift the alluring blush was natural.

More recently, he found that he not only wanted a

woman to share his bed, he wanted one he could enjoy conversing with as well. Finding such a woman had been impossible among the available mistresses.

He grunted a laugh. Perhaps it was just that he'd lived so devilishly, so fast, and for so long that for a time he'd become disenchanted with mistresses, drink, and gambling. Now that he was twenty-eight, maybe he was finally ready to enjoy all life had to offer again, but in moderation this time.

Since he had to attend the entire Season because of his sisters' debut, perhaps he would give serious consideration to the possibility of searching for such a lady who could stimulate his intellect as well as his primal passions. Surely there would be a bevy of young ladies at the balls to choose from. Perhaps he'd find one who stirred him as much as Miss Swift had just now.

She'd had no compunction about talking freely with him—except, of course, when it came to telling him why she couldn't chaperone his sisters. Now that he knew her problem, he wasn't surprised she was so reluctant to divulge her personal and financial circumstances to him. Surely it was an embarrassment for her to have to do so, though it shouldn't have been. Her situations weren't her fault.

It couldn't be easy for a young woman to take care of herself and a sibling without the aid and protection of a male relative or guardian. Knowing she had done just that, and that she seemed to be doing a reasonably good job of it, impressed the hell out of him.

She had done very well holding her own with him too. That was no easy accomplishment. He wasn't sure he understood it himself, but the more she said she couldn't chaperone his sisters, the more adamant he became that she would. She kept telling him she had never been a chaperone, but he'd already made up his mind by then that she was the one for Sara and Vera.

Nothing else had mattered to him.

Including the fact that she was probably right when she said that most of Society wouldn't consider her the proper age to be an acceptable chaperone. He could imagine the horrified expressions on all the widows' and dowagers' faces.

He smiled.

They all knew him well. They should expect no less. Miss Swift's determination to resist him demonstrated the kind of strength needed to keep an eye on his spoiled sisters at the Season's parties and other festivities.

At first he didn't know why he was so hell-bent that she be the one to chaperone the twins other than he desired her.

He *wanted* her.

No matter how unwillingly. It was that simple.

There was no use in denying it, because it wouldn't change the fact he wanted her. In bed. Beneath him. Softly gasping with pleasure. Desire stirred low in Griffin's body. He almost gave in and welcomed it so he could enjoy the satisfying feeling. But this was not the time for that. So once again he pushed away the yearning for her that beckoned enticingly.

He hadn't been drawn to a woman in the way Miss Swift charmed him in a very long time. It wasn't surprising she captivated him and now his thoughts. He was a man after all. She was enticing. Strong, shapely, and lovely. But he wouldn't act on those primal urges she'd aroused so wantonly inside him. He couldn't. She was now a part of his staff. Under his protection and his care. He'd never attempted to seduce anyone in his employment, and he wasn't going to start with her.

However, he had no doubt he would enjoy lively conversations while in her presence.

With that thought firmly planted in his mind, he settled

his hat on his head and walked briskly in the rain to the other side of the street where his carriage waited. His driver jumped down and opened the door for him.

"St. James," he said as he climbed inside.

Settling himself on the plush velvet cushion, Griffin doffed the hat he'd just donned and knocked off the rain before laying it on the seat beside him. He felt the landau pull out into the street and take off at a jaunty clip. Seconds later the carriage lurched violently and then jolted to a quick shuddering stop, throwing him forward.

"Damnation," he swore, catching himself with his hands on the opposite seat as his hat tumbled end over end to the floor.

The only thing that would have made his driver stop so quickly was if a person or animal had run into the street in front of them. Intent on finding out what the devil happened, he reached for the door, but it was suddenly jerked open and he grasped only air. Rust Rathburne, the Duke of Rathburne, bounded inside and slid onto the cushion opposite Griffin. Sloane Knox, the Duke of Hawksthorn, climbed in behind Rath and plopped onto the seat beside him. So it wasn't anything quite so horrendous as a person or dog in danger of being run down after all but a foolish stunt by his friends.

Griffin's driver was left standing in the open doorway, looking bewildered while rain drizzled down on top of his hat.

"Park, and I'll let you know when I'm ready to leave," Griffin told the shivering man.

Turning to his friends, he said, "Do you want to tell me what the bloody hell made you cause my driver to almost wreck my carriage and harm my horses?"

"You know that wasn't our aim," Hawk said, removing his hat and running a hand through his dark brown hair to smooth it down. "Just as we alighted from my coach, your driver took off like bats from a chimney at dusk. We had no idea he'd react so quickly to stop the horses when we waved to him."

"Waved?" Griffin questioned skeptically.

"It may have been a bit more than a wave," Rath admitted rather sheepishly, wiping droplets of rain from the side of his face. "I didn't mean to scare the daylights out of the poor man. It doesn't appear there was harm to the horses."

"You best be glad of that," Griffin said, as he picked up his hat from the floor and laid it on the cushion beside him once again.

"He is," Hawk agreed, and then quickly added, "I mean *we* are. But that aside for now, we've been searching for you for almost two hours."

"You are a difficult man to find," Rath added.

"Since when? I have one home in St. James and another in Mayfair and belong to only two clubs." Griffin rolled his shoulders and settled back into his seat once again. "I can usually be found at one of those four places when residing in London."

"We have been to all four," Rath answered dryly.

"And we were on our way back to your house in St. James when we saw your coach. Perhaps we should have followed you rather than stop your driver."

"Perhaps so," Griffin agreed, glad there was no mishap and not really upset with his friends.

"We needed to talk to you," Hawk said. "We've heard a rumor we thought we should let you know about as soon as possible."

Griffin looked at the serious expressions on the faces of the two men and knew they'd also heard about the possibility of someone seeking revenge on his sisters. He'd suspected it would only be a matter of time before the rumor was spread around Town and he was right. This was just the sort of gossip the *ton* relished and loved to chew on.

He'd known Hawk since their early days at Eton, and Rath since Oxford. Rath was a year younger than Griffin and Hawk when he entered Oxford, but he'd been an easy fit into their friendship. He was more reckless than the two of them, and proved it every day by suggesting one daring escapade after another that always ended up with the three of them in trouble with the headmaster and sometimes their fathers too.

Unlike Rath, Hawk's clothing and hair were always presentable. Like Griffin, Hawk was studious, organized, and somewhat sensible—most of the time. Rath was the opposite. His dark eyes and shoulder-length black hair made him look more Greek than English, though he was a British aristocrat through and through. His hair always looked as if he'd just crawled out of bed and needed a brush. His neckcloth was never properly tied and his coat didn't always match his waistcoat and trousers. He cared little for fashion and it showed. His casual appearance had never bothered any of the ladies. In fact, from what Griffin could tell, they all were drawn to him because of it.

It was an anomaly that England had three unwed dukes all relatively close to the same age. That by itself was enough to make the scandal sheets light up with rumors when they all started attending the Season almost ten years ago, and the gossip hadn't stopped since.

The rakes didn't see as much of each other as they once had now that they were older. All the responsibilities that came with such noble titles kept the three busy with their estates as well as matters before parliament and London's elite. There were endless numbers of people who wanted a moment of their time for a favor, a business deal, or a night of entertaining in their homes.

Both Hawk and Rath were tall, broad-shouldered men

with faces most ladies would consider handsome. And like Griffin, they had stayed away from most of the social gatherings of Polite Society for the past few years, attending only a few well-chosen events.

This year had to be different for Griffin.

"Your sisters might be at risk for pranks or mischief during the Season," Hawk said.

Griffin nodded. "I was made aware of the rumor last night."

Rath frowned. "And you didn't think it important enough to find us and tell us about it?"

"My first priority was to determine if the rumor was credible."

"And did you?"

"Yes. I was on my way to St. James when I noticed the—" Griffin stopped, realizing he didn't want to mention Miss Swift and his unscheduled stop at the employment agency to his friends. That was none of their concern. "As soon as I arrived back home, I was going to send a message asking that you both come over later today. Tell me what you heard and from whom."

"I was told Sir Welby overheard some gentlemen discussing the fact your sisters were making their debut," Hawk said. "One of the men said something to the effect that the Rakes of St. James always get away with everything. They've never had to pay a price for their scandalous behavior years ago and it was time they did."

"Another said they needed to be brought down a peg or two and wouldn't it be fitting if something happened to ruin one of the Duke of Griffin's sisters' first Season," Rath finished for him.

"That's precisely what I heard," Griffin mumbled under his breath, once again damning Miss Honora Truth for resurrecting their prank from the past. He had no doubt that her scandal sheet started this line of thinking when she reminded the whole of London about the wager that ruined the Season almost ten years ago.

"Apparently someone thinks turnabout is the clever thing to do," Rath added. "And your sisters are fair game now that they're ready to make their debut in Society."

Griffin would move heaven and hell to see that didn't happen. The twins had nothing to do with what the three of them did, and he would protect his sisters from this mischief at all cost.

"I know Sir Welby is almost blind," Hawk offered, "but I don't understand him not recognizing any of the men. Not one. Seems unbelievable to me. He said it was late afternoon and the lamps hadn't been lit."

"White's doesn't have the best of lighting even when they are," Griffin added. "I talked with Sir Welby, and he assured me he wouldn't recognize the blades again if they walked right in front of him."

"Do you think there's the possibility that maybe he knows but doesn't want to say?"

Griffin looked at Rath. "That crossed my mind. He's always been an honest, unassuming fellow, but at this point I'm not going to discount anyone."

"Surely he gave you more information than we have heard," Hawk said. "Did he say how many men there were?"

Griffin shook his head. "Maybe four or five. He couldn't be sure. When he turned to look at them, they were laughing and leaving the table. Some other gentlemen were just entering the taproom. Apparently the two groups mingled together and all he saw was a blur. He had no idea how long they had been there or how deep they were into their cups."

"So he doesn't know if they were serious or just talking to impress each other."

"No. But either way, I will treat this the same. I can't

take the chance it was the bottom of a brandy bottle talking and not a true penchant to get at me."

Rath's dark brown eyes stared at Griffin as he asked, "So what are you going to do?"

Miss Swift came easily to his mind, and an unexpected calmness settled over him. He liked the tilt of her chin when she questioned him, her softly rounded shoulders that moved so gently when she walked, and the determined set to her beautiful lips when she wasn't speaking. The enticement she'd stirred inside him had stayed with him and made him want to think about her.

Reluctantly, Griffin sobered. This wasn't the place to think about the woman who had captured his attention by not trying. *Trying?* he thought with a silent chuckle. She not only didn't try, she rebuffed him time and time again.

He stared at his friends with determination and said, "I will keep my sisters safe."

"So do you think you should wait until next year for their debut?" Rath asked as he absentmindedly rubbed the condensation on the window with the knuckles of his gloved hand.

"I considered that, and while I would like to, it wouldn't be fair to them. It's all they've talked about for more than two years. And if someone is planning revenge, then they would only have to wait as well."

"There's probably any number of men who want to get even with us," Rath said.

Hawk nodded.

"Sir Welby was certain none of the older bachelors were in the group," Griffin added. "Though his eyesight has failed him, he feels sure he would have recognized the voices of men who'd been around White's for years."

"It looks as if there are some things we can assume," Rath offered. "That at least one or more of them had a sister who made her debut the year we made the wager."

"Or possibly a cousin or daughter," Hawk added. "And there is the possibility that these fellows are jackanapes who simply want to be a part of mischief much like we used to do."

"All could be true," Griffin agreed. "And if brothers, they could be younger or older brothers."

"We know there were twelve young ladies making their debut when we sent the notes, but I'm not sure I can recall all their names."

"I'm certain I don't," Rath admitted. "Between the three of us we should be able to come up with most of them and with some reasonable possibilities of who might be plotting this retribution too."

"If we don't, you'll have no way of knowing who is seriously interested in pursuing one of the twins to make a match and who would only be out to ruin her reputation or her Season."

Rath inhaled loudly, deeply. "Lady Sara and Lady Vera had nothing to do with what we did."

"That doesn't matter to whomever is planning this," Griffin said. "I'm sure they look at it as their sisters, cousins, or daughters were innocent too when we pulled our foolish prank. It's been said that a man will wait forever to exact his revenge."

Rath and Hawk looked at Griffin but stayed quiet. They knew what he said was true.

Hawk slowly drummed his fingers on his knee. "I thought there might come a day when we could actually live down that foolish time in our lives."

"It's not likely to happen now that Miss Honora Truth has decided that bringing it up would make the sales of her gossip sheet soar to the skies," Rath muttered with a fierceness.

"Why didn't we think about the fact that our sisters

were going to grow up and become young ladies one day?" Hawk asked.

"That's right," Rath said to Hawk. "You have a younger sister too."

"She'll make her debut next year."

Griffin, Hawk, and Rath hadn't been dubbed the Rakes of St. James because of the work they did for the church, but Griffin could only answer for himself. From the time he left his studies and the strict environment of Oxford, he'd only been interested in whatever gave him pleasure. All else be damned. He had all the money and women he wanted, and he went through plenty of both. At the time, the future never entered his mind.

"I know what the two of you are thinking." Rath's gaze swept from Hawk's to Griffin's. "And you're right. I have no sister and the wager was my idea."

"We all agreed to do it," Griffin stated without hesitation. "None of us is any more or less to blame."

"He's right," Hawk said. "We were all too foolish to think of others at the time."

"Too young, too arrogant, and too wealthy for our own good," Griffin finished.

"The way this story has lived far past most scandals is still a mystery to me," Rath complained.

"It didn't help that the gossip sheets decided to revisit it just as my sisters came of age."

"Damnation, how old were we? Eighteen? Possibly nineteen. There's not a father, brother, or cousin out there who didn't do stupid things when they were that young."

"But most of them didn't get caught in the middle of their mischief," Hawk reminded him. "We did."

"It's not like we laid a hand on any of the young ladies. Or that there was any real harm done. When all was said and done the only thing we did was prove that every young lady, no matter how good or how poor her prospects for a match are, no matter how lovely or unpleasant or how shy or companionable she is, wants a secret admirer."

"And is willing to meet him—in secret," Hawk added. "I supposed their fathers and brothers didn't like knowing that."

Rath blew out a disgruntled sigh. "No, but we accomplished what we set out to do. Prove that whoever wrote that drivel about how a gentleman woos a lady was wrong."

Hawk brushed the rain droplets off the sleeve of his coat. "There is no use in our rehashing that. We can't change the past." He looked at Griffin. "What do you want us to do now to help?"

Griffin gave them a rueful smile. "I've been waiting for one of you to ask that all-important question."

Leaning forward, Rath rested his elbows on his legs, stared at Griffin with his dark intense eyes, and said, "Tell us what it is you want and consider it done."

"That's exactly what I wanted to hear," Griffin said. "You can marry Lady Sara, and you, Hawk, can marry Lady Vera."

"Wait," Rath said, holding up his hands and leaning back against the seat cushion again. His gaze swept from Hawk's to Griffin's. "That's not what I had in mind."

Of course not, Griffin thought.

"Me either," Hawk immediately agreed while shifting his tall frame in the small seat. "You know we can't do that."

Griffin deliberately hesitated and searched the eyes of his friends. It wasn't often he had the opportunity to see these two men squirm like worms in hot ashes. He wanted a few moments to savor their worried reaction before asking, "Why not?"

"It would be like marrying our own sisters," Rath argued, running his hand through his long black hair again.

"You know they adore both of you." Griffin continued with his ruse. "And would marry either one of you tomorrow if you'd only ask. It would solve the problem quickly and effortlessly. No one would dare try anything if they were engaged to the two of you. And, I might add, they bring a very handsome dowry with them."

"Lady Sara and Lady Vera are beautiful," Hawk said, rolling his shoulders and shifting uncomfortably once again. "They will be without question the most sought after young ladies the *ton* has to offer this year."

"And they are truly sweet, desirable, and all the rest." Rath paused. "But I won't go into the rest since they are your sisters."

"That's best, Rath," Hawk chimed in quickly. "All you need to know, Griffin, is that we can't marry them."

"So when you said you'd be willing to do anything, you didn't actually mean 'anything'?"

"No, no," Rath defended firmly. "That's not true. We did and we still do. But you have to agree that we would not be saving them by marriage to us."

"We would not make good husbands for your sisters," Hawk added. "And you know it."

Griffin did know. So he chuckled and said, "You two are such cowards, but you're right. I don't want the two of you marrying my sisters. You don't deserve them." He laughed again when he saw relief wash down their faces.

"When it comes to thinking about marriage," Rath said with an amused smirk, "I willingly admit that it scares the hell out of me to think of a wife to protect and one day having a son like me. However, though I dislike attending all the balls of the Season, I will this year so that I can help you keep watch over Lady Sara and Lady Vera and make sure they come to no harm."

"I think we all feel that way about the parties. There's so blasted many of them," Hawk grumbled. "And while I

have no desire to attend all of the parties either, I will. I'll
do all I can to facilitate getting to the bottom of whoever
is behind this foolish notion of ruining Lady Sara and
Lady Vera's Season."

"That's really all I wanted to hear," Griffin said with a
nod. "I'm hoping in the light of day with clearer heads, the
bucks decided they really don't want to take on three
dukes. Join me at St. James for a drink. We'll put our memories to the test to come up with a list of possibilities of
who might want to engage in this ill-conceived plot."

His friends agreed and soon left the carriage. When the
door shut behind them, Griffin reached up and knocked
twice on the roof, signaling his driver to proceed. He then
relaxed against the seat and allowed his thoughts to drift
back to the past.

Being the firstborn and only son of a duke, his parents
celebrated him the day he was born and never stopped.
If he wanted it, it was given to him. If he wanted to do
it, he was allowed. If he didn't want to do it, he wasn't
forced to. The only thing his father required of him was
that he respect and learn how to manage the entailed
property of the dukedom. That had been a relatively easy
accomplishment.

But when his father died and Griffin became duke, instead of treasuring and respecting the title, he abused it and
chased only what he desired, and then voraciously in-
dulged in it. Drinking, gambling, and ladies of the night
were the cravings of his heart.

The beginning of that wasteland of extravagant behavior was what led to the catastrophic wager that stunned all
in Society and still haunted him and his friends.

It all started because of a book: *A Proper Gentleman's
Guide to Wooing the Perfect Lady.*

He blew out a huffed laugh and watched his breath chill
in the frosty air of the coach.

Griffin never doubted they'd rightly deserved the "Rakes of St. James" name. They had no boundaries and no discipline. Week after week they attended card parties that were littered with willing women and overflowing with brandy and anything else they desired. They wagered and gambled continuously for weeks on end, winning prized horses, estates, and fortunes—losing a little along the way too.

In the evenings they'd make their rounds to the Season's dinner parties and balls. They would dance, charm, and woo all the innocent young ladies, making them think they could be tamed, or caught. But none of the rakes had any intentions of making a match. They only wanted to hone their skills with mistresses, cards, and dice. As soon as they left the gatherings of innocent ladies of Polite Society, they spent the rest of the night and most of the next day in a gambling hell on the east side of Bond Street.

Now, Griffin was restless. No, it was more than that. He was bored. Bored with cards, dice, racing, shooting, and hunting. All of it. He was even bored with the parade of beautiful women that seemed to have no end.

In truth, he couldn't remember half of the things he'd been accused of that Season because he'd kept his face in a bottle of brandy, port, or a tankard of ale. His eyes were always blurred and his head had kept a constant pounding. Thankfully they didn't think, drink, or behave like that anymore.

He couldn't say he missed those days. He didn't. Somehow they'd all three managed to live through the debauchery, though they hadn't lived it down as he'd hoped. *Miss Honora Truth's Weekly Scandal Sheet* had seen to that by being the first to stir up the past again.

At various times, they'd all tried to find out who wrote that column about the wager. Each one of them had failed miserably. They had finally concluded the writer must be one of the older, trusted employees at the publishing company that concocted the drivel. The owner, who'd made it quite clear he would take the writer's identity to his grave, used the made-up name so no one could find out who the real author was. Griffin had long since ceased reading or caring what was written about him, though it was a very different story now that his sisters were mentioned.

There were things he and his friends did in the early years that were far worse than that wager, but no one had found out about those. And it was a good thing no one had, or Miss Truth would be writing about that too.

One drunken night, they'd decided that they should each select a young lady, find a way to slip into her bedroom without her or anyone else in her house knowing about it, and bring back something to prove he had been there—a monogramed hairbrush, a bow, a ribbon, or a reticule they would all be able to recognize as belonging to the young lady. They were all such reckless, heartless rakes at the time. It was never to harm or to seduce the young lady. It was only to test their skills of getting in and out of the room without anyone knowing.

Griffin stretched out his booted feet and leaned against the cushion as his thoughts took him back to that fateful night that earned him and his friends the name "Rakes of St. James." They had been laughing at the ridiculous suggestions in *A Proper Gentleman's Guide to Wooing the Perfect Lady.*

On the list of things a proper gentleman should never do was to send a young lady a love note signed *Your Secret Admirer.* That's all Griffin and his friends needed to read. If they were told they shouldn't do something, it was a given they would.

Rath's idea was to send a secret-admirer note to all the unmarried ladies of the ton. Griffin and Hawk had readily agreed to the lark. Over another bottle of brandy they'd decided there were too many ladies and it would be far too much work. In the end they sent secret-admirer letters only to the young ladies who were making their debut Season. There were twelve. That was more manageable.

And turning it into a wager would make the prank more interesting. They each put in one hundred pounds. The one who had the most young ladies show up for the assignation with their secret admirer would win the money.

It was so easy—until it was over. Their success that night ended up being their downfall.

In the letter to his four, Griffin had asked them to meet him by the fountain in the back garden of the Grand Hall. Rath had told his four to meet him on the south portico, and Hawk had instructed his to meet him by the pavilion. Much to their astonishment, all twelve young ladies showed up to meet her secret admirer. But no admirer showed. Just four ladies at each place who eventually started talking to each other as young ladies were predisposed to do. It was then they realized they had been duped.

None of the rakes could have expected that there would be no winners that night.

Only losers.

The carriage stopped, pulling Griffin from the past. He looked out the small window. He was home. The sooner his sisters were married, the better. Once they had husbands they would no longer be tainted by his scandal.

He would gladly take whatever revenge anyone wanted to do to him for his crass behavior so long ago, but he would do everything in his power to keep his sisters from being hurt because of him.

Chapter 6

Do choose your words carefully. You never know
when they might be said back to you.

⚭

MISS MAMIE FORTESCUE'S DO'S AND DON'TS FOR
CHAPERONES, GOVERNESSES, TUTORS, AND NURSES

A short time after the duke left, Esmeralda locked the front door of the building. The stuffed coin purse weighted the pocket of her skirt as she headed to the back of the building. She climbed the stairs to the living area and smiled at Napoleon's familiar woof. She heard his nails clicking rapidly on the wood floor as he raced toward the entrance to greet her. No matter how quietly she tried to come up the stairs, he always heard her and stood his ground at the entryway, waiting for her each afternoon.

She opened the door and the blond Skye Terrier jumped up to greet her. "How are you this dreary afternoon, Napoleon?"

The dog woofed several times and licked Esmeralda's hand as she knelt down to rub him. She patted his head and brushed her hand down the back of his warm, damp coat.

Damp?

Why was Napoleon wet?

At first it puzzled Esmeralda, and then a prickle of concern shot through her. It could only mean one thing, and Esmeralda didn't like it. She now knew why Josephine had been so nice about bringing her tea each afternoon. She was trying to keep Esmeralda from coming above stairs and realizing that she was sneaking out the back door to take Napoleon for a walk. Esmeralda rose. A strong desire to tap her foot in frustration gripped her, but she resisted the urge.

"Enough playing," Esmeralda said, brushing the active Napoleon away from her skirt. "Off with you for now."

"You're up early this afternoon," Josephine said, skipping happily into the small drawing room as if she didn't have a care in the world. "I was getting ready to put the kettle on to steep you a cup of tea. I wanted to bring it down to you."

After a quick glance at her half-sister's wet shoes, Esmeralda stared at the youthful face of the happy twelve-year-old. The two of them looked nothing alike, and their differences had nothing to do with the almost-sixteen-year span in their ages. Esmeralda's hair was honey blonde and Josephine's was a gorgeous shade of bright golden-red. On sunny days it fell thick and straight down her back, but on rainy days like today there was a beautiful wave to its long length.

Josephine's eyes were the most vibrant shade of green Esmeralda had ever seen. Her complexion was fair with a light smattering of pale coppery-colored freckles feathered across the bridge of her nose and cheeks. Josephine was slim but sturdy and had all the handsome features of her father's Irish heritage.

Esmeralda walked farther into the room and said, "I do appreciate that you've started doing that for me, but tell me, do we have a leak in our ceiling?"

Josephine kept an innocent expression on her face as she looked all around the room. Esmeralda's gaze followed hers. The drawing room wasn't large, but it had double windows in the front and a single one at the back that let in late afternoon sunshine on clear days. They had a few nice pieces of furniture that had been handed down from Josephine's father's family. A floral-print settee and an armchair were beginning to show wear but were far from unsightly, and the small tea table was in excellent condition. Two brass sconces and a painting of an Irish hillside dotted with sheep were the only things hanging on the walls.

"I haven't seen a leak," Josephine replied as her gaze traveled up to the ceiling, sweeping from side to side in search of a wet spot. "Why? Did you see a puddle on the floor?"

"No, but Napoleon's hair is wet. Much like it was this morning when we took him for a walk in the rain."

Her sister stilled. There was no mistaking she knew she'd been caught doing something she shouldn't have done. Her eyes widened and her mouth formed a small O.

"Did you disobey me and go out by yourself again?" she asked even though she knew the answer.

Josephine clamped her lips together tightly and settled them into a wide line of defiance as she folded her arms across her chest.

"Well? What do you have to say for yourself?" Esmeralda added when an answer wasn't forthcoming.

"I'm not going to answer that."

Napoleon barked and grumbled in his throat as he jumped on Esmeralda's skirt again, hoping to regain her attention. She gave him a couple more pats on the head then shooed him away again.

"Why not?" she asked her sister.

"You won't like what I say."

"That may be," she answered as her foot began to tap. "However, I insist on having an answer from you."

"I don't want you angry with me, Essie."

Esmeralda's anger plummeted. Josephine had always known how to go straight to Esmeralda's heart. She didn't want this tension between them either, but this was too important for her to ignore. Disciplining her sister should have never been her job, but there was no one else to do it since her sister's father died. Esmeralda supposed she'd always been a nervous Nellie where her sister was concerned, and it had only gotten worse after Josephine's father had passed so suddenly.

"If you went out alone again, I have good reason to be upset with you. Napoleon has proven he can wait until I get home to go out, so now tell me, did you take him?"

Refusing to answer, her sister stayed tight-lipped and stern-faced. Stubbornness was another trait she'd inherited from her Irish father.

"Josephine?"

"See, you're already angry with me and I haven't even answered you yet," she accused with her eyes flashing rebelliousness.

"I'm not angry at this point but I will be very soon if you don't start talking." Esmeralda felt compelled to defend herself. "I am getting quite annoyed with you for refusing to respond to my question."

"All right, I went out." Josephine paused briefly and added dismissively, "But I wasn't alone."

Taking her sister's words as truth, she stiffened when she heard this. "Who was with you? Mrs. Chiddington? Did she come for a visit?"

"Napoleon was with me."

"Oh," Esmeralda said on an exasperated sigh. "You know Napoleon is not a chaperone."

"He is better than a chaperone," Josephine contended, throwing her arms down beside her. "He's my friend and a guard dog. He wouldn't let anything happen to me."

"You know I've told you before that it's not just the danger of walking the streets alone," Esmeralda insisted, knowing that while it wasn't the best address in the busy shopping area, they were in a well-respected section of Town that was fairly safe from footpads and mischief-makers. Otherwise, she'd have never agreed to lease the agency from Mr. Fortescue. Taking the man up on his offer to keep the agency open had not only given them a means of support, but a safe home as well.

"How many times do I have to tell you it's not proper for a young lady to be out without a companion?"

"I'm not a lady," Josephine countered petulantly. "I'm a girl."

"Who *will* be a proper young lady one day, and we can't have your character tainted any more than—" Esmeralda caught herself and stopped just in time. She was about to say "any more than it already was."

Josephine was the granddaughter of a viscount, but also the daughter of a penniless Irish poet. Esmeralda didn't think Josephine understood the ramifications of that yet, and Esmeralda wasn't ready to have that discussion with her.

"Nobody pays any attention to me anyway." Her arms snapped back up to cross over her chest again in a contrary stance.

"You don't know that. How long have you been sneaking out of the house in the afternoons?"

Josephine pursed her lips for a moment or two, then said, "Not long. Only a few times and just since the weather turned warmer so Napoleon's paws wouldn't freeze."

"All right," Esmeralda said, thankful her sister hadn't been slipping out all winter. "But you must not do this again. On this I will be firm and have your promise."

The seconds ticked by, Josephine's gaze staying on Esmeralda's. As if sensing what was going on between the two sisters, Napoleon wandered over to stand beside Josephine. She lowered her arm and bent down to pat him on the head.

"We can stand here all night if you wish, but I will have your promise before either of us leaves this room for the night," Esmeralda said, using the firm tone she would use with an unruly five-year-old.

"All right. I promise. But I don't like it."

"You don't have to." Esmeralda wasn't happy about having to force Josephine to give the promise either, and quietly added, "Thank you," hoping that would be the end of the uncomfortable conversation.

"We get tired of staying inside, waiting all day for you to come up and go outside with us."

"If that's the case, perhaps I'm not giving you enough needlework to do."

"Needlework is for old ladies who have nothing else to do, Essie, and you know it," she countered.

"Very well. Since you don't like working with a needle and thread, then we will concentrate more on your sums, reading, and poetry."

"I hate poetry too, and you know that. I only write it to make you happy."

That wasn't the first time Josephine had said she hated poetry, and Esmeralda wondered if it was in some way a retaliation against Josephine's father for dying and leaving her. Myles Graham had written many poems for his daughter. She'd always seemed happiest when sitting on her father's lap, listening to him read his latest poem. But there was no way of knowing, because Josephine refused to discuss her father. It was as if she believed that if she didn't have to think about him, she wouldn't miss him. At least it was only the poetry she said she hated and not Esmeralda.

"I can be flexible on this as well," she said, trying to find some way to let Josephine know she wasn't trying to be difficult. "You can do more of whichever task it is that you enjoy the most."

"Walking outside," she shot back quickly as Napoleon wandered over by the cold fireplace and laid down.

Esmeralda wrapped her shawl tighter about her chest. They hadn't had a fire in more than a week because there was no coal or wood because there was no money. There was oil in the lamp, so she walked over to the table and turned up the flame. It may be cold but it didn't have to be dark and dreary too.

She wished Josephine could have all the proper things the granddaughter of a viscount should have—a large, warm home to grow up in, servants to wait on her, lessons on the pianoforte, someone better in French than Esmeralda to teach her the language—but none of those things were within Esmeralda's power to give unless she wanted to swallow her pride and ask her cousin for help. And she and Josephine hadn't been that cold and hungry yet.

The dashing Duke of Griffin crossed her mind, and her stomach fluttered deliciously. Those romantic feelings were such nonsense, yet she didn't know how to stop them. And in truth, she didn't want to. They were a welcome reprieve from her worries.

Maybe it would do her and Josephine good to get away to the duke's house for a few weeks. It had been a cold winter and she didn't blame her sister for wanting to spend more time outside. Esmeralda would love that too. But if she had been out with Josephine and Napoleon this afternoon, she would have missed His Grace and other potential clients who came to her agency for help securing employees for their households.

"Since we don't have to take Napoleon out, I'm going to make your tea," Josephine mumbled and turned away.

"Wait," Esmeralda said. "We'll have a cup in a few minutes. I have something to tell you."

Josephine huffed. "It's probably something I don't want to hear."

"No, silly girl. It just so happens this is something wonderful. Or I think it is and on such a dreary day as this, it's a good time to hear something lovely."

"If you think it's lovely, I probably won't."

Obviously, Josephine wasn't ready to forgive her for being so firm.

"I'll tell you what it is and then you can decide if you think it's to your liking. How's that?"

Josephine returned to the silent treatment and didn't answer.

"You and I have the opportunity to live in a different place for a few weeks."

"What do you mean, Essie?" she exclaimed, jerking her hands to her side once more. "We've hardly lived here a year. You promised this would be our home for a long, long time and we wouldn't have to move again. You promised."

"You misunderstood. It's not that we're moving. We're not. This is our home and will be. It's more like we'll be visiting. And it's only for a short time. Six weeks at the most."

"I don't want to go. Besides, Napoleon doesn't want to go and I won't go anywhere without him."

"You won't have to," Esmeralda said, mentally thanking the duke again for agreeing Napoleon could come.

"He was invited as well. But he will continue to be your responsibility. Besides, you must go. There is no alternative. I cannot leave you here alone."

Josephine's bottom lip formed another pout.

Esmeralda forged ahead and said, "I have been employed by the Duke of Griffin to be the chaperone for his twin sisters for the Season."

"Chaperone."

"I know it's not your favorite word," Esmeralda admitted.

"No, but it must be yours." Josephine rolled her eyes in disgust and then said something else under her breath. Esmeralda wasn't sure what it was, which was probably for the best.

"I didn't think you were going to work in homes anymore after Papa died."

Esmeralda had promised Josephine she wouldn't. That's why when Mr. Fortescue had offered her the prospect to maintain the agency, she jumped at the chance. Women were seldom afforded such opportunities. And it was the perfect setup with the agency below stairs and the living area on the first floor. The only problem had been that the man hadn't been honest with her about the monthly income from the business.

"That was my plan. But the duke specifically wanted me. Perhaps because he wanted someone near to the ages of his sisters, who are eighteen. I'm not sure of his reasons. I couldn't say no once he agreed that you and Napoleon can come with me. That was a great concession on his part."

Unimpressed, Josephine challenged Esmeralda with her eyes and stuck her lip out even farther.

It was time for Esmeralda to stop explaining and start getting ready for her new position. "Now I have a lot of planning to do. I must figure out who is available right now to have the agency open each day while we're away. I don't want to miss any opportunity that might come our way while we are at the duke's house. And, I must read up on the duties of a chaperone. Oh, and I need to find out the names of all the eligible bachelors."

Suddenly Esmeralda's mind was swirling with things she must get accomplished in a very short time. While Miss Fortescue had schooled her well in all the forms of service, she was wishing she had some practical experience right now to go along with her knowledge.

"But, I must put all that aside for now." She paused and looked down at her sister. "The first thing tomorrow we must go and be fitted for new clothing. Wouldn't you like a new dress to wear?"

"Why?" Josephine asked in a determined tone. "I will never get to go for a walk on the street for anyone to see me in it."

"Josephine, you know that's not true. You are simply trying to make me feel horrible about a decision I had to make for our future. I won't let you. If this works out well, and I can earn the bonuses the duke promised, I will be able to hire someone like Mrs. Chiddington from down the street to come and be with you and Napoleon each day. Yes, to be your chaperone, but she could also go for walks with you in the mornings and afternoons too when the weather is good. A young lady must always have someone with her at all times."

"But what will I do during the day while you are doing your chaperoning?"

"Well, I haven't seen the duke's house, but I'm sure it has a garden," she offered, trying to find a way to be persuasive. "Perhaps a big one with paths, nooks, and I bet it will have fountains."

Her sister's eyes widened a little and her expression sobered. "A real garden?"

It seemed unwise to be suggesting something she had no idea would come to pass but since she'd finally gotten her sister's attention, she couldn't back away from the possibility.

"I can't imagine he wouldn't have. I feel sure he will allow you and Napoleon to spend as much time in it as you would like. But you'll also have to do the same things you do here. You will work on your needlework, sums, and reading. There's a good possibility the duke has a vast library too. I don't think he would mind if you read some of his books."

"I don't like to read. I'd rather daydream and come up with my own stories. Napoleon and I go on many adventures that way." She turned and looked at the dog, who had curled up by the fireplace. His only reaction was to move his pert ears.

"Then it will be a wonderful idea for you to write a story about all the exploits you two will have."

Josephine walked closer to her. "And you really think the duke will let us play in his garden? He won't make us stay inside all the time like you do?"

"I'm certainly going to ask him if you may go outside any time you wish."

"All right, Essie," Josephine said in the same cheerful voice she'd used when she'd first entered the room. "I guess I'll go."

Esmeralda's body relaxed and she smiled. Now she could start to make plans.

Chapter 7

Don't ask anyone to do something you are not
willing to do yourself.

~❧~

Miss Mamie Fortescue's Do's and Don'ts for
Chaperones, Governesses, Tutors, and Nurses

It was a hell of a dark night for Griffin to be huddled
in the shadows watching a man's back door. Griffin
wore his hat low on his forehead and his cloak high
around his neck. Still, the icy chill of damp air seeped
into his bones, making him wish he'd thought to stuff a
flask of brandy into his pocket.

He'd moved slowly between dark unfamiliar houses
in search of the one he was looking for. Shifting banks of
fog had whirled and scattered before him as he had walked.
Many were the times as a boy, and later as a young man,
when his father didn't know he was out, Griffin had made
his way through the lighted streets of Mayfair in the cold
dead of night. He knew every house, yew hedge, and
garden along the way. This quiet area of London was new
to him. Clouds shielded any glow of light from the moon
and stars but even in the pitch-darkness Griffin could see

the houses were smaller and less affluent. Lamplights, cobblestone lanes, and garden walls were nowhere to be found.

His first thought had been to approach the man at White's to find out what he knew. In mulling over all the possibilities of what might be said between the two, he'd decided it was best to see him in private. Sir Welby might be blind, but the barkeep wasn't. Griffin planned to get the information he wanted from him.

Time passed slowly.

The air grew colder. Leaves rustled noisily as wind whistled softly around the corner of the house and whipped at Griffin's cloak, forcing him to wrap it tighter about his shoulders. From somewhere on another street he heard the lonely baying of a hound and was reminded that the captivating Miss Swift would be bringing a dog with her to his house. He coughed out a soft laugh. He'd gone to great lengths to obtain her.

Thoughts of her made him smile. She knew how to play her hand better than any man he'd dealt with. She'd held him off until he was willing to give her anything she wanted just to hear her say yes. The arrangement he'd made with her might be unorthodox, but he didn't expect it would cause any problems even though his aunt Evelyn had strongly disagreed with his decision to hire Miss Swift.

When Griffin heard the faint rattle of harness and wheels and the clipping sound of a horse's hooves on a hard-packed street in the distance, he straightened. At last he heard the shuffling of feet and was soon rewarded with the figure of a man hunched against the biting cold walking up to the doorway he'd been watching for the better part of two hours.

Griffin's footsteps were silent as he stepped out of the shadows and said, "Holsey."

"Arrah," the old man moaned as he jumped back and threw up his hands as if to thwart an attack.

Hellfire!

He hadn't meant to scare the barkeep senseless. There wasn't much light but he could see the man was shivering from fright. "It's Griffin, Holsey, I mean you no harm."

"Your Grace." The man gave him a low bow and in a shaking voice murmured, "I thought you were a footpad out to rob me of my purse. What are you doing out here this hour of morning?"

"I've come to see you about an important matter. I didn't want to talk to you at White's, and it couldn't wait."

"Ah, important you say?" He wiped his mouth with the back of his woolen-gloved hand. "Did you want to come inside? I can stoke the fire and put a kettle on for you."

"No. I don't want to keep you and this won't take long."

"What can I do for you?"

"I understand you were working the taproom last night when Sir Welby was there. The time was between seven and nine. I want to know who else was in there at that time."

"I don't know, Your Grace," the barkeep said without hesitation.

Griffin frowned and shifted his stance. "Think back, Holsey. It wasn't tonight but last night. You know Sir Welby always sits at the table nearest the door so everyone will speak to him when they enter and leave. You had to have seen him, served him."

"I don't remember him being there." Holsey's voice was shaky again. He pulled a handkerchief from his pocket and wiped his nose. "I don't know who was there."

Griffin hadn't expected the bartender to be so unequivocal about his answer.

"You've heard the rumor going around about the

possibility that my sisters might fall prey to a jokester out to ruin their Season, haven't you?"

"I haven't heard that, Your Grace."

Cold and frustrated, Griffin was finding it difficult to hold his temper, but managed to quietly say, "That's impossible. Damnation, man, all of London has heard it by now. It's only a matter of time until someone has the courage to create a wager and register it in the books at White's and other clubs."

"I'm sorry to disappoint you, Your Grace. Especially since you've been waiting here for me, but I don't know about any of that."

How could that be? Perhaps his information was wrong and it was another barkeep who was there.

"You were working in the taproom, right?"

"Yes, Your Grace."

"Good. Once again, all I need to know is who else was in the taproom while Sir Welby was there. You won't be implicating anyone just telling the truth of who was present."

"I can't help you, Your Grace. I don't know."

Griffin's hands fisted in frustration. If the bartender had been a younger man, Griffin might have grabbed him by the neck of his coat and scared the hell out of him again. Perhaps he was just waiting for Griffin to line his pockets. He shouldn't have expected the man to give over the information without some compensation.

"There will be a handsome reward for you if can recall a few names for me."

Holsey's breathing grew louder, and Griffin's tensed. The man was considering his offer.

"It would be a fine day for me if I could collect it, Your Grace," Holsey said slowly as he shook his head. "But I can't. It wouldn't be right. I started to work in the kitchen at White's when I was still a lad. It was a good job to have for a youngster like me. A fine establishment to work in.

That was a long time ago, but I can recall my first day as if it was only yesterday."

"That's all well and good, Holsey," Griffin said, growing more irritable by the moment, "but it doesn't help me find out who wants to hurt my sisters."

"And I can't help you, Your Grace. I took an oath not to see anything or hear anything no matter what was said or done or who said or did it. I've never forgotten that. If I've learned one thing from serving gents like yourself, it's that a man's honor is the most precious thing he has be he royalty, commoner, or servant like me. I must have honor as a representative of White's. That place has been good to me over the years. If there's one thing I believe more than anything else, it's that if everyone doesn't trust me, then no one will trust me."

The man's words hit Griffin hard. He believed that too. Despite his reputation as a one of London's most notorious rakes, Griffin wasn't a man without honor. He took a step away from the man and tipped his hat.

"Go on inside, Holsey. I won't bother you about this again."

Griffin turned away, knowing that a man's honor was a hell of a thing to fight.

Chapter 8

Don't jump to conclusions before the first word
is uttered. Contrary to popular opinion, instant
reactions are not usually the best ones.

~∾∽~

MISS MAMIE FORTESCUE'S DO'S AND DON'TS FOR
CHAPERONES, GOVERNESSES, TUTORS, AND NURSES

Esmeralda stood with her back to the low-burning fire
in her office, reading yet another of the seven books
Miss Fortescue had filled with words of wisdom throughout her forty years in service to the elite members of Polite Society. The ink had started to fade in the earliest of
the volumes and several pages in one of the books had
been damaged by moisture and mildew. The rest were in
excellent condition.

For the most part, the woman's handwritten words of
tried and true wisdom were an easy and uncomplicated
read. The best way to describe her books was as a common-
sense approach to doing your best to serve your employer.
The difficulty was that it was so easy to forget common
sense when you found yourself flustered, angered, or in
dire straits. If Esmeralda could put all the woman's

rules, suggestions, and knowledge to memory, perhaps one day she would be as successful with Polite Society as Miss Fortescue had been. But for now, that was a distant dream.

Esmeralda lowered the book and turned to face the fire. It was heavenly having warmth in the rooms again. She held one hand down to the fire, enjoying the heat against her skin. The small pieces of coal gave off an inviting glow.

The duke had given her the money for clothing and other items she would need to be properly dressed for her position as chaperone. Not for coal. But she hadn't been able to resist the splurge when she discovered how much money was in the velvet pouch. Because she hadn't used the ridiculously overpriced French modiste he'd suggested, Esmeralda had enough funds leftover to pay her coal debt and have more delivered.

With the help of Mrs. Chiddington from down the street, she had found a competent dressmaker who had acceptable fabrics, enough trimmings, and two daughters who helped her with the sewing. There would be no trouble getting the three gowns and matching velvet capes, two carriage dresses, gloves, unmentionables, and all the rest made in time for her departure to the duke's house.

She'd had Josephine help her pick out ribbons, lace, and a strand of glass beads that looked a little like a string of pearls that she could use to adorn her hair for the balls. For daily outings to the park or afternoon card and tea parties she would make do with her black velvet bonnet and coat. They weren't the height of fashion anymore but still in reasonably good condition.

She smiled to herself, found her place in the book once again, and continued her reading. *"Don't take part in the gossip of other household staff. Don't listen to it and don't repeat it. Do remember the lady of the house has entrusted her children into your care. Don't disappoint her by giving wings to idle words or listening ears."*

The door to her office opened, so Esmeralda turned to greet whoever had come in and saw the Duke of Griffin striding inside. Much to her dismay, her first thought was *Yes*. He was the most handsome man on earth. Just the sight of him sent her heart whirling like a spinning wheel again. But the second thought that entered her mind was that he'd come back because he'd changed his mind about hiring her.

That knotted her stomach and clogged her throat with fear. If he no longer needed her, what was she going to do? She had very little left of the money he'd given her. Would he force her into a workhouse? What would happen to Josephine and Napoleon? They had no one else to care for them.

She snapped her book shut quickly and curtsied. "Your Grace."

"Miss Swift." He took off his hat as his gaze swept past her to the fireplace before settling on her face. "Am I interrupting anything other than your reading?"

"No," she said, gripping the book tightly in her hands and lowering it to the front of her skirt.

"That's good," he said.

Different thoughts scattered crazily in her mind. What could she say to him about how she'd spent all of his money? How could she justify what she'd done? If she were a weaker woman, she would faint from the very idea of having to tell him some of it had gone to heat the house and for new clothing for Josephine too.

But she wasn't weak. Esmeralda had proven that when shortly after her mother died she'd applied for a position with Miss Fortescue and was immediately accepted. Without her mother to guide Josephine's father, Esmeralda knew she couldn't depend on him to make enough money from his poetry and stories to take care of the family, and she'd been right.

She took a step toward the duke. A more tentative step than she'd wanted, but she wouldn't let him know she was trembling inside. It was one thing to tell yourself to be strong and brave, but quite another to actually be that way when you were staring eye to eye with a duke.

"Have you decided you don't need me?"

His brow tightened. His deep blue eyes watched her intently. "You amaze me, Miss Swift."

"Do I?" she questioned cautiously.

"Yes. I have never seen anyone who has tried so hard to keep from working for me."

Her stomach jumped again. "Well, I—"

He walked farther into the room. Stopping in front of her, he tossed his hat into a chair. "Usually I have people standing in line wanting to be of service to me; others pleading for my assistance in one way or another. Here you are still trying to get out of being employed by me. Let me assure you that won't happen. We have an agreement. It is a good one for both of us. I won't let you break it."

Thank goodness!

Her fears about her position in his household put to rest, she simply said, "You are persistent."

"With you, I'm forced to be. Now tell me, do you have any new demands to make today?"

Demands?

She had done that, hadn't she? But only because, at the time, she'd hoped to persuade him to use someone else in the agency.

"Of course not. I didn't know you were coming by. Why would you think that?"

Humor twitched the corners of his mouth. "I was thinking perhaps you were going to tell me that you discovered

Napoleon has a sister after all and she must come with you to Mayfair."

Esmeralda smiled too. And a soft, short laugh escaped past her lips. "I have no such ultimatums to make today. I thought maybe you had re— I mean, I didn't expect to see you again until I arrived at your house, but no matter about that now."

"Did you find someone to take care of your responsibilities here in the agency while you are away?"

"Yes," she said, feeling the tension slowly ebbing from her body and her runaway heartbeat returning to almost normal. She had a feeling that, in his presence, it would never be normal. "Everything has been arranged satisfactorily."

"Let me guess," he said, folding his arms across his broad chest. "It will be Miss Pennywaite who replaces you."

Her eyes widened in surprise. "How did you know?"

"From what little I heard of your conversation with her the other day, I think it was clear she doesn't have the fortitude to handle a strong-minded child and that you'd have to replace her."

Esmeralda would have used the word "spoiled" instead of "strong-minded," but kept her thoughts to herself and said, "You're right, she doesn't. Though she tried hard to overcome her feelings of inadequacies in knowing how to calm her charge and prevail."

It wasn't so much his handsome face that kept Esmeralda staring at him, it was all of him. The wide shoulders, broad chest, slim hips, and the powerful-looking legs ensconced in shiny black knee boots. Her gaze dropped to the medallion at his throat that held his cloak together. The design was beautiful and fancy with lots of swirls and curls. After a moment, she realized the inscription was a G.

In a rare moment of make believe, Esmeralda envisioned herself walking up to the duke, unhooking the ornamental pewter disk at the base of his throat, and letting the black cape fall to the floor. She imagined slowly untying the casual bow of his neckcloth, unwinding it, and allowing it too to flutter to the floor. She imagined closing her eyes and reaching up to place her lips against his as he gathered her into his strong, warm embrace.

Anticipation rose in her chest.

She made a move to step closer to him before she caught herself, coughed, and cleared her throat, hoping the rising heat she felt in her body wouldn't travel up to her cheeks and tell on her. What kind of madness had come over her? What in heaven's name was she doing thinking about kissing the duke?

Exhaling a deep breath, she walked over to the desk, laid Miss Fortescue's book down, and said again, "Miss Pennywaite wasn't able to be successful in her duties, but I had another very capable governess waiting for a position, so it all worked out in the end."

Perhaps it was just her guilty conscience, but with the way his eyes questioned hers, she could have sworn he knew exactly what she'd been thinking before she put the book down.

"At least you gave her a second chance to succeed," he said.

"Yes. She will do a good job here. I've asked her to have weekly reports delivered to me and told her that she could contact me at your house should there be an emergency. Is that acceptable to you?"

"Quite."

"Thank you. Now, was there something you needed from me today, or did you simply want to make sure I would keep my word and chaperone your sisters?"

"Both. The main reason I'm here is at the behest of my aunt, Lady Evelyn."

Esmeralda knew about Lady Evelyn the same way she knew about most of the elite few who made up the *ton*— from what she'd gleaned from the social pages and ladies who worked for the agency. When they came in each month to pay their fee, most of them had a morsel or two of gossip about their employers or what they'd heard about others to share as well.

Lady Evelyn was the only sister of the duke's father. She had been married to an older gentleman who died a few years after they'd wed. She'd never had children and had never remarried. Since the duke's mother had died shortly after giving birth to the twins, Lady Evelyn had moved into the duke's house to see to it that the girls were properly brought up as befitting daughters, and now sisters, of a duke.

"My aunt takes her responsibilities for the twins much too seriously at times," he continued. "She was quite perturbed when I told her that I had hired you without consulting her or anyone and without questioning you in detail about your family."

Esmeralda's back arched with indignation. "Was she?"

"She wanted to know if you are related to the Swifts who come from Derbyshire, and Sir Timothy Swift's family in particular. I had to admit I didn't ask."

Esmeralda bristled tightly though she tried to hide it. It shouldn't bother her that Lady Evelyn wanted to make sure she was from a family reputable enough to be employed by a duke. It was the proper thing to do after all. Still, it rankled. It may be unfair, but ever since Esmeralda's mother had been disowned by her brother, Viscount Mayeforth, for marrying beneath her, Esmeralda had dislike for the favored few who held the livelihood of so many in their hands. Her mother had lived an impoverished life when, at the very least, she should have lived comfortably with an allowance from the viscount.

"You mean Lady Evelyn wants to make sure I didn't come from the streets."

The duke's blue eyes darkened and one corner of his mouth twitched slightly. "No, Miss Swift. That's not what she meant."

Esmeralda wanted to say more but, thinking better of it, gave him a look that conveyed her doubt instead.

He took exception to it by saying, "That never entered her mind. She knows you were properly assessed by Miss Fortescue and that she would have never accepted anyone who wasn't qualified in all areas."

Perhaps Esmeralda was being too prickly and should just thank her lucky stars that his aunt was only asking about her father's family. It was easier to answer questions about the Swift family than her mother's. So far she'd managed to keep it to herself that her first cousin was Viscount Mayeforth. She wanted it to stay that way. She had no desire to let anyone know she had a connection to that family. And, if he was like his father, *he* wouldn't want anyone to know either.

Still, she asked, "Will it be good or bad if I am related to Sir Timothy?"

He folded his arms across his wide chest. "You are a continual challenge, Miss Swift. No matter the direction of our conversation, you manage to find a way to confront me." His gaze lingered on hers.

"Perhaps that's because I am provoked first."

He looked surprised. "That may be in some instances, but in this conversation that wasn't my intention. However, it will be good if you are related to Sir Timothy."

"In that case, the man had ten sons by three different wives over a period of thirty-five years. How could I not be related to him? Half of Derbyshire is. He was my father's grandfather."

The duke nodded. "And so Aunt Evelyn thought. She'll be pleased to hear she was right."

Stiff and on the defensive, Esmeralda asked, "Would she like for me to go for a visit with her so she can make her own assessment of me? I'm quite willing to have her question me at length about any concerns she might have."

"Take my word for it. My aunt wants nothing more than to look you over from head to toe and test your knowledge on a number of different subjects, but she won't be receiving you."

"Oh," she said, her feelings giving rise again to her previous thoughts of being put in her current place in Society.

He lowered his arms and stepped closer to her. Their eyes held steady. "Not for the reasons you are thinking."

Esmeralda's breathing increased. "You don't know what I am thinking, Your Grace."

"I do," he said softly. "Deny it if it pleases you to do so. I won't press the matter."

Her breath caught in her throat, yet she managed to say, "It would do no good."

"I'm willing to admit to that. I'm already well-acquainted with how hardheaded you are—and opinionated too."

Her shoulders and her chin lifted. She had to be. "I'm not sure those would be considered attractive traits."

He smiled. "I admire those qualities, Miss Swift, and they were just what I was looking for. It appears the stress of preparing two young ladies for the Season was more than Lady Evelyn's constitution could bear. She's come down with an extremely difficult case of the hives, welts, and most likely shingles too, according to her physician and apothecary. They have both assured me she will get better with bed rest and time. However, the unsightly rash has spread to her face, around one eye and halfway down her cheek. As you can imagine, she doesn't want anyone outside our family and her maid seeing her."

Esmeralda saw strain in his forehead and around the edges of his eyes. His aunt's condition worried him. "That's dreadful. I hope it's not too painful for her."

"Regrettably, it is at times. But not as bad as it could be. I've told her if she would just stop worrying about the twins' Season she'd get better, but she's been a mother to them all their lives. She finds it difficult not to worry over the simplest of things."

"I'm sure you're right."

"I am, but she won't listen to me, insisting I bring these to you." He brushed his black cloak aside and from the pocket of his dark brown coat he withdrew a small leather packet. He handed it to her. "Since it became clear Lady Evelyn wouldn't be well enough to attend the Season with the twins, she has been making notes for whoever would be taking her place at all the parties. After you look over this, you should be well-versed on all that she expects of you."

The folder was heavy. There was no small amount of paper inside.

"I will do my best not to disappoint her."

"I've never had any fear you would."

Esmeralda laid the packet on the desk behind her. "Did you tell her I would be bringing my sister and Napoleon?"

"I did."

Was that all he had to say about something so unconventional? "Was she all right with it?"

"She has no choice, Miss Swift. It is my house. But that said, I told her all that we'd discussed about the two and assured her there were no concerns about them interfering in your duties. She said as long as you do a proper job of caring for Lady Sara and Lady Vera she doesn't care if you bring an elephant with you to the house."

Esmeralda laughed. It amazed her that she was annoyed with him at one moment and laughing with him in the next. "You are teasing me, Your Grace."

The duke smiled and chuckled softly. "The twins were only weeks old when Lady Evelyn came to live with us to care for them. Since that time her only goal in life has been to see to it that Sara and Vera each make a good match. She would like to see that happen in their first Season. After they are wed, she will consider her obligation to my father fulfilled and so will I."

"And now she has to miss the Season. That must be very hard for her to accept."

"It is, but as most of us have found out, life doesn't always turn out the way we want it to."

"I will attest to that, Your Grace. Though sometimes fate allows us choices and we must make good ones."

With what looked like a nod of reluctance, he answered, "I wish I had learned that a little earlier in life, Miss Swift. It could have saved me a lot of difficulty."

"That can probably be said by all of us." She let her gaze briefly scan up and down his face before settling on his gorgeous blue eyes. "There's an old adage that makes regrets a little easier to bear."

"I'm not certain that's true, but which one were you thinking about?"

"Better late than never."

He gave her a rueful smile. "Ah. You are clever to recall that one."

"I am practical."

"And that should serve you well in my house. If you have questions, we will look into them when you arrive in Mayfair. Now, I'll take my leave so you can continue with your reading."

Without further words, the duke picked up his hat from the chair, turned, and strode out.

Esmeralda walked back to the fireplace. It wasn't what she wanted, but there was no denying the duke fascinated her. Despite all efforts for it not to happen. Her mind immediately went back to her earlier fantasy of kissing the duke. She liked the way it made her feel inside when she thought about what it would be like to have his lips pressed against hers, exchanging breaths and sighs.

She wondered if his arms would be as strong as they looked, his chest as hard and muscular as it appeared. Which of the womanly feelings that he had awakened inside her would she experience if she was wrapped in his capable arms, held firmly against that broad chest with his lips pressed so lightly upon hers? Would it be the tingling sensation that skipped along her breasts, the warm tightening low in her abdomen that reached all the way down to the core of her womanhood, or would it only be that elusive, magical, and breathless stirring that made her legs go weak and her body tremble?

"What did it matter?" she whispered to herself.

She would never know and shouldn't even want to know. She was not a part of his social world now and never would be again. Maybe, if her life had been different, if she had been a debutante rather than a chaperone there might have been a chance for her to try to win the duke's favor and receive that kiss she desired.

Even then, capturing the heart of such a magnificent duke would have probably only been a dream.

A thrilling dream.

My Dear Readers:

I've heard it's never a good thing when a young rake's wicked ways come back to haunt him. But let's ask the Duke of Griffin, one of the notorious Rakes of St. James, shall we? With the Season less than a week away it appears all of London Society is in a twitter. While the duke is still trying to live down the ill-fated wager he made years ago, rumors have started swirling around Town that the chickens have finally come home to roost for the embattled duke. And it just may be his twin sisters, Lady Sara and Lady Vera, who bear the brunt of his past misdeeds.

MISS HONORA TRUTH'S WEEKLY SCANDAL SHEET

Chapter 9

Do be patient in all things. There's a reason
"patience" is called a virtue.

Esmeralda didn't mind sitting as long as she had something else to occupy her while she was doing it. Which unfortunately she didn't. No needlework to stitch, no book to read, no foolscap or quill and ink for writing. Just waiting.

And more waiting.

By the hands on the fancy brass clock sitting on an elaborately carved and perfectly decorated side table she knew she'd been at the duke's house for more than an hour now. It shouldn't surprise her that he had left her sitting tight. He was a duke after all and she just a lowly worker. However, the master of the house's tardiness was about to get the best of her usually good disposition.

She, Josephine, Napoleon, and a large overstuffed trunk had been picked up by a handsomely dressed driver wearing a dark red coat trimmed with black braid and shiny brass buttons running up the front panel and cuffs of his sleeves. The carriage was a sleek, black-lacquered barouche with the Duke of Griffin's seal painted in red on the sides of the doors. Josephine had never ridden in anything as ornate as the coach, and she kept saying she felt as if she were a princess. Esmeralda hated to admit it to herself, but she felt a wee bit like a princess too, despite the fact she thought the lavish conveyance much too grand a ride for a mere chaperone, a girl, and a dog.

Sparks, the tall, portly butler with thinning gray hair and a stern expression on his flat, round face, had met them at the door and had immediately taken charge of the luggage, Josephine, and Napoleon. He'd shown Esmeralda to the drawing room and told her to wait there for the duke, who would be joining her shortly.

That's where she still sat. Twiddling her thumbs, crossing one foot over the other and back again, rearranging her reticule, pressing the wrinkles out of her gloves, and anything else she could think to do to keep from getting up and snooping around the beautifully appointed room. There were grand paintings on the walls, exquisite figurines on the tables, and large Asian-inspired urns and sculptures of Greek gods and goddesses placed around the room.

Apparently the duke's idea of "shortly" was longer than hers. Or perhaps the butler never got around to alerting the master of the house that she'd arrived. Whatever the reason for his delay, it didn't really matter—waiting was a tedious position to be in.

It didn't help her impatience that she was eager to talk to His Grace. Just yesterday she'd read in Miss Honora Truth's latest gossip sheet that Lady Sara and Lady Vera may be set upon by some unscrupulous men in an effort to get even with the duke for an astonishing prank he and his friends pulled off many Seasons ago. She couldn't help but wonder if he'd known that danger was lurking when he'd asked her to step into his aunt's slippers and chaperone the twins.

If he had, why hadn't he mentioned it? And was there more she needed to know before the first ball?

Esmeralda touched the lace that covered her hair. She'd already checked it twice since removing her bonnet when she arrived. It seemed to be in place. Checking it gave her something to do.

A fleck of white lint on the skirt of her new dress caught her attention and she quickly brushed it away. While the fabric and cut of the dark gray, lightweight wool wasn't of the finest quality available, it was more than acceptable for Esmeralda's position as a chaperone. The pale gray cuffs and satin band at the high waist gave the dress a bit of fashion flare without stepping over the line and into extravagance. She ran her gloved hand up and down her sleeve a couple of times. She'd forgotten how lovely it felt to wear fine clothing. That was another reason to be grateful the duke, no matter how arrogant, had walked into Miss Fortescue's employment agency rather than another's.

She'd studied all the notes Lady Evelyn had sent to her, and felt she'd have no difficulty following her instructions—once she could put faces to all the names. There were five young bachelors that Lady Evelyn was especially interested in for the twins and there were several that she didn't want them to consider or to spend time with at all. Two of the latter were the duke's friends, the Duke of Hawksthorn and the Duke of Rathburne and part of the trio called the "Rakes of St. James." That made Esmeralda smile. She couldn't help but wonder if the duke knew that his aunt wanted the twins to avoid those two gentlemen at all parties.

Just when she thought she couldn't bear to sit for one more second and would have to get up and stretch her back and legs, she heard a noise coming from the front of the house. She looked expectantly toward the doorway. Someone was humming. She couldn't make out the whispered words but it was clearly a feminine voice and not the duke or his butler. A floorboard creaked and then another.

Esmeralda kept her gaze glued to the entranceway. Moments later, a tall willowy young lady with shiny brown hair and a pleasing face walked into the room. She came to an abrupt halt when she saw Esmeralda.

"Oh," the young lady said. "I didn't know anyone was in here." Her fan-shaped brows drew closer together for a second and then arched up in wonderment.

There was no mistaking that she was one of the duke's sisters. Not only were her eyes the same sparkling shade of blue as her brother's, but she carried herself with the same commanding presence as the duke. She wore a simple morning dress that was far from simple. It was exquisite. The fabric was superb quality. The detail of the stitching along the sash at her waist and the band at the sleeves was sewn by someone with a steady hand and a sharp eye.

Esmeralda rose. "I'm sorry I startled you."

"No, you didn't," she said, though it was obviously not the case. "Who are you?"

"I'm Miss Esmeralda Swift," she said calmly, though for some reason she had a death grip on the drawstrings of her reticule as she curtsied. She hadn't expected to be nervous, but suddenly she was.

That would never do. One of Miss Fortescue's golden rules was "Don't show you are nervous." She slowly loosened her hold on the braided cord and relaxed her breathing.

A smile brightened the young lady's face. "How lovely of you to come calling on us. We haven't had any visitors since we've been in Town, but of course we've only been here a week." She strolled farther into the room. "Auntie Eve said we shouldn't seek anyone out." She sighed and then gave Esmeralda a most pleasing smile. "We must wait for them to call on us, and now you have."

Esmeralda wondered if perhaps the young lady had misunderstood her name so she said again, "I'm Miss Swift."

The friendly smile stayed on her face. "Oh, I'm sorry, Miss Swift. I forgot to introduce myself to you. I'm Lady Sara. I'm so glad you stopped by today. My sister and I are eager to get to know some young ladies and start our Season."

Lady Sara didn't recognize Esmeralda as her new chaperone. That put Esmeralda in a quandary. Why? Did it mean the duke hadn't told his sisters about her? Or that she was coming this morning to start her position as their chaperone? If she was correct, Esmeralda didn't know if she was horrified or amused by his failure to do so.

"Please sit back down. I'll arrange for some refreshments to be brought in while we visit. It will only take a moment to tell Sparks and then I'll be right back."

"No, no, Lady Sara. Please don't go to that trouble."

"But I must," she beamed. "My goodness, it's no trouble at all. It may be a little early in the day for a social visit, but I don't mind you bending the rules. I think most of them are stuffy anyway, don't you? But never mind that now, you're our first caller to stop by and welcome us to London. I've been absolutely famished for a guest. I adore my sister and my aunt but I've been dying to meet someone else, so I'm certainly going to treat you properly. Now sit back down."

"But you see, I'm not here just for a visit." She paused, not knowing exactly what she should say. *Where was the duke?* "There are other reasons I'm here."

"How wonderful. I look forward to hearing what they are. Now, please do make yourself comfortable. Go ahead, I insist."

"Sara," another female voice called from the front of the house. "Did you find the book for me?"

"I haven't found it," Lady Sara answered, walking over to the door way and looking out. She motioned to someone. "Come into the drawing room." Lady Sara looked back at Esmeralda. "It's Lady Vera. I know you want to visit with her too. She will be as pleased as I am that you dropped by to introduce yourself to us."

"No," Esmeralda said, stepping forward. "I-I think you might misunderstand who I am."

Suddenly, Esmeralda considered another of Miss Fortescue's golden rules and felt like groaning. She was failing miserably at "Don't get flustered. You must be in control of whatever situation you find yourself in." It had never dawned on her that the duke wouldn't have mentioned her arrival to his sisters.

What kind of brother was he?

Obviously the kind who couldn't be bothered with minor details!

"I don't know where I could have left it," Lady Sara's twin said as she entered the room and stopped as abruptly as her sister had at the sight of Esmeralda.

Esmeralda stared at her in astonishment too.

The two young ladies looked identical right down to the way their hair was parted on the left and swept up in a pile of curls on top of their heads. She'd never seen two people look so much alike. If they hadn't had on different-colored dresses Esmeralda wouldn't have been able to tell them apart. Their height, eyes, nose, and lips were the same. Their carriage, countenance, and the way they looked her over from head to toe were exactly the same too.

Esmeralda had seen twins only once in her life, and

they had been young boys whose hair wasn't cut the same style. Because of that, it had been fairly easy to tell them apart.

"Who are you?"

"I've already asked her that. She's Miss Esmeralda Swift. Our first visitor."

"Lady Vera," Esmeralda said and curtsied as she studied their faces carefully, hoping to see a distinguishing mark on one that the other didn't have. She found nothing. Not a mole, a freckle, or a twitch. It wasn't natural for two people to look so much alike.

Her annoyance with the duke grew. Not only had he left her on her own for way over an hour, he'd not given his sisters her name. It was just like the titled not to give a fig about the feelings of the less fortunate.

"I'm sorry, my ladies," she said with as calm a smile as she was capable of giving under the circumstances, "I am not here to visit with you."

"Oh," Lady Sara said, her smile fading. "I must have misunderstood. I thought you had come calling on us."

Hearing the disappointment in her voice, Esmeralda felt compelled to add, "That is to say, I'm not here to visit you in the manner that you are thinking about."

Esmeralda's hand tightened on the braided cord of her reticule again. She didn't know what to do. The only thing she knew for sure was that she didn't want to make a mistake on the first day and tell the duke's sisters why she was there if he wasn't ready for them to know.

While at first she hadn't wanted this position because of the responsibility of Josephine and Napoleon and her lack of clothing, now that she had it, she would not willingly give it up. This was too important to their future. If the duke was satisfied with her, she felt certain he'd be willing to give her an excellent reference so that she could obtain a position with another family when this one ended.

She didn't want to upset him by saying or doing something she shouldn't.

So what was the right thing to do?

Lady Vera frowned suspiciously at Esmeralda and asked, "Does Sparks know you're here?"

"Yes, of course. He showed me into the drawing room and asked me to wait here for His Grace. Perhaps we could summon Sparks and ask him to let your brother know I have arrived."

"So you are really here to see the duke?" Lady Sara asked.

"Yes."

"Is the duke here?" Lady Vera asked her.

"I thought so," Esmeralda said, though now she wasn't so sure. "I should say I assumed he was when Sparks asked me to wait here for him." A feeling of dread threatened to settle over Esmeralda, but she shook it off and admitted, "I really don't know."

"He has been stopping by more often because Auntie Eve is unwell," Lady Sara offered.

"Stopping by?" Esmeralda questioned.

"He doesn't live here with us, Miss Swift," Lady Vera said. "Did you think he did?"

"Yes." Confusion swarmed inside Esmeralda. Her first day was not turning out like she'd thought. "I did assume that."

"Oh, no," Lady Sara said. "Whenever we come to Town, he resides at his town house in St. James."

That was a piece of information Esmeralda would have found useful if the duke had taken the time to tell her. No wonder he wasn't fearful that Josephine and Napoleon would bother him. He wouldn't be here!

Oh, he was an impossible man to figure out. She didn't know why she wanted to try.

"He says it is to give us more room and privacy," Lady Sara added.

"But we know it's really because he wants *his* privacy," Lady Vera said, giving Esmeralda a smile that said she was quite pleased with herself. "He can't be the notorious bachelor he's known for being if his sisters and aunt are in the same house with him, now can he?"

"I suppose not," Esmeralda whispered.

"Vera, hush that kind of talk," Lady Sara admonished. "You are not being polite."

"Oh, don't be such a persimmon," Vera countered testily. "You know very well what I'm saying is true."

Esmeralda was beginning to believe the duke had purposefully not told his sisters she was the new chaperone, preferring to leave the delicate task to her. What a dastardly thing for him to do.

"Well, then perhaps he isn't here," Esmeralda said, hoping to quell the argument brewing between the sisters before it began. "I'm sure he will be soon."

Lady Vera walked closer to her. "Why don't you tell us why you want to see our brother?"

Lady Sara admonished her sister again, by saying, "Vera, that's not a very nice question to ask a guest."

"It's certainly not rude. She is here in our home, asking to see our brother. I think it's a perfectly natural thing for us to want to know." She turned back to Esmeralda. "Besides, I may be able to help you in some way since he's not available."

"How can you help her?" Lady Sara questioned.

"I don't know yet, Sara. She hasn't told us what she wants. Now, if you will be quiet long enough, maybe she will."

Esmeralda knew she might as well learn how to handle the twins and their tit-for-tat bickering right now because she aimed to see to it that they spent the next six weeks together. And the best way to do that was to stick to another of Miss Fortescue's rules: "Do be forthright at all times."

"All right, my ladies. I suppose since the duke didn't tell you who I am, I will have to tell you."

"That won't be necessary, Miss Swift. I am here now and will do it."

Esmeralda whirled toward the entrance to the room. The duke leaned casually against the door watching her. *Handsome as ever,* she thought grudgingly as her gaze met his across the room.

Much to her consternation, the rhythm of her pulse quickened and her stomach fluttered deliciously, but that didn't keep her from murmuring under her breath, "And about time."

Chapter 10

Don't let little things annoy you.
Concentrate on the larger issues in your position.

⤞⤝

Miss Mamie Fortescue's Do's and Don'ts for
Chaperones, Governesses, Tutors, and Nurses

Esmeralda didn't understand why she was so delighted to see the duke, when at the same time she wanted to strangle him for making her wait so long—and for other things too! If his sisters weren't in the room, she would immediately take him to task for not telling them she was coming to be their chaperone, and that would be just the start of what she had to say to him. She would ask him why he hadn't told her he didn't live there, and ask why he hadn't mentioned there were rumors the twins could be subject to some type of trickery, meanness, or revenge against him.

"Griffin," Lady Sara said, rushing over and giving her brother a quick kiss on his cheek. "We didn't hear you come in."

"I arrived before you came below stairs. I've been with your aunt since I arrived."

Lady Vera rushed to his other side and affectionately took hold of his arm. "This lady has come to see you. Sara thought she was here to see us, but she's not. I have to say she wasn't very forthcoming about why she wants to see you."

The duke looked at Esmeralda and said, "That doesn't surprise me."

"I want to have a real visitor soon," Lady Sara complained. "London is full of people, and yet we haven't had a visit from anyone."

"You know that is because your aunt is not well," he said. "After the first week of balls and parties you will have so many visitors you'll be begging for a rest from all the activities."

"That's all she talks about," Lady Vera complained.

"I'm sorry if it bothers you that I want to see someone other than you all the time."

The duke left his sisters grumbling with each other and walked over to Esmeralda. He wore a dark blue coat, light blue waistcoat, and fawn-colored riding breeches stuffed into his boots. She'd never seen a more powerful-looking and commanding man. And she had never met one who made her insides feel as if they were melting.

"Good morning, Miss Swift."

She curtsied. "Your Grace," she answered, and then under her breath added, "Were you standing outside the door eavesdropping on my conversation again?"

He gave her a mischievous smile. "I might have overheard some of what was said."

"Were you waiting for your sisters to come down so you could see how I handled them?"

"Why would I want to answer that question and possibly incriminate myself?"

"Why indeed?" she murmured as the twins walked over.

"The truth is," the duke said, turning to his sisters, "that

Miss Swift *has* come to see you two, so I hope you made her feel welcome."

"Of course we did." Lady Vera glanced at Esmeralda and smiled before looking back to her brother.

"Good, because Miss Swift will be taking your aunt's place and be your chaperone to all the balls, dinner parties, and afternoon card games. Everything you will attend for the Season."

The twins looked from Esmeralda to each other, clearly stunned.

"When you said you would employ someone to chaperone us, I didn't expect anyone quite so young," Lady Sara said softly.

Esmeralda was sure that their aunt and everyone else in Society would also be expecting the twins' chaperone to be older. But she wasn't, and they would just have to get used to that fact. Now that she had accepted this position, she fully intended to see it through to the end and, if all went well, collect the promised bonus as well.

"Me either," Lady Vera agreed, giving Esmeralda another once-over. "How long have you been a chaperone?"

She looked at the duke. "Not long. And I'm older than I appear."

"How old are you?"

"Vera, you don't ask someone's age."

"Why not, Sara? It's not rude. It's a simple question, and no one minds telling their age. It's not impertinent."

"I don't mind answering," Esmeralda said, once again hoping to avoid an argument between the two. "I'll be twenty-six in a few weeks, and I don't think that is considered young by anyone's standards."

"You're probably right," Vera said in a tone that let Esmeralda and Lady Sara know the subject was settled.

"We were expecting someone as old as Aunt Eve," Lady

Sara offered. "Most chaperones are. But I think we should like it that you are more our age than our aunt's."

"Miss Swift's age is not important; that you listen to her and do everything she says is," the duke said. "Show her the same respect you would your aunt. If I hear differently, I might decide send you back to Griffin, and wait until next year to make your debut."

"I don't believe you." Lady Vera challenged her brother with a determined look. "You want us to marry so you can finally be rid of us."

"I do want that," he conceded with an affectionate smile. "But it matters not to me whether it is this year or next. You will be back at the estate in Griffin with each other for another year while I will be in London enjoying my life as usual."

"You are teasing us," Lady Sara said.

He gave her cheek a loving pat. "If you doubt me on this, give Miss Swift trouble and see what happens."

"You are being a terrible bore, Griffin, and a bully too," Vera accused.

"That's because I'm your older brother and it's my job to be stern and look after you as our father would have. Now, Lady Evelyn has asked to see you both."

"Immediately?" Vera asked.

"Yes."

"But we want to stay here and get to know Miss Swift," Lady Sara complained.

"You will soon, but I need to talk to her first, and your aunt needs to talk to you."

Lady Vera looked over at her sister and gave her a smug smile. "What our dear brother is trying to tell us in a most tactful way is that Auntie Eve can't wait to find out what we think of our new chaperone."

"But we haven't had a chance to find out for ourselves yet."

"Go," the duke said to his sisters. "Miss Swift will be in the book room waiting for you when you come back down."

The twins walked out, grumbling to each other. Esmeralda turned to the duke, folded her arms across her chest, and asked, "Why didn't you tell your sisters about me before I arrived?"

He quirked his head and said, "I did."

Astonished, she said, "You couldn't have. They didn't know who I was and I didn't know what to say."

Looking as if puzzled by her statement, he said, "I told them I was going to employ someone to take Lady Evelyn's place as chaperone." He paused, his forehead wrinkled. "Perhaps I neglected to say I'd actually done that, and also your name."

"Perhaps?" He was unbelievable. He apparently didn't believe certain rules of civility applied to him.

Why should that shock her yet again?

Unperturbed by her comment, he simply said, "I do have duties other than taking care of my sisters, Miss Swift."

"I'm sure," she quipped. "Fencing, shooting, billiards, and maybe an occasional boxing match too."

He grinned attractively. "You forgot cards, racing my Thoroughbreds, and reading the morning newsprint."

Esmeralda harrumphed. "You know, Your Grace, I don't think I will have any trouble at all managing your sisters, but I'm not so sure the same will hold true for you."

He gave her a satisfied smile. "I would be disappointed in myself if you could manage me, Miss Swift."

She had no idea where she got the brazen audacity to talk so boldly to the duke, but knew she couldn't make a habit of it even though he'd given her permission to do so the first time they'd met. He would have limits of what he would tolerate from her.

"True words, I'm sure. Yet if our circumstances were different, I would still try."

"If our circumstances were different, I would want you to."

Much to her consternation, his softly spoken words made her heart trip. She quickly changed the tone of the conversation by asking, "Do you have any special instructions for me?"

"Lady Evelyn's maid, Harper, will be your messenger while you're here. She will deliver everything to you that you need, and if you have questions for Lady Evelyn, all you have to do is let Harper know. She'll relay them. Harper has organized my desk in the book room for you. All the invitations, notes, queries, or whatever you might need will be left for you there."

"I don't want to intrude in your private area. I can keep up with all correspondence in my room."

"No need. I won't be using the area while you are here."

"All right," she agreed. "And since that is now settled, there is something else I wanted to discuss with you"— she paused—"if you have the time."

"You will be taking care of my sisters. I will always have time for you."

Esmeralda's stomach tumbled deliciously. "*I will always have time for you.*"

Oh, why was he always saying exactly what she wanted to hear? The duke was dangerous. With a simple turn of phrase, he could make her lose all perspective. It was as if he knew exactly what to say to make her want to melt into a puddle of wonderful feelings right before his eyes. Why did such innocuously spoken words from him seem, at times, so intimate and heavenly to her ears?

"Yesterday," she said, swallowing past a shaky sigh, "Miss Truth's tittle-tattle said there might be someone out to ruin the twins' Season. Is there any validity to that claim?"

A fleeting expression of apprehension crossed his face. "There might be."

"You must have known this when you visited me a couple of days ago. Why didn't you mention it?"

"I was having a hard enough time as it was trying to get you to agree to help me. I didn't want to give you one more reason not to accept my offer of employment."

"If you thought this news would scare me off, you're wrong."

"I'm pleased to hear it, though considering how difficult it was to obtain your services you'll understand why I couldn't be sure."

"Has your aunt heard this rumor as well?"

"She wouldn't miss reading the weekly offerings from all the scandal sheets in London. It gives her great pleasure to inform me what they say whether or not it concerns me or one of my friends. I indulge my aunt and listen respectfully because it gives her such pleasure to fill me in on the latest gossip."

"It's kind of you to do that," Esmeralda said. "But do you actually think Lady Vera and Lady Sara could be pursued for meanness by an unscrupulous man? I mean, I find it hard to believe anyone would dare to ruin a duke's sister."

"There are some young men who would dare anything, Miss Swift."

Of that she had no doubt. And perhaps she felt like most everyone else. There had been no retribution to the rakes for what they'd done that Season.

"Yes, I suppose that's true."

"The source of the rumor looks to be reliable, but I have no proof anyone will be foolish enough to try anything. It may be something as simple as playing them for a fool. I don't know. That is why your job is so important. Every man who comes near them is a potential threat to their happiness. I won't take that possibility lightly."

"I agree you shouldn't. Do they know about this yet?"

"No." He paused as if thinking about what to say next. "I wish they didn't have to find out. I would rather they have as normal a Season as possible and be free to choose the man they want to marry without having to worry if his attention is true or false."

"It does seem unfair that they should be sought out for retribution rather than you and your friends."

"You don't pull your punches, do you, Miss Swift?"

"I am only stating the truth of what most people are thinking."

"Including you?"

A braver person might have answered affirmatively, but she would not be ensnared in that trap today. She would answer with some of his own words. "Why would I want to answer that and possibly incriminate myself?"

He lowered his voice. "You learn quickly."

Esmeralda didn't know her heart could beat so fast. "It's not hard when the teacher is a master."

"I could teach you many things, Miss Swift."

"Right now, all I need to know is when you plan to tell the twins."

He smiled. "For now, I don't plan to tell Sara and Vera at all."

"What? You can't mean that?"

"I do."

"Why?" she questioned. "I'm sure, as they get to know other young ladies at the balls and parties, they will hear this gossip. They'll be asked about it. I think they'll be upset you didn't share this with them."

"Probably, but I think it will upset them more if I tell them there is a rumor that someone is out to make mischief."

Forgetting her earlier determination to be more cautious with her words, she said, "I'm sorry, Your Grace, but that simply doesn't make sense."

"That's because you don't understand," he said calmly, appearing unruffled by her bold statement. "My sisters have been sheltered at Griffin for most of their lives. If I tell the twins about this rumor before the Season starts, they will assume I'm worried that something terrible will happen to them. If they think I'm worried, they'll be frightened. I don't want that. I know they'll hear about this gossip. When they do, they'll ask about it. I'll say that I heard the vile talk and that I think it's rubbish. I have dismissed it as scandalmongering and paid it no mind, and neither should they. I'll expect you to say the same should they come to you. That should calm their fears and allow them to continue to enjoy their Season."

She understood his reasoning, but still didn't agree with it. "I'll abide by your wishes, of course." She hesitated, then added, "Not to argue your point."

"But you will," he said before she could finish her thought. "I expected no less from you, Miss Swift."

She ignored his sarcasm. "Good. It's a valid one. And I know you didn't ask my opinion, but I'm not sure it's wise to keep this from your sisters. I agree that it's rational thought that they will take their cue from you and act as you do, but there is that old adage that says forewarned is forearmed."

He quirked his head and straightened, though his gaze didn't leave her face. "You make too much sense, Miss Swift. Your point is valid too. "

"Then perhaps you should listen to me," she said without any qualms she was going too far.

An attractive grin lifted the corners of the duke's mouth. "I can see you are used to giving orders around the employment agency. It's no wonder Mr. Fortescue thought you the best person to manage it for him. But your instructions and commands will not work on me."

She had no idea if that was a compliment or a slight, so she chose to disregard it and say, "I only have your sisters' best interests at heart."

"And that is why you are here."

"Do you have any idea who these men might be?"

"Only suspicions at this point."

"Don't you think you should let me know who you think they are so I can be aware if I see them with your sisters?"

He blew out a scornful breath. "If the number was smaller, perhaps so. There were twelve young ladies that we sent letters to that Season. Of the twelve, five have older and younger brothers. Some of the others have only younger or older brothers. Seven have fathers who are still living, and all twelve have numerous male cousins and uncles. So narrowing the field is not going to be easy until I have more information."

"Oh my. I can see that. Perhaps there is other information you can go on."

His brow furrowed with interest. "What has crossed your mind?"

"I would assume that if the young lady is married and happy with her life, none of the male family members would be bent on rehashing that unbecoming story to seek retribution. Do you have any idea how many ladies fall in that category?"

"No, but you may have something there. That should be easy enough to find out, and I do believe it would narrow the field considerably." He smiled. "That's very sound reasoning, Miss Swift."

She acknowledged his approval of her assessment with a smile of her own. "If a lady hasn't married these ten or so years, then perhaps her father or brother or whoever takes care of her would be more inclined to blame you, and the stunt, or scheme"—she paused—"I'm not sure how to refer to what you did."

She watched a flicker of something that looked very much like unease cross his face before he said, "I wagered on a prank. That's the way I thought of it at the time."

"Yes, well, others didn't feel that way."

"I know that now. I was young and foolish. The wager was never meant to harm anyone."

"However, it's quite possible someone could believe that the *prank* was the reason for a young lady's lack of marriageable prospects."

"You have no problem laying what you believe on the line, do you, Miss Swift?"

"I've found it's always easier to be blunt about someone else's misfortunes rather than delving into one's own."

"That's true. The wager happened so long ago, it's maddening that it's circulating once again. Of all the scandals London has seen in the past few years, I don't know why Miss Honora Truth decided to resurrect this one from the ashes of the past."

"Of course you do," Esmeralda said confidently. "Your sisters entering the marriage mart must have made it an easy choice for her. She wanted to make a name for herself in the gossip columns, and it's worked."

"If the writer is a she. I have my doubts about that. I can't help but think Miss Truth is actually a man at the publishing company hiding behind a woman's name. But no matter the gender, if the wager hadn't been brought to light again, my sisters wouldn't now be at someone's mercy." He blew out an audible breath. "It's not like any of the young ladies were actually harmed."

"But they were," she countered earnestly.

"How? Not one lady was touched by any of us."

"Not by your hands, but all of them were touched by the scandal. They put their reputations at risk and went to meet a secret admirer—a stranger. Surely you understand how improper it was for them to do that. After all, wasn't that the purpose of the prank? Besides, you really don't know how many of the ladies you might have harmed in some way, do you?"

Frustration clouded his eyes again. "I don't know anything for sure, Miss Swift," he argued. "But by the saints, why should meeting a secret admirer cause a young lady's reputation to be ruined if there never was an admirer to meet?"

"It could be that some gentlemen might have thought that because the ladies went to meet a secret admirer, they could be tempted to do so again, or maybe that they had actually done it before. It could have caused some beaus to second-guess the young ladies' virtue. You can't deny that they put it all at risk by being willing to meet a man, an unknown man, in secret."

"I will concede that it's a good possibility we did more damage than any of us realized at the time or since."

"And I will concede that getting all twelve young ladies to fall for the same prank at the same time was quite a feat that hadn't been done before, nor has it since."

"No one else has been as foolish as we were at the time."

"I never heard. How did the story manage to get in all the gossip columns?"

"It was our own fault. No one was to ever know. We'd done other questionable things and hadn't been caught."

"I'm sure."

A grunted laugh passed his lips. "Yes. That would surprise no one. I've never pretended to be a saint."

She smiled. "It would have done you no good to have done so. How did the prank become public knowledge?"

His eyes took on a faraway quality, and she could see he was remembering back to that time all those years ago.

"After the secret admirer letters went out, we each had our own hiding place where we could watch to see how many young ladies had come to meet us. The one who had the most ladies show up would win the wager. But believe me the money wasn't important. We all had such a desire to best the other no matter what we were doing. It was having the right to boasting that fueled us. And that was our downfall."

"So you went around bragging about what you'd done?"

"No," he said adamantly. "Not to others. As I said, no one was to know but us. We never talked about our wagers with anyone else. We usually met in the reading room at White's as it's seldom used in the wee hours of the morning. Deep in our brandy bottles as we were that night, we didn't check to make sure the room was empty. As fate would have it, Mr. Howard Drayton had fallen asleep in one of the chairs facing the fire. We didn't see him. After we'd all had a good laugh about the outcome, Drayton decided to make himself known to us. He said he wouldn't expose what we'd done if we'd each pay him a tidy sum each month to keep his gambling pockets plump. You can imagine how we felt about that."

"You didn't pay him?

"Hell no." He paused and searched her eyes. When he saw no censure for swearing, he continued. "In hindsight, perhaps we should have given in to his demands, but it went against our nature to be intimidated to that point. We knew it would do no good to threaten him because he had the prince's ear."

"I don't recognize his name. Where is he now? Is it possible he is behind this?"

"Not unless he is doing it from the grave. He was killed in a duel about three years ago. Accused of cheating at cards. But in any case, for now at least, I will stand by my original plan not to tell my sisters about the rumor and wait for them to come to me."

"As you wish."

"I'll be over each evening to escort the three of you to the parties, remain there with you, and then I'll see you home each night."

"Very well," she said, knowing she had no more arguments to make. "We shall be ready."

"Good," he answered. "Should you need anything, or if anything happens you think I should know, tell Sparks to find me and I will come to you."

I will come to you.

His words created a slow curl of sensation in her stomach. "I understand and will do so, but I don't foresee any complications arising that should require your immediate attention."

"Then I should leave you to get settled in."

She thought he was going to move away from her, but instead he stepped closer, lowered his voice, and said, "You didn't use the dressmaker I suggested."

That statement took her aback. Her first thought was to deny it, but that would have been foolish, not to mention dishonest. The truth was always the best answer even when it might be the hardest thing to say.

"No," she admitted.

"Why?"

The word wasn't accusing in any way. It was so softly spoken, it was almost sensual. Her breathing increased. "I found her much too expensive, and I'm far too practical to overspend when it isn't necessary. But how did you know?"

"I told her not to let you have anything in the color gray."

Shocked, she whispered, "You didn't."

"I did. I told you, I take care of my own, Miss Swift. You are a part of my household."

Her chest tightened. The muscles in her abdomen quivered enticingly. *I take care of my own. I will come to you. You are a part of my household.* More innocently spoken words that sent all of her senses reeling, and reminded her that he was standing so close she could feel the heat from his strong body, smell the shaving soap that had bathed his face, and hear his calm, steady breathing. She must find a way not to be seduced by words that were never intended the way they fell on her ears.

He was gently caressing her with his gaze. But then perhaps she was caressing him with hers too.

Somehow she managed to ask, "Is there a reason you don't want me wearing gray?"

"It's a matronly color."

"And it suits perfectly for my position here in your household as chaperone."

"Then perhaps gray is the best color for you after all, but the square of white lace covering your hair must go."

Without thinking she reached up and touched the small scarf, then slowly let her hand slide down the side of her head. "It makes me look older."

"I know." He bent his face closer to hers. "You have no need to look older when you're in this house, do you? We all know your age."

"Very well, I'll do as you ask."

His face moved closer until he touched his nose to hers. Not knowing what to say or do, she was rigid. He caressed her nose with his for a moment or two before letting it glide across her skin where he pressed his cheek against hers.

What the duke was doing was highly inappropriate behavior, but the thrill of his light touch was so new to her she couldn't back away from him. For a moment, Esmeralda thought she might swoon, but then, with his lips resting so close to her ear, he whispered, "You know I'm attracted to you, don't you, Miss Swift?"

No, she didn't know. She only knew how she felt. Her breath turned hard and choppy. Her heart started twirling like a spinning wheel again. Something wonderful and eager unfurled and fluttered deep inside her. All she had to do was turn her head, and their lips would meet. She would then know what it would feel like to be kissed.

"And you are attracted to me."

"No," she lied without hesitation. She had to. She couldn't expose herself to him and become more vulnerable than she already was. She had to think of Josephine and not the disturbing and sensuous and confusing feelings going on inside her at his nearness.

He kept his lips at her ear. His tone was soft and melodious as he said, "Yes, Miss Swift. You are. I sense it. I feel it. I know it. But I don't mind you denying it."

She silently prayed he wouldn't ask her again to admit that to him. It would be her undoing and she would probably collapse into his arms and beg him to kiss her before she fainted.

"But you also know I can't do anything about our attraction to each other, don't you?" he continued in the soft husky voice that was mesmerizing her.

Her heart was pounding so fiercely and her breathing was so shallow, she couldn't say anything. She was past talking unless she whispered *Kiss me now!*

The duke straightened and looked down into her eyes. "You are under my protection, and that means I must protect you from myself as well."

Somewhere deep inside herself she found the courage to back away from him and found the breath to say, "I'm glad to hear that, Your Grace. Now, if you don't mind, I would like to get settled in my new position."

He nodded once. "I'll leave you to it," he said and turned away.

Chapter 11

Do be willing to give in when it's clear
you have lost the argument.

❧

MISS MAMIE FORTESCUE'S DO'S AND DON'TS FOR
CHAPERONES, GOVERNESSES, TUTORS, AND NURSES

Griffin turned to leave Miss Swift but stopped dead in his tracks. Thank God he hadn't given in to his overwhelming desire to kiss her. A red-haired girl with sparkling green eyes and cheeks lightly dusted with freckles was in the doorway staring at him. A short-legged, long-haired blond dog stood quietly beside her.

It surprised him that he hadn't heard the two approaching. He was usually aware of his surroundings at all times. Perhaps he'd been concentrating a little too much on Miss Swift. For the dog not to have made a peep of sound meant he was either very well trained or too old to be interested in the goings on of people.

"Your Grace," Miss Swift said, rushing up beside him. "May I present my sister—"

"Miss Josephine," he interrupted. "I've been expecting to meet you."

The girl curtsied and said, "I wanted to meet you too, Your Grace. It's a pleasure. May I present my friend Napoleon?"

The dog's tail wagged back and forth. Griffin knew the animal wanted to rush and sniff him, but Napoleon stayed right beside his owner waiting for the command.

"You may," Griffin said and bent over and held down his hand to the short dog. Taking that as a cue, Napoleon sniffed Griffin's hand, licked around his fingers, and then barked once. "He's well trained," Griffin said as he straightened and looked back at Josephine.

"Essie said we couldn't keep him if I couldn't train him to behave properly. But it didn't take long. He already knew most things."

He glanced over at Miss Swift. She looked worried, but she shouldn't be. He didn't mind that her sister had come as long as his sisters were taken care of. Looking back to Josephine, he said, "You do know that Napoleon is not a name that is held in high regard throughout most of England, don't you?"

"I know," the girl said as casually as if they were talking about the weather. "But I like the name. And I think it's a good name for a dog."

Griffin smiled. "So do I."

Josephine sighed quietly as she looked up at him and added, "You're tall."

"No, Josephine," Miss Swift admonished, stepping in closer to her sister. "It's not your place to say things like that to a duke."

Griffin held up his hand to stay Miss Swift's objection as he looked down at Josephine and said, "You're short."

"Yes, but I'm still growing. I'll get taller one day. You're as tall as you will ever be."

Griffin chuckled. "That I am. And what about Napoleon? Is he still a growing pup?"

"No, he's old like you."

He heard Miss Swift suck in another gasp as he responded, "I suppose at twenty-eight I am getting old." Griffin hadn't expected the girl to be so outspoken, but he should have, given the boldness of Miss Swift. Though she looked nothing like Miss Swift, they had the same daring personality.

"Do you have a dog?" the girl asked.

"Not here in London. I have a spaniel at my home in Griffin, and rest assured, he is not named after a defeated French emperor."

Josephine smiled up at him, and Griffin had no doubts the girl knew exactly what she was doing when she named her dog.

"What's your dog's name?" she asked.

"Jasper."

"That's a good name for a dog. Is he the reddish-brown color of most jasper stone?"

"As a matter of fact, he is."

"I like my room. Napoleon likes it too. Thank you for letting us stay here with Essie."

That was the second time she'd called Miss Swift "Essie." He approved of the nickname she had for her sister and wondered if Miss Swift ever called her "Josie" or "Jessie." *Probably not,* he thought. With flame-red hair and deep green eyes, "Josephine" fit the girl perfectly. He wouldn't shorten it either.

"May I ask you something?"

"No, you may not." Miss Swift spoke up again. "Enough of this chattering, Josephine. His Grace has been very patient with you, but you have taken up enough of his time."

Griffin glanced over at Miss Swift and said, "Did you forget I grew up with two sisters in the house demanding their older brother's attention and that of his friends whenever they were around? You are worrying too much.

When she has a question, let her ask and I'll answer—if I can."

"All right."

He then returned his attention to Josephine, and in a good-natured voice with a grin on his lips asked, "Do you ever get to say what you want to when she's around?"

Josephine stared up at her sister and preened delightedly before looking at Griffin and saying, "Not often. She talks a lot."

He chuckled. "That's what I was thinking. You have permission to ask me whatever you want whenever you want."

"You might regret saying that to her, Your Grace," Miss Swift offered.

Griffin took note that Miss Swift was a little miffed that he'd given her sister the same permission he gave her to speak freely to him. She had a choke hold on the braided cords of the little velvet reticule she held. And he had to admit that Miss Swift's show of displeasure was very enticing to a man who already wanted to pull her into his arms and kiss her until she sighed with passion.

"I believe I told you that I like a woman who knows her mind and isn't afraid to speak it."

"Do you have a back garden?" Josephine asked.

Clearing his wayward thoughts and his throat, Griffin said, "That's an easy question to answer. I do."

"May I take Napoleon outside to play in it?"

When was the last time anyone had asked such a simple request of him? To play in his garden. He couldn't remember a time in recent years. Being a duke, there was always someone wanting something from him. Usually the requests were from someone in Parliament, another peer, his overseers or accountants, and sometimes his tenants. And the favors were usually much harder to accomplish than saying a simple *yes* to a twelve-year-old girl.

"I don't see why not."

"All by ourselves?" she asked with eager excitement showing in her face. "Essie won't let us go outside alone where we live."

"Your sister is probably right about that. It's not safe or proper in a business district."

"That's what she says."

"But while you are here at my house, you and Napoleon may play in my garden as often and long as you wish without supervision."

Her eyes brightened like stars. "Thank you, Your Grace!"

Griffin quickly looked over at Miss Swift. "That is if it doesn't interfere with anything your sister has planned for you. Her wishes must come first."

"They always do," Josephine said.

"In that case, I'll speak to Sparks so he'll know you have permission to treat this house as your home while you are here. One other thing. My gardener, Fenton, will probably be out there most days. He might have other men with him sometimes." He glanced over at Miss Swift. "The man prides himself on his talents to produce the biggest and best blooms in the Royal Horticulture Society. Other gardeners often stop by to see what he's growing for the May Day Fair."

"I like flowers too, but we won't bother Mr. Fenton," Josephine said. "I promise."

"I didn't think you would, but I wanted you to know his name should you be out when he's working."

Another big smile spread across her face. "Thank you, Your Grace. May we go out now?"

"I'm fine with it." He looked at Miss Swift again.

"Yes, of course, you may," she said to Josephine.

"But you don't have permission to open the gate and go outside the garden," he said. "Understand?"

"Don't worry, we won't. Thank you, Your Grace."

Then, suddenly, without warning, the girl rushed him, threw her slender, still-childlike arms around his waist and hugged him tightly for about two seconds before turning loose and stepping away. Napoleon took that as a sign he should show appreciation too. He jumped up on Griffin's leg and barked.

"Josephine!" Miss Swift exclaimed. "You shouldn't have done that. Napoleon sit!"

The girl's action surprised Griffin as much as it did Miss Swift, but he didn't mind. Though he'd much rather it had been Miss Swift's arms around him. He patted the girl's head a couple of times and then the dog, who had obeyed his master and rested on his haunches.

"You must never touch the duke again," Miss Swift reprimanded Josephine.

"I wanted to thank him," she argued convincingly. "I hug you when I thank you."

"That's because I am your sister. It's not the proper way for you to thank a duke."

Josephine rolled her big green eyes up at him and said, "I'm sorry, Your Grace."

"I never mind a hug from a young lady, Miss Josephine. You did nothing wrong in showing your gratitude." He nodded his head toward Miss Swift and said, "Your sister is too prickly."

"She sure is." Josephine gave Griffin another big smile and whirled away. "Come on, Napoleon, I'll go get my coat and we'll go outside and play."

As the two ran down the corridor, Miss Swift turned to him. "She shouldn't have been so familiar with you. The only justification I have is that her father was a very affectionate man. I'm sure she didn't realize that was inappropriate. We haven't been around a lot of men for me to explain to her that it shouldn't be done."

"You are fretting for no reason, Miss Swift. It was only a hug, and a brief one at that. No explanations or apologies are necessary. My sisters have been hugging me since before they left the nursery."

"That's kind of you to say. I do appreciate you being so nice to her about it."

"I like hugs, don't you?"

With those few words spoken so casually, the atmosphere around them changed in an instant. The intense yet gentle look in his eyes made her breaths come fast and choppy. "I, well, of course I do."

"Then, tell me, Miss Swift, when was the last time you were hugged?"

She didn't know for sure. *A long time,* she lamented to herself, but softly asked, "What?"

Griffin found himself wondering if she had ever been held in the arms of a man and kissed. Passionately. The way he wanted to hold her and kiss her right now. It didn't matter whether or not she had, but for some reason, he wanted to know.

He inched closer to her. "You heard me. When was the last time you were hugged? From someone other than your sister, or your mother or father."

Her eyes grew wide. "I'm not exactly sure," she hedged, not wanting to tell him the truth that she hadn't ever been.

"Recently?"

"Probably not. But I really don't see how that is any of your concern, Your Grace."

It wasn't, but he still wanted to know. "I'm curious."

"And I'm not going to answer such a personal question or continue further on this subject. I'll just say I'm pleased you're not upset with Josephine's fresh behavior and leave it at that."

He was right when he'd thought that Miss Swift would know just how to keep him in line. That was good, because with the least bit of encouragement, Griffin could so easily cross that line of what was acceptable where she was concerned. She reminded him that she was not available for him to pursue.

He watched her inhale. He had no doubt she knew what he was thinking. He'd wanted to kiss her. Hellfire, he'd wanted to since the first time he saw her. Everything about her had drawn him to her when he first saw her, and that hadn't changed.

Suddenly there was barking from the front of the house. An ear-piercing scream shattered the stillness. It was followed by a loud crash and then something rumbling down the stairs.

Chapter 12

Don't worry about things you can't control.
Do control the things you can.

❧

Esmeralda almost jumped out of her skin as her gaze flew to the duke's. He was alarmed too. Fearing it was Josephine tumbling down the stairs, she dropped her reticule to the floor and took off running. The duke must have thought the same thing, because he rushed past her as she cleared the doorway.

Entering the corridor, Esmeralda saw a tabby cat scampering off the last step of the stairs. Napoleon was right behind the cat, barking like a fiend. Josephine was behind the dog, screaming his name and running after him. Thankfully she wasn't harmed, but a small broken table lay at the foot of the stairs.

"Josephine, what happened?" Esmeralda ask breathlessly, but there was no time for an answer.

The cat darted into a room off the vestibule with the barking dog right on its tail.

"Napoleon! Stop! Sit!" Esmeralda added her cries to
halt and calm the dog as she, Josephine, and the duke all
tried to go through the door at the same time.

They bumped shoulders, elbows, and hips. Six arms
and six hands all pushed and tangled together in the trio's
haste to get inside and catch the animals. Josephine shoved
her way through two of them first and squealed in horror
again as Esmeralda and the duke skidded to a halt beside
her. The cat had jumped on top of a table and sent a figurine flying to the floor where it shattered into hundreds of
pieces.

At the same time, Napoleon rounded a chair and side-
swiped a large urn. It teetered from side to side. Esmeralda and the duke stumbled over each other in a rush to
save it, but the large vase toppled to the floor with a loud
thud and broke into several pieces before either of them
could reach it.

Esmeralda thought she might stop breathing. But there
was no time to even do that as the cat quickly altered his
course and dashed right toward her. As she reached down
and grabbed the cat, he scratched at her. His claws dug into
the bodice of her dress, and he shrieked as if he thought
all the hounds in hell were giving him chase. Napoleon's
front paws landed on Esmeralda's skirt as he jumped to
reach the cat. The duke scooped up the barking dog and
moved him away from the cat.

Horrified, Esmeralda called, "Napoleon! Quiet!" The
dog instantly stopped barking and scrambling to get down
from the duke's arms. He quickly turned around and licked
the duke's chin and lips before the duke had time to move
his face away from the excited dog.

Anguished by all that had happened, and knowing
that any chance she had of keeping her position in this
household had just evaporated, Esmeralda advanced on the
duke and exclaimed, "This is all your fault, Your Grace!"

"My fault?" the surprised duke countered as hastily as she'd spoken. "How is that possible, Miss Swift? I was in the drawing room with you when all this commotion started."

She glared at him and said, "Because you didn't tell me you had a cat in the house."

The air between them crackled with tension as he advanced on her. Napoleon woofed and squirmed to get near the cat again, but the duke held him firmly. His blue gaze pinioned hers. "I didn't know."

Searing disappointment in her inability to keep this debacle from happening made her bristle at his annoyed tone. "Don't be ridiculous," she said.

"I'm not," he answered, holding the squirming dog tighter.

Esmeralda knew she was behaving irrationally. She should listen to her inner voice and quiet herself. She shouldn't be accusing the duke of anything, but fear made her unable to stop herself. She'd lived in Viscount Mayeforth's house long enough to know how servants who broke things were treated. She knew how uncompromising and how unforgiving the titled few were.

"How could you not know? This is your house."

His head tilted defiantly. "It is my house, but I don't live here. My sisters do."

"Then maybe you should spend more time here with them so that you know what's going on in it."

"It looks as if I will need to if this is an example of what's going to happen while you're here. If anyone is at fault, Miss Swift, it's you. You told me this dog was trained to obey your sister."

"No dog will obey its master if its sees a strange cat. The temptation is too great."

"Oh, I know all about great temptations, Miss Swift. I'm having a few of them myself right now."

"So am I," she countered, infuriated that she'd lost the opportunity to make a better life for Josephine and for herself. She was more than upset that Josephine wouldn't get to experience a little of what it would be like to live in a fine house and play in a large garden.

"Why are you two yelling at each other?" Josephine asked.

Esmeralda and the duke looked over at Josephine. Her lips quivered and tears had pooled in her eyes. Esmeralda's heart broke.

"We're not," they said in unison.

"It's my fault Napoleon knocked the table down the stairs and broke the urn. Not yours."

"It's no one's fault," the duke said, keeping his intense gaze on Esmeralda as he continued to control the excited dog. "It was an accident."

"May I be of assistance to you, Your Grace?" Sparks said calmly from the doorway as Lady Sara and Lady Vera skidded up to flank him.

Lady Vera gasped as she surveyed the broken pieces scattered around the floor. "What happened?"

"Oh my!" Lady Sara cried as she covered her mouth with her hands. "How did the cat get out of my room?"

"This must be the girl and her dog," Lady Vera said. "Auntie Eve was just telling us about them."

Her anger spent, despair settled around Esmeralda. She could have never imagined anything so catastrophic would happen. And all because of a cat. She swallowed hard and opened her mouth to tell the duke they would leave immediately, but he spoke first.

"Lady Vera, Lady Sara, this is Miss Swift's sister, Miss Josephine, and her dog, Napoleon."

In the midst of all that happened and with tears in her bright green eyes, Josephine had the presence of mind to curtsy to the young ladies after the introduction and say a greeting.

Lady Vera stepped farther into the room. "I thought you must have been teasing Auntie Eve when you told her their names were Napoleon and Josephine."

"I was not teasing, and I'm in no mood for teasing right now, Vera," the duke said. "They will be living here with Miss Swift for the Season. I suppose I should have mentioned it when we were talking earlier."

"That's highly irregular," Vera offered. "That a chaperone would bring her sister and her dog with her."

"They are here because that's the way I want it," he answered.

"Well, all right. I don't mind." Vera huffed. "But if Miss Swift could bring her dog to Mayfair, why couldn't we bring Jasper with us to London?"

Esmeralda watched the duke's jaw tighten. She was waiting for an opportunity to enter into the conversation so she could excuse herself, Josephine, and Napoleon and get out of the house with the least amount of fanfare as possible.

"I've never kept you from bringing Jasper," the duke said. "If you wanted to bring him, all you had to do was do it."

"I didn't think you would allow us to."

"Why didn't you ask? He's as much, if not more, your dog than mine. I would have told you to bring him." He turned to his other sister and asked, "Sara, is that your cat?"

"Not exactly," she timidly said, looking at the excited tabby in Esmeralda's arms.

"Then what, exactly?" he asked pointedly.

"I saw him in the front of our house yesterday, so I picked him up and brought him inside to give him some milk. I was going to put him back out when it grew dark, but instead, I ended up keeping him in my room all night.

My maid must have let him out. I'm sorry, Griffin. I should have asked for permission before keeping him, but he was so friendly."

"He's clean and looks well fed," the duke offered, as Napoleon tried to lick his face again. "I don't think he's a stray. He obviously belongs to someone, and they are probably looking for him to return."

"Don't be angry with her, Griffin," Lady Vera said, coming to her sister's defense. "She had no way of knowing there would be a dog in the house today."

He inhaled deeply and looked at Josephine. "I'm not angry with anyone."

"You sounded like you were," Josephine said.

"You're right, I did. I'm sorry about that." He looked over at Esmeralda. His gaze swept down her face. "And I think your sister is sorry too. Aren't you, Miss Swift?"

If only he knew. "Immensely sorry, Your Grace, and Josephine."

"I'm sorry too," Sara said softly to Josephine. "It was my fault about the cat, but I like your dog."

"He's usually a good dog."

"He will be again," the duke said, walking over and handing Napoleon to Sparks. "Take him outside." He then turned to Josephine. "Go with him," he told her as he took the cat from Esmeralda's arms and gave him to Lady Sara. "Sara, put him back out the front door where you found him so he can find his way back home. Do not bring him back into this house as long as Napoleon is here. Vera, go tell Lady Evelyn what happened before the stress from all the noise has her rash spreading to the other side of her face. I'm sure she's desperate to know what all the uproar was about." He then turned to Esmeralda and said, "You stay there."

Esmeralda groaned silently as she nodded for the tearful Josephine to follow Sparks out and then watched as the twins quietly left the room too. She should have known that working for the duke, earning the kind of money he'd promised, was only a dream. A very fine dream that had filled her with the kind of excited anticipation she hadn't had since before her mother died.

Why had she let herself believe their lives would be different, better than before they met the duke? Why had she agreed to try? She should have never said yes to the determined duke. Getting her hopes up and Josephine's too only to have them dashed caused a great hurt deep in her soul.

Esmeralda's mind was a blur of many thoughts, her body a mixture of emotions out of control. One word from the duke, and Mr. Fortescue wouldn't let her continue managing the employment agency. She and Josephine would have to leave the building, and they didn't have anywhere else to go.

She remained stiff and solemn as the doorway cleared and the house fell silent after the footsteps faded and the doors were shut. Bracing herself for the words she knew were coming, she lowered her chin and moistened her dry lips. The only good thing was that she hadn't had time to unpack, so they could leave quickly.

When she was brave enough to shift her gaze to the duke, he was smiling.

Her world had been turned upside down and he was smiling?

She felt as if her heart sank to her feet and filled them with lead. He was going to enjoy throwing them out! Oh, why had things gone so horribly wrong?

"That cat gave Napoleon quite the chase," he said

Her chest was too heavy to move. Her stomach jumped so fast she could hardly breathe as a lump of cold emotion settled thickly in her throat, making her "What?" sound more like a croak.

He chuckled. "That was the most excitement I've seen around this house in years."

Was he laughing? Perhaps she could find amusement in the dog chasing the cat if not for the fact she didn't want to lose this position. Didn't he know how much this meant to her?

She tried to keep her upper lip stiff as she said, "I don't find this comical, Your Grace."

His expression challenged her. "You don't?"

"No," she said softly.

"Not after we knew it wasn't your sister tumbling down the stairs? I admit that gave me cause for alarm too."

Regret consumed her. Unable to give a verbal response, she shook her head.

"How about when all three of us were trying to get through the doorway at the same time. Surely, you think that was a little amusing, don't you? I do believe your hand hit me in the face twice and Josephine elbowed me in the ribs and stepped on my foot."

He was doing a good job of trying to make her feel better, but Esmeralda was in no mood to stay around and have him beguile her with all he found delightful about the incident.

"I'll gather our things together and we'll leave as soon as possible."

"What?" He walked over to her. The smile faded from his expression. "Leave? What do you mean? After all I had to promise you in order to talk you into taking this position? Now that you are finally here, do you really think I'm going to let you leave?"

They stood toe-to-toe. His gaze penetrated hers. "I didn't think you would want me to stay now."

"Why?" Fierce concentration settled on his face. "Because in the heat of the moment we raised our voices to each other?"

"No, not just that," she declared. "I understand that the

tension of the incident got to both of us. Look." She pointed to the urn. "Napoleon broke a table, a vase and a figurine, in case you don't remember. I can't possibly pay for those things."

His features softened. "You won't be asked to. Neither were prized possessions or held great value. How many more times are you going to try to get out of working for me?"

Through a catch in her breath, she managed to say, "You mean you really want me to stay? I mean, all three of us? You're not going to throw us out?"

He ran an open hand through his hair and shook his head. "Throw you out? Did you really think I would do that?"

She nodded.

"I'm going to have to change your opinion of me, Miss Swift." His voice was soft, soothing. "I want *you* to watch over my sisters. I don't know how I can make that any clearer to you."

"What if Napoleon breaks something else?"

His gleaming blue eyes held steady on hers. "What if he does?"

Her skin peppered with goose bumps at his intense gaze, at his closeness. It truly didn't seem fair that she was so susceptible to his nearness, to his very presence.

The duke placed his fingertips under her chin, nudging it upward. A thrill of something, which could only be described as feeling like a lightning strike, bolted through her, heated her with a shocking, shimmering, delicious warmth.

"What if he does?" he asked again as his palm cupped her jaw with a gentle sweetness that beckoned her to relax and welcome his touch.

She watched his lips as he talked, and all she could

think was that she wanted to feel his lips on hers. She wanted to be caught up in his strong embrace, held against his powerful chest. What madness! To change the direction of her thoughts and those traitorous desires springing up inside her, she said, "You will be unhappy."

"No. You will be. I won't." His thumb lightly rubbed up her cheek, to the corner of her mouth and then across her lips.

Her lips tingled. Her breasts tightened and her stomach quaked at the boldness and the intimacy of his thumb caressing her.

"Accidents happen," he said softly. "It's over."

His touch was reassuring and so much more. It was comforting, delicious, and persuasive. She knew the prudent thing to do was recoil from his hand, his nearness, but she simply didn't have the will to deny herself the closeness and feeling of his warmth.

"I rather enjoyed you taking me to task about the cat," he said huskily, keeping his hand on her jaw, his fingers brushing her cheek so lightly.

He bent his head closer to hers. Much too close. And still closer. She held her breath, thinking surely he was going to kiss her. And she was going to let him.

Instead, he whispered so close to her lips she felt his warm breath waft across hers, "I don't believe I've ever had a young woman yell at me."

"No," she countered earnestly. "I didn't yell at you. Did I? I mean, I might have raised my voice—a little."

The edges of his mouth twisted into an attractive smile. "A little?"

Her chest heaved with embarrassment over what she'd done, over desperately wanting him to kiss her so badly she was ready to initiate the kiss herself.

After a long intake of breath that ended on a shaky sigh, she noticed that the fire had burned low, giving peaceful warmth and a golden glow to the morning shadows that filtered through the windowpanes. "In that case, I should apologize."

"No need for that," he said as his fingertips slowly caressed their way down her neck to the hollow of her throat and back up again to her cheek. "I told you to always feel free to speak your mind to me. That's one of the things I find so appealing about you."

Esmeralda found everything about him appealing. His thumb ran across her lips again and, dear heavens, the sensations that spiraled through her made her tremble with a need she'd never had before, a need she didn't understand. She was certain he could sense her shaking, sense her silently begging him to kiss her.

"You may regret saying that."

"I don't think I will. Besides my voice was loud too. No harm was done. Servants break things. It's part of life."

Servants.

That word brought her up short, and she stiffened. That was all she was to him. All she would ever be. A servant to help his sisters. How could she have forgotten?

She had to swallow the bitter taste of it and remember it every time her heart started beating faster at the sight of him. Every time she wanted to be caught up in his strong arms. Every time she dreamed about his lips on hers. Every time she heard him say, *I want you, you're a part of my household, I'll always have time for you,* or similar innocent phrases that delighted her senses and made her feel special, she must remember she was a servant. She was in his life as an employee, not as a member of Polite Society, not as a guest in his house.

And not as his social equal.

She turned her head away from his touch and stepped away from him on shaky legs, angry at herself for forgetting that she was nothing to him but a person to look after his sisters.

"Thank you for being so understanding about that, Napoleon, everything." She lifted her chin and her shoulders. "Is there anything more that you need from me this morning? If not, I'd like to get started on my work."

He looked as if he was going to speak, but stopped himself and dropped his hand to his side. "Do you see any reason the twins won't be ready for the first ball?"

"No, none at all," she said, pulling herself together quickly and returning to a professional stance. "But I just realized I do have one question for you before you leave."

"All right."

"It's about the five on Lady Evelyn's list of acceptable gentlemen for Lady Vera and Lady Sara to consider for a possible match. Am I to assume they have been cleared of having any interest in the mischief of ruining the twins' Season?"

"No one has been ruled out."

"So that includes your friends the Duke of Rathburne and the Duke of Hawksthorn?"

A glint of admiration shown in his eyes. "I seldom have to admit this, but I was wrong. Those two have been ruled out. They adore my sisters and would never seek to harm them. They will help us watch over Vera and Sara at the parties."

"Good. I'm glad I'm clear on that."

"Anything else?"

"That's all."

"Then once again I'll bid you good day, Miss Swift."

Chapter 13

Don't get caught in the middle of a family matter
by voicing your opinion. Do be mum on
your view of things.

‹›‹›‹›

MISS MAMIE FORTESCUE'S DO'S AND DON'TS FOR
CHAPERONES, GOVERNESSES, TUTORS, AND NURSES

Esmeralda couldn't watch the duke walk away. She stared at the broken figurine and urn. Her shoulders slumped with relief as she let out a heavy silent sigh. The sensations he'd created inside her were confusing at best. She couldn't believe the duke's touch had stirred her to the point of madness. That she was aching for him to wrap her into his arms and kiss her with all the passion she was feeling couldn't be anything but madness.

She closed her eyes and expelled a deep breath.

He was right when he'd said she was attracted to him. She was. Immensely so, but there was nothing to do about it but fight it, deny it, and make sure she kept it to herself. What she was doing for her future and Josephine's had to be at the forefront of her mind. She'd been given another chance. She must not lose it over silly notions of kissing and these mysteriously feminine feelings he aroused inside her. That she even kept the post was a miracle considering all the damage Napoleon had caused.

Perhaps the duke wasn't as set in his beliefs and as unforgiving as Viscount Mayeforth had been. In any case, it would only be for six weeks at the most. Surely she could keep her wits about her, keep Napoleon under control, and her feelings for the duke at bay for that long.

Shaking off the lingering effects of his touch and her desires for more, Esmeralda walked down the corridor. She looked into the open doorways as she passed, stopping to give a closer look to the dining room. A highly polished table was surrounded by chairs covered with a golden-colored brocade that matched the draperies. Placed in the middle of the long table was a large silver urn with a lion's-head handle on each end. Past that room was a small music room. A pianoforte and a harp stood in one of the far corners. Chairs were lined around the walls, as if a musical might be planned for that evening.

The last room on the left was the book room, the duke's private study. The first thing she noticed when she stepped inside was its warmth. A fire was burning, but the heat that enveloped her came from a far different source than the small leaping flames. It had been from the look in the duke's blue gaze, the expressions on his face, and his nearness when he touched her. She looked around and smiled. There was something intimate about having free reign of the duke's private study. But her practical side reared up. Those were the things she must find a way to put out of her mind and remember she was a mere servant to him.

Both sides of the room were lined with shelves stuffed with books of all sizes. She hadn't seen that many bound copies all in one place since she and her mother left Viscount Mayeforth's house almost fifteen years ago.

On the back wall were twin windows. The chocolate-colored draperies were pulled back and sunshine streamed inside, making the dust particles shimmer in the air. A small round table and lamp sat between two comfortable-looking, upholstered armchairs. It was easy to imagine herself curled up in one sipping warm chocolate, reading until the sun faded, then lighting a lamp and continuing until darkness covered the sky.

Esmeralda was suddenly filled with sweet memories of her youth. When she lived in a spacious house like this instead of working in one. When she had servants instead of being one. For a few moments she allowed herself the time to indulge in those happy remembrances of a life with no worries, no responsibilities, and no thoughts of the future except to attend the Season and fall in love with a handsome gentleman. She'd missed those days of her youth, and she could never get them back.

Because her mother had made the choice of love over family and left Polite Society behind, Esmeralda now had a different future than she was brought up expecting. She supposed it was impossible to keep all her memories at bay. And now she'd added another to her storehouse of the past. The duke's intimate touch and all the thrilling sensations it awakened inside her.

At that thought she laughed. She supposed one never got too old to daydream and think about love, to want the touch of a handsome prince and to see desire for her in his eyes. Surely there was nothing wrong with permitting herself the fantasy of enjoying them all once in a while.

But for now, she reminded herself again, she could only go forward and see to it that Josephine had a good life.

Taking a steadying breath, she walked over to the desk. Stacks of papers and cards were lined up in meticulous order under headings. *Accepted invitations. Declined invitations. Alternate Invitations.* Placed on the desk in front of the chair was a note addressed to Esmeralda. Beside it was a daily appointment calendar that started with the first ball of the Season.

She skimmed down the pages that held all the events they would be attending as well as the times for afternoons and evenings. Their days would be busy, but thanks to Lady Evelyn's thoroughness it would be very easy to follow exactly what to do. Esmeralda picked up the letter addressed to her and broke the wax seal.

> Dear Miss Swift,
> The duke told me he has explained why employing you was necessary. So I will dispense with further mention of it and so will you. He assures me you are capable for the duties for which you have been positioned. The only thing left is for you to prove that you are.
> If you have studied my previous notes that the duke delivered to you, you know what I expect from you.
> Each morning I will hear from Lady Sara and Lady Vera about the evening before and will have Harper deliver further instructions to you for the day.
> I await your questions.
>
> Lady Evelyn

That note was about as direct as could be, Esmeralda thought.

From a distance, Esmeralda heard Napoleon barking and Josephine squealing with delight. She laid the note down on the desk, walked over to the window, and looked out. Josephine was running and holding a long length of ribbon out behind her. It fluttered and flapped in the wind as Napoleon chased after her, nipping at the flowing piece of satin. Her red hair bounced and swayed around her shoulders. The skirt of her new dress tangled around her legs.

Esmeralda smiled as she pressed her forehead against the cold windowpane. For a few weeks her sister would have a little taste of what her life would have been like if she could have grown up as the granddaughter of a viscount. "Thank you, Your Grace," Esmeralda whispered softly into the quietness. "For giving Josephine this gift to enjoy being outside and playing with her dog."

"Miss Swift."

Startled, Esmeralda whirled. Only by what she was wearing did Esmeralda know which twin was standing in the doorway. "Yes, Lady Vera." Esmeralda moved away from the window.

"Were you talking to me?"

"No, to myself," she answered honestly. "An annoying habit of mine, I'm afraid. I hope your aunt is all right and that she wasn't disturbed too greatly by all the barking and crashing."

Lady Vera continued on into the room. "She wasn't. She's fine. I knew she would be."

"That's good to hear."

"She's much stronger than Griffin thinks she is. But then he does like to take care of everyone. His duty I suppose. Auntie Eve said she assumed there would be mishaps and mayhem with a dog and a child in the house."

"I'm going to do my best to see it doesn't happen again."

"I told her it was really quite comical, though she was surprised to hear you and Griffin were having a tiff about it."

Esmeralda blinked slowly and whispered, "Oh dear."

"She wasn't overly concerned, but glad to get the news that no one had fallen down the stairs."

"I was glad of that too."

"There is no reason for Griffin to worry so much about her. Perhaps other than she is getting old, and now sickly. He worries too much about everything, if you ask me." She paused. "But I suppose you didn't."

Nor would Esmeralda ask Lady Vera anything about the duke or anyone else in the household. Miss Fortescue's rules on getting mixed up in a family's affairs were quite clear: "Don't do it."

Remaining neutral, she answered, "I may not always ask, so please feel free to tell me anything you want me to know."

"I will." Lady Vera wandered over to the desk. She looked down at the neatly stacked cards. She picked up the appointment sheets and asked, "Will we really attend this many parties?"

"Yes. I assume the afternoons where nothing's planned, you and Lady Sara will be free to accept rides or walks in the park with gentlemen who show interest in you."

Lady Vera's eyes brightened and she laid the papers down. "You mean with all the handsome beaus who will be seeking my hand."

"Yes," Esmeralda said on a laugh. "And perhaps some young ladies might invite you to go to the park with them, as well, so you can talk about all the gentlemen."

"Oh, I can't wait for the Season to begin," Lady Vera said anxiously. "I've decided I agree with Sara. I think I should like it that you are our chaperone instead of a stuffy old woman who will be constantly sniffing into her handkerchief and telling us what we can and cannot do."

"I don't believe I'll have need to keep a handkerchief at my nose, but other than that, I'm not sure I'll be any different from an older woman, Lady Vera. There are rules you must adhere to no matter who is your chaperone."

"Perhaps you're right about the rules," she said as she picked up the letter that was addressed to Esmeralda from

Lady Evelyn. "I don't get the sense you are the condemning sort."

"I am in no position to condemn anyone nor would I even if I were."

"I thought as much." She looked down at the note and skimmed it before replacing it on the desk. "You know I love my sister, don't you?"

That was an odd thing for her to say, but Esmeralda answered, "Yes. That goes without saying."

"Good," Lady Vera said pleasantly. "Then you will understand that though I know many gentlemen will seek my hand, I have already set my cap for Lord Henry."

From Lady Evelyn's notes, Esmeralda knew Lord Henry Dagworth was the Earl of Berkwoods' youngest son and one of the five gentlemen Lady Evelyn had mentioned as a highly favored prospect.

"So you've already met him?"

"No, of course not." Lady Vera moved from behind the desk. "How could I have? Auntie Eve would have never permitted that. But she assures me he will be at the first ball and I will meet him there."

"Yes. Most likely. I mean, I'm sure he will be. Do you mind telling me why you have already settled on him before you've met him?"

"Because I know everything there is to know about him. He's the one I want. That is, I know everything Auntie Eve has told me. She has gone into great detail about all the eligible gentlemen she feels will be suitable for us to marry. She has met them all, and she said he is the most handsome by far." Vera smiled dreamily.

Esmeralda couldn't imagine a man more handsome than the Duke of Griffin, but of course she couldn't tell his sister that so she remained quiet.

"I simply can't wait to meet him and dance with him."

"And you know for certain you want to marry Lord

Henry and not any of the other eligible bachelors you haven't met?"

"Yes," Lady Vera said without hesitation.

That comment took Esmeralda by surprise. She hoped Lady Vera wasn't setting herself up for a broken heart. "There will be many young ladies other than you and Lady Sara making their debuts, as well as ladies who made their debuts in years past but haven't made a match. They will be looking at Lord Henry too, you know. Being an earl's son, and if he is as handsome as you say, many of them will be trying to gain his attention too."

"Yes, I know," Lady Vera said as if she didn't have a concern in the world. "I know all about the ladies and their pushy mamas, but I'm not worried about any of them."

Her tone was so nonchalant that Esmeralda knew Lady Vera believed that she would have no competition to win the young man's heart.

"Auntie Eve has assured us we will have our pick of all the gentlemen because we are daughters of a duke. None of the other young ladies who are making their debut this year are. I've decided he's the one I want."

"All right. Do you know if Lady Sara has already decided on someone she is interested in?"

"Yes," Lady Vera said as if she was shocked Esmeralda had to ask. "She also expects to win the heart of Lord Henry."

Oh no. That couldn't be good.

Lady Vera added, "That's why I want you to see to it that she doesn't and I do."

Chapter 14

Do find someone you can trust to share your
thoughts. You'll never regret having an ally
in the house.

~~~

MISS MAMIE FORTESCUE'S DO'S AND DON'TS FOR
CHAPERONES, GOVERNESSES, TUTORS, AND NURSES

Griffin strode through the door of his Mayfair home.
He took off his hat and placed it on the side table. He
started removing his gloves, then stopped and listened.
There was no sound of chatter or movement in the house.
Just the ticking of the clock that stood beside the door. That
was odd for a place that had five females, a dog, and several servants in it. The first glove off, he tossed it on the
top of his hat.

It had been only three days since he'd seen Miss Swift,
but he couldn't stay away any longer. He wanted to see how
she was managing. A short laugh passed his lips. There
was no use lying to himself. He knew she was managing
just fine. With her strength of mind, how could she not?
Besides, Lady Evelyn would have sent for him if there
had been any problems.

Griffin had come over because he wanted to see Miss Swift.

The second glove landed on the hat, and he remembered once again how close he'd come to kissing her right there in his drawing room—with Josephine looking on. He should have never touched her, because now he wanted to touch her soft skin, brush her full lips with his own.

But he couldn't.

He wouldn't stoop to seducing one of his staff, no matter how desperately he wanted to. Contrary to what all of Society thought, he had a code of honor that he wouldn't break. He had changed from the reckless youth he had been. He would want Esmeralda, but he would not have her.

"Esmeralda," he said aloud. He liked the way her name sounded when he said it.

Yes, he would think of her as "Esmeralda." And though it would be difficult, he would show restraint and not take her in his arms until she was out of his employ.

Unhooking the medallion at his throat, he swung the heavy cloak off his shoulders.

"Your Grace," Sparks said, hurrying down the corridor. "Let me help you with that."

"Not necessary, Sparks. I have it. Tell me, why is the house so quiet? Is everyone in the garden?"

"No, Your Grace. Only a few minutes ago, Miss Swift took Lady Sara, Lady Vera, Miss Josephine, and Napoleon for a walk. In Hyde Park, I believe."

A rare stab of disappointment struck Griffin. So Miss Swift wasn't at home. It was probably for the best.

He handed his cloak to the butler and said, "It's a nice day to be outside."

"Yes, Your Grace. May I get you something to drink?"

"No, thank you. I'm going up to see Lady Evelyn." With that, he turned and headed up the stairs.

Griffin knocked on the door and waited for the reply for

him to enter. He opened the door to his aunt's bedchamber and walked inside, closing it behind him. Lady Evelyn sat in a straight back chair in front of a window, which was opened a few inches. To his surprise she was wearing a dark plum dress. Her gray-threaded hair had been arranged neatly on top of her head, and secured with silver combs.

She smiled. "This is a pleasure. I didn't know you were going to stop by today, Your Grace."

"A pleasure for both of us then," he said even though he was sure there was a grimace on his face. "I didn't know I was going to find you out of bed, dressed, and sitting in a chair in front of an open window." He grabbed a brown velvet robe from the foot of her bed as he passed and laid it on her lap as he stopped in front of her. "Do you think that it's wise for someone who has been as ill as you have?"

Her aged, blue eyes stared purposefully into his. "What? Being up or sitting where I can get some fresh air for the first time in over a week?"

"Both."

"Probably not." She faced the window again. "I decided if I was going to be in pain anyway, I might as well be in pain sitting up enjoying spring air and this glorious blue sky instead of spending yet another day looking at these four walls." She cut her eyes around to him again. "They don't change much, you know."

He shook the robe down to cover her legs and then bent on one knee and tucked it snugly around her feet. "Then I will have Sparks change out the furniture, the paintings, mirrors, and all the rest of it so you'll have something new to look at."

She smiled and patted his cheek affectionately as he rose and seated himself in the chair opposite her. "You'll do no such thing. I rather like the familiar. It's comforting. Besides, I knew it was getting close to time for Fenton's flowers to start blooming and I wanted to see if any of them had. Unfortunately, they haven't. None that I can see from my window anyway. I suppose he'll enter his Persian irises in the May Day Fair again this year."

"He has enough planted that at least one of them should bloom on the right day so he can."

"Good. I know he wants to win for the fifth year in a row."

"I have no doubt that he will."

Griffin looked at the angry, welting red rash of blisters that covered one side of his aunt's face from her hairline to her jawline. It was a devilishly hard thing to look at. The pain she endured must be great, yet she had never once complained about suffering.

"I think you are looking better today," he lied without guilt.

"You say that every time you come. I appreciate it, though you and I know it's not true."

"If not today, it will be one day soon," he said, though he admitted to himself that he really hadn't seen much improvement in the past few days. The only good thing was that, once the rash had made it down to her jawline, it hadn't gone any farther.

"I suppose it will." A wistful sigh passed her lips. "The doctor, the alchemist, and the apothecary who visit me almost daily say that it will go away. They just don't know when. In the meantime, I will continue to drink their concoctions and bear their foul-smelling creams and ointments on my face. So don't stop saying I'm looking better. It does cheer me, even if it's untrue."

"Well, at least you haven't lost your ability to brighten my day."

She gave him a wilted smile that ended on a long-held sigh. "Nor shall I. I hope."

His aunt's undaunted spirit reminded Griffin of Esmeralda. She and his aunt had the same outspoken disposition. They would get along well together, if his aunt could accept visitors. Once again he thought about the possibility of meeting someone during the Season, someone who appealed to him and stimulated his body and his mind.

"All ladies should be as forthright as you are, Lady Evelyn. Unfortunately most of them are too timid. So tell me, what has you feeling so down today?"

She laughed softly. "Life, I suppose. If not for the twins coming to visit me a couple of times each day, and your visit too, I think I'd go mad."

Griffin picked up her hand. It was cold. He kissed the back of her palm and then pulled the robe over her hands. "You know I won't allow that kind of talk."

"And you know I don't usually either." She looked out at the blue sky again. "I'm feeling sorry for myself today, so if you don't like it, you can leave me."

"Does it have anything to do with the house being so quiet? Sparks told me that Miss Swift has taken Sara and Vera to Hyde Park to spend the afternoon."

"And her sister and that dog."

Griffin smiled. "You're still ill-tempered with me about hiring her and meeting all her demands without consulting you, aren't you?"

"Of course I am." She slid her hand out from under the cover and rearranged the robe on her lap in a testy manner. "Everything about her is highly unusual."

"I'm not known for doing what's expected."

"And you probably never will."

"What did the twins have to say about her?" he asked.

"Exactly what you told them to: She's lovely and clever but they'd much rather have me and will I please get well quickly and join them at the parties."

Griffin laughed. "I said no such things."

"I know. I was making it up. It matters not to Sara and Vera who escorts them during the Season. It only matters to me."

"So that's what's bothering you?"

She looked out the window and sighed again. "Isn't it obvious? It was my place to see the twins through the Season, and I've let them down and they will be with a stranger."

"Listen to me," he said firmly. "You've not let anyone down. Least of all the twins, so don't mention that again."

"That's good of you to say, and I know that someone had to fulfill my duties for me. In truth, I probably wouldn't have liked it any better if you'd been able to secure one of the Queen's ladies-in-waiting to chaperone them." She paused. "But if you had, I'm sure she wouldn't have brought along her sister and her dog."

"Look on the bright side," Griffin said with a grin. "How many people in London would ever have the opportunity to entertain Napoleon and Josephine in their home for a few weeks?"

She turned back to him and gave him a weary smile. "How many would want to?"

Griffin chuckled. He could never get the best of his aunt, so he said, "There is still hope that one of these treatments you're using will dry up your rash and you won't miss all of the Season."

In the bright sunshine streaming through the windowpane, he could see the furrow in her brow had deepened, the wrinkles around her eyes and the lines marring her upper lip were more pronounced from the pain she'd suffered.

"How can I help?" he asked.

"You could try feeling sorry for me and treating me like the old woman I am."

"You wouldn't like that," he said and pulled the edge of the robe up over her cold hands again.

"You're right. I wouldn't. So stop doing it." She pulled

her hands out from under the cover. "I was glad she suggested it, though."

"Who and what?" he asked, though he had a pretty good idea what she was referring to.

"Miss Swift asked if she could accompany the twins to the park for the afternoon. It was a good idea, so I agreed because I've been indisposed. I know Vera and Sara were ready to see something other than the inside of this house and the back garden. And, on such a glorious spring day as this, it was the perfect time. I insisted they both keep their parasols open at all times. The last thing we need is for their noses or cheeks to be too rosy for the first ball of the Season."

"They are very good about following your instructions."

"As far as we know. Now tell me, are you any closer to finding out any more about the rumor that is circulating about the twins being in danger from a scoundrel?"

"Not much," Griffin said as he leaned against the window frame. "I talked with the barkeep who worked in the taproom the night Sir Welby heard the men talking. I will get nothing from him. Whatever he knows will go to the grave with him."

"Sounds as if he was simply being discreet."

"My thoughts too. I can respect a man who stands by his honor, but I am determined to find out who is behind this. Perhaps there are others who might remember who wandered in and out of the taproom that evening around that time."

"Perhaps you should speak to someone on Bow Street and let others try to find the answers for you."

"What kind of man would I be if I let another handle this for me?"

"The intelligent kind. The first ball is in two nights. You haven't much time."

"I'm well aware of that. But Rath and Hawk will be there helping me and Miss Swift keep watch on Sara and Vera. If any man shows with mischief on his mind, we will be ready."

"By the saints, Griffin, you can't let those two rakes near your sisters. They'll be ruined for sure if anyone thinks either of those two have designs on the twins."

"The last I heard titled gentlemen were much preferred over younger sons. I told you Rath and Hawk have mended their ways." He paused. "Well, Hawk for sure."

"I don't believe you." She sighed heavily and pulled the robe up to cover her chest.

"They have no designs on Sara and Vera, and you know they don't. They will continue to treat them as if they were their own sisters."

"Well, as with this blasted rash I have on my face, I can do nothing about it."

Griffin reached over and closed the window. He spread the draperies wider to allow more sunshine to come through. "Auntie, you know you can trust me to take care of my sisters."

"Oh my, yes, I can trust you"—she looked up at him with tired eyes—"to tell me only what you want me to know."

"Your rash has done nothing to dull your sharp tongue. Very uncommon for one who has been so ill. Now would you like me to help you back over to the bed?"

"That's what I have a maid for. You can ask Harper to come up on your way out."

"And that sounds as if you are dismissing me, so I'll say good-bye."

He reached down as if to kiss the side of her forehead that was clear of the rash, but she held up her hand to stop him and turned her head away.

"Are you off to the park?"

Oh yes. He wanted to see Esmeralda. "I thought I might as well look in on my sisters and see how Miss Swift is handling them."

"Yes, I thought you might. I took it upon myself to tell the cook to have a picnic basket ready in case you happened by. They'll be wanting refreshments by the time you get there."

"You are always one step ahead of me."

"I try to be. Now, be off with you. Don't tarry long or you might miss them."

Griffin sauntered out of his aunt's room. He wasn't worried. If he missed them in the park, it didn't matter. He would find them walking home. He didn't intend to let the day pass without seeing Esmeralda. There was something about her that just made him feel good and eager about life again.

Chapter 15

Do be on guard at all times. You never know
who might be watching you.

～✦～

MISS MAMIE FORTESCUE'S DO'S AND DON'TS FOR
CHAPERONES, GOVERNESSES, TUTORS, AND NURSES

It was the warmest temperature London had seen in months. Days of gray and rain had finally ended. The dry air felt fresh, and smelled fragrant. Spring had finally arrived. Esmeralda walked into Hyde Park with a smile on her face. The twins were on her left, Josephine with Napoleon flanking her right. A few wispy white clouds scattered across a brilliant blue sky. Trees, shrubs, and bushes were beginning to show their vibrant green coat of new leaves. Cool breezes lingered in the air and fluttered the pale yellow and pink ribbons on the twins' parasols. Heat from the sunshine made it an absolutely lovely day for a stroll.

Though the Season hadn't officially started, the park was buzzing with pedestrian, horse, and carriage traffic. There were conveyances of all sizes and shapes rolling along the pathways and the open spaces. Milk wagons, peddlers' carts, and fancy coaches all mingled together in the park. Families, couples, and gentlemen on horseback littered the landscape as far as she could see. Children played, couples walked side by side, and groups of people sat on blankets, enjoying refreshments, chatter, and the beautiful day.

Lady Sara's and Lady Vera's dispositions were much improved from earlier in the day. They chatted excitedly to each other as people passed them. Gentlemen doffed their hats and ladies smiled with nods of friendliness. The twins didn't seem to mind that they had to stop once in a while for Napoleon to scratch and sniff the ground. They twirled the shafts of their parasols in the palm of their hands and kept watching and talking. Seeing them, no one would know many harsh words had passed between the sisters in the past few days. They appeared such loving and happy young ladies. And they were most of the time, but they could also be unkind to each other.

Esmeralda had found it was best to awaken early so she could have Josephine dressed, fed, and working on her studies before the twins were up and ready to begin their day. On her first morning, everything had gone quite nicely until Lady Sara and Lady Vera had walked into the drawing room shortly after noon dressed exactly alike, challenging Esmeralda to identify them by name. Her vision might as well have been blurred. She couldn't have said for sure who was who if someone had been holding a loaded pistol to her head and threatening to shoot her if she got it wrong.

Over the past three days, the sisters had argued about the silliest of things as far as Esmeralda was concerned. They would get into squabbles over who could read the fastest, who had the finer embroidery stitch, and who could curtsy the lowest. They even had a spat over who was going to play the pianoforte first. That had ended rather badly with a shouting match that escalated into Lady Vera pushing Lady Sara off the stool.

Earlier in the day when Esmeralda had heard the two quarreling over the placement of ribbons in their hair she knew she had to do something drastic before she shot one and drowned the other. *For the love of heaven!* What did it matter if a ribbon was moved half an inch to the left or the right if it was at the back of your head and you weren't going out for anyone to see it anyway?

The duke's sisters were in need of something to entertain them—other than each other. Esmeralda knew that in a few days or a few weeks she couldn't change the habits they'd developed over eighteen years. Though, if she were going to be with them longer, she might be tempted to give it a good try.

The day was gorgeous, so she gathered her courage and sent them to ask Lady Evelyn if she might take them for a walk in the park. Thankfully, their aunt had readily agreed to the idea.

Not long after they entered the park, Lady Vera found a rather stout but short limb. She asked Josephine if Napoleon would fetch it if she threw it as far as she could. Josephine wasn't sure because it wasn't a game they had ever played. After a short deliberation, the trio decided to put the Skye Terrier to the test. They watched, laughed, clapped, and cheered when the short-legged dog went running after the stick and promptly came back carrying it his mouth. Esmeralda wondered if it was a dog's instinct to chase after a stick or something that was thrown or if Napoleon's previous owner had taught him to play that game.

Lady Sara quickly lost interest in the merriment and walked over to Esmeralda. "I'm looking forward to our first ball, but I'm quite anxious about it too."

"Why is that? You will be one of the most beautiful and

charming young ladies there, and not to mention one of the most sought after too."

"I know," Lady Sara managed to say without sounding boastful. "I can't wait for it to get here, but when I think about dancing with a gentleman, my stomach starts feeling like it has a ball of knitting yarn in it that's jumping around and won't be still."

"That's just excitement and nerves," Esmeralda reassured her. "After the first dance, you'll be fine."

"I've never actually danced with a man. Have you, Miss Swift?"

"No," Esmeralda answered, sounding a little more wistful than she'd intended. She wouldn't be dancing at the ball, but she was looking forward to watching all the beautifully gowned ladies being twirled across the dance floor by splendidly dressed partners.

"Our dance tutor was a woman," Lady Sara offered. "She was very good. Auntie Eve assured us it will be different when a man is our partner and he takes our hand and leads us through the steps of the waltz or when we hold hands and make a canopy for the other dancers to sashay underneath."

Esmeralda thought of the duke's hand on her cheek, his thumb on her lips. It was as if the breeze had stilled as his warmth enveloped her. Oh, yes. She could attest to the fact that it was a very different feeling when a man touched you.

"I do hope Lord Henry asks me to dance," Sara continued. "And I want to be the first lady he asks."

Lord Henry?

Oh, no. This couldn't be a good thing.

What was Esmeralda going to do? Maybe Lady Vera was wrong and Lady Sara had no interest in Lord Henry. How had it happened that both young ladies wanted to catch the eye of the same young man?

She wondered if Lady Evelyn suggested that they both set their caps for the Earl of Berkwoods' son in hopes one of them would win his favor. Could it be that they both simply wanted him because Lady Evelyn pronounced he was the most handsome? No, Esmeralda quickly convinced herself, that couldn't be the case. The twins weren't that shallow. Perhaps it was simply because they were twins. If they looked alike, they probably thought alike and had the same feelings. Maybe it was natural for twins to be attracted to the same man. Whatever the case, Esmeralda couldn't see this as ending well.

"I'm sure most of the eligible men will ask you to dance. There should be enough time for you to accept each one."

"Auntie Eve said she used to attend balls where everyone danced until dawn, so I should have opportunity to dance with them all." Lady Sara sighed. "But Auntie said Lord Henry is the one who makes all the young ladies swoon each year, and I really want to know what it feels like to swoon."

Esmeralda smiled. She knew exactly what it felt like to swoon. She had thought she might faint when the duke was so close to her she could almost feel his lips on hers.

"Since you haven't met him, you know there's the possibility you will see someone you are attracted to more than the earl's son. Handsome is not the only thing that attracts a young lady to a gentleman. You'll want him to be kind, have a good wit, and be affable too."

"Aunt Evelyn says he must also come from the right family, have a plump allowance, and not be given to too much wine or gambling."

Esmeralda's spine stiffened. Yes, first and foremost, the right family. How could she have forgotten? That was the mistake her mother had made. Apparently, the twins didn't intend to fall into the trap of loving a man their family disapproved of.

"Have you thought about the possibility he may not be ready to marry? At twenty-four, he's still quite young. I don't want you to be disappointed if he's not ready to make a match."

Lady Sara frowned. "Oh, but I will," she said earnestly. "I'm the daughter and sister of a duke. Auntie Eve said I should have my pick of all the gentlemen, and he's the one I want."

Oh, dear.

If there was yelling and a shove when they both wanted to play the pianoforte, what would happen when they both started vying for the same young man's attention? That was a road Esmeralda didn't want to go down until she must. She would hope that one of the twins would be swept off her feet by a different bachelor and avoid the fight that was sure to come if their expectations didn't change.

"Look over there, Lady Sara. A crowd is gathering. What do you say we get your sister, Josephine, and Napoleon and go see what everyone is watching?"

"I think it's a juggler. Did you bring some coins we can toss to him?"

Esmeralda smiled and opened the black knitted reticule that swung from her wrist. "I believe I do have a coin or two in my purse. I'll give it to you and let you take care of tossing it in the man's hat."

"Oh, that would be wonderful, Miss Swift," Lady Sara said, smiling from ear to ear and taking the coin. "Auntie Eve would never let us get near someone like that. I knew I was going to enjoy you being our chaperone."

A few minutes later they were standing on their toes behind about thirty people. They moved from side to side, twisting their heads this way and that, trying to see through the throng to watch a man throwing six balls into the air while another man was off to the side setting up a puppet tent.

"It's not fair," Josephine complained as more people crowded around them. "I can't see."

"We can't break in line," Esmeralda told her. "Do you want me to see if I can lift you up high enough to see over their heads?"

Josephine folded her arms across her chest and pouted. "I'm too heavy for you to hold."

"Maybe not. We won't know unless we try. Here, jump up into my arms and let's see."

Lady Vera took hold of Napoleon's leash and pulled it from Josephine's hands. "That's nonsense. There's no reason all these adults should stand in front of a child. Come with me, Josephine. I'll walk you up to the front and find someone to let you stand in front of." She looked over at Esmeralda, smiled, and in an authoritative tone said, "Napoleon will lead us. Everyone likes dogs. And we won't be breaking in line; someone will step aside and let us in. Watch."

"If you're going," Lady Sara said, "I want to."

Making a waving motion with her hands, Esmeralda said, "All of you, please go ahead." She quickly glanced at her surroundings. "I'll stand over there and observe from that rise."

Esmeralda kept her gaze on the twins as she walked the short distance. After they melted into the crowd, she knew exactly where the girls were because of the twins' parasols. It was fascinating to see how effortlessly the juggler kept the leather balls in the air. But he soon tired out and stepped aside. Then the marionette show began. She couldn't hear everything that was said, but judging by the laughter and clapping, all were enjoying the puppets' antics.

The crowd grew larger as time passed and, unexpectedly, she realized someone had moved very close to her. Someone warm. Comforting. Someone too close. An arm brushed against hers as they clapped. Her body tingled. She knew it was the duke who had come up beside her.

Esmeralda turned her head and stared up at him. Her stomach turned a slow, easy summersault. Joy filled her at the sight of him. He was so divinely handsome she was tempted to throw her arms around him, hug him close, and tell him how good it made her feel just to see him.

"Hello, Miss Swift."

Pushing all those delicious feminine feelings aside, she asked, "Your Grace, is something wrong?"

He glanced over the crowd in front of them and said, "Not as far as I can see. Why?"

She frowned and pursed her lips before saying, "That's too bad. I was hoping there was."

"You're upset that nothing is wrong?" An inquisitive expression settled on his face. "Why is that?"

"I was hoping there was something amiss so it wouldn't feel as if you were here in the park to check up on me." Her gaze briefly darted to the basket in his hand and the blanket thrown across his arm. "That is what you're doing, isn't it?"

He gave her a good-natured smile. "That's exactly what I'm doing."

She didn't want to get caught up in the magical feelings that always assailed her whenever they were talking, so she looked away and gave her attention back to the parasols and puppet show. She would have loved to have been offended by his arrival, but she wasn't. As hard as it was to admit, no matter the reason, she was happy to see him.

"Any other gentleman would have denied such a breach in common decency and here you are almost boasting about it."

"Ah, but I knew you would have seen right through my attempt to be so noble. So why do it, right?"

"Still, you could have tried in order to save my feelings."

"That's true. I'll do my best to be more gentlemanly next time I want to see if you have everything under control."

"I will have to give you high marks for being honest about why you have followed us here."

"That's a good sign, at least. Tell me, did the twins come below stairs dressed alike for you this week?"

Her head snapped around and her gaze caught his. "How did you know? Did you tell them to do it?"

"Me? No. Believe me, those two don't need coaxing from anyone to be mischievous. It's been one of their favorite things to do since they were little girls. Guests of the Griffin family have always been treated to the twins dressing differently on one day and then dressing identical on another. It was probably Lady Evelyn who first gave them the idea. They get an enormous amount of delight out of confusing people about who is who."

"The girls did seem to relish seeing me perplexed. Maybe it would have been easier if I were more familiar with them."

He grinned. "How did you do?"

"Quite well, oddly enough. I knew I had a fifty-fifty chance of getting their names right, and luck was with me. I called the right name each time I needed to."

"I'm not surprised you were so intuitive, but I bet *they* were."

His praise pleased her. She smiled and remained quiet.

"Most of our guests would end up being so flustered by seeing double that they wouldn't try to get their names right. They would just say 'my lady.'"

"Unfortunately, I wasn't given that option."

"After you've been around for a few more days, you'll be able to tell them apart no matter how they are dressed."

"It's already getting easier."

"Good. They may look exactly alike at times, but they have different natures. Vera's nature is more forceful and cantankerous. Sara's sweeter."

Esmeralda started to say she agreed completely, but then thought better of it, and simply replied, "But both are lovely."

The duke faced her. "Did Miss Fortescue teach you how to be so diplomatic?"

"No," she answered with a teasing smirk. "It's my nature."

His smile was natural as he said, "And a temperamental nature it is at times."

She frowned. "I'll ignore that comment."

"But you know it's true. I'm glad you suggested bringing the girls to the park and so is my aunt. And I see you brought Josephine and Napoleon along too.

"You don't mind, do you? I supposed I should have cleared it with you first."

"I don't mind. I can see you aren't neglecting Sara and Vera. They are enjoying the show too."

"I think so. Vera showed Josephine how to play throw and fetch with a stick. Napoleon was already quite familiar with what to do, so his former owners must have taught him. And the twins were very accommodating to him on our walk over here. They didn't get upset when Napoleon wanted to check out every doorway, hitching post, and tree along the way."

He chuckled. "Living a protected life at Griffin for so many years, Sara and Vera have had few occasions to enjoy friendships or relatives their own age. It will be good for them to have you as their chaperone. Except for me, my aunt, and the servants, they've had only each other to get to know. It's made them close, but it also, regrettably, causes a fierce competitiveness from time to time."

Including the pianoforte and Lord Henry, Esmeralda

wanted to say but decided that Griffin didn't need to know about the earl's son.

"I'm rather glad they have someone else in the house to interact with now other than each other."

"And that will change after they meet young ladies at the various parties."

"Which reminds me," he added. "I looked into your suggestion of finding out which young ladies who were a part of the wager hadn't married and also had brothers, uncles, or fathers."

"Who did you come up with?" she asked anxiously.

"Only two names."

"But didn't Sir Welby think there were more than two at White's?"

He nodded. "He did but admitted he couldn't be sure of anything other than the comments that perhaps the way to get back at me was through my sisters. If you listen carefully enough in a taproom, you can overhear a lot of conversations."

"But you're saying we have two young men to watch carefully, right?"

"Yes. For now, anyway. Sir Charles Redding and Mr. Albert Trent are the only gentlemen who have sisters who received a secret admirer letter but never married."

Esmeralda repeated the names in her mind. They weren't on any of Lady Evelyn's lists. And they wouldn't be. She wouldn't consider either of them high enough in the heel to offer for the twins.

Why did Esmeralda keep forgetting all she'd been taught when she was living in her uncle's home? She knew all about the snobbery of Polite Society. She just hadn't been a part of it for a long time. And now she was on the other side of it.

"I will keep a steady eye on the two should they get near Lady Sara or Lady Vera even for a dance."

The duke's eyes swept up and down her face. Fluttering began in Esmeralda's chest. It was madness that whenever he looked at her with that intimate intensity radiating from him, she wanted him to pull her into his strong arms, nestle her to him, and kiss her eager lips. She knew he was attracted to her. He had admitted that. But surely she was more aware of his every breath than he was of hers.

"Did you know that out in the sunlight your eyes lose all their brown coloring and are golden?"

With that question, Esmeralda felt the atmosphere change. The noise of the crowd faded away, the cool breeze stilled, and the sun heated her face. It was as if she and the duke were the only two people in the park.

"How could I possibly know that? I have never seen my eyes outside a house."

"I thought perhaps someone might have told you—your parents, possibly a beau?"

"I'm sure you've had countless ladies tell you that your eyes are as blue as a summer sky."

He ignored her comment and said, "You skillfully deflected my question, but I'm not going to let you get by with that."

She evaded him again by saying, "Did you ask one? I thought you were making a statement."

He gave her an amused smile. "It's always a challenge with you, Esmeralda. I like that."

She gasped. "You can't call me by my given name."

"I can and will when we are alone and no one is around to hear but you. Now, here is a direct question for you, Esmeralda. Have you ever been kissed?"

Her immediate instinct should have been to shy away from such intimate conversation once more and insist he call her Miss Swift at all times. It was on the tip of her tongue to tell him she was outraged he'd ask her something so personal, but staring into his striking gaze as it brushed down her face to her mouth, she knew she didn't want to resist him in that way or any way.

Maybe she wanted him to call her Esmeralda and to know that her lips had never been touched by another's. Maybe she wanted him to know she'd welcome his kiss.

Still, her practical, survival nature came to her rescue and she resisted what her heart desired and said, "I've not had time nor opportunity for such things as hugs and kisses."

"Twenty-five and never been kissed." His voice was low, and soft. "I find that very intriguing."

His hold over her intensified. There was something about his unobtrusive interest in her that stirred her womanly passions to an anticipation she couldn't have known existed.

Her throat ached with an increasing need that was always denied—to feel his lips caress hers. Perhaps he found it intriguing she'd never been kissed, but she found it discouraging that she'd never had the opportunity to know what it felt like to be kissed. She wanted to know.

Putting all her sensible, inner declarations aside, and willing her voice not to quiver, she asked, "Are you offering to change that, Your Grace?"

Chapter 16

Don't think about romance. It has no place for a
person in the line of service.

~∼∼

MISS MAMIE FORTESCUE'S DO'S AND DON'TS FOR
CHAPERONES, GOVERNESSES, TUTORS, AND NURSES

Esmeralda felt the duke's breath kick up a notch,
matching her own. She didn't know where the question
or her nerve to ask it had come from. It was impertinent,
rash, and downright brazen, not to mention something
that had never crossed her mind to say before it tumbled
from her lips with a confidence that belied her inner
feelings.

And impossible too!

Yet, for a split second she thought he was going to drop
the blanket and the basket and do exactly what she desperately wanted him to do right there in the park in front
of the world. However, he remained still and said, "You
only dare to ask that because you know I can't."

"Do I?"

"Yes."

His voice had been husky and caressing, leaving no

doubt he meant what he said. And she understood. They were both born in the same world, but he didn't know that because she now lived in a different society. Fate wasn't likely to change their futures. He was a man of honor and had sworn not to touch her while she was under the protection of his household. It was becoming clear each time they met that it wasn't what either of them wanted, but that was the way it had to be.

Knowing she needed to stop the intimacy swirling between them, she took a step back, changed her demeanor and her tone to one she would use on an errant child, and asked, "Then why would you bring up kissing, Your Grace?"

The corners of his mouth tightened. So did the corners of his eyes. He hadn't liked her change in attitude or her question, but he had to know it was best. What was happening between the two of them needed to be stopped.

"Curious."

She kept her firm countenance and expression. "And is that curiosity now satisfied?"

"It will have to be," he answered much in the way she'd asked.

She inhaled deeply, trying not to allow the sudden disappointment she was feeling to overtake her. "That's reassuring. As I said, I know little about kissing, and I doubt a man like you could teach me, so we don't have to discuss kissing again, do we?"

He snorted a short laugh and moved to make up the distance she'd just put between them. Lowering his head so close to hers for a second she thought he was going to forget his honor, forget where they were, and kiss her anyway.

Instead he whispered, "You don't think I can teach you? With a challenge like that thrown at me, oh yes, Miss Esmeralda Swift, we will talk about kissing again. Have no fear about that. It must wait until you are no longer in my employ, but we will discuss it."

His tone suggested a promise. That had her legs once again feeling weak. The thought of a kiss from him, no matter how distant in the future, thrilled her, but somehow she had to keep him from knowing that. The duke was far more than she had bargained for, and she had to be careful. She didn't want to leave her heart with him when she left his employment.

"Griffin!" Lady Sara asked as she ran up to her brother and bussed his cheek. "What are you doing here?"

Esmeralda expelled her deep breath and stepped away from the duke.

"I didn't know you were going to join us today," Lady Vera said, brushing the air beside his other cheek while Napoleon barked once and then started sniffing around his feet.

"Neither did I, but I hope my arrival won't spoil your afternoon." He reached down and patted Napoleon on the head while he asked, "How are you, Miss Josephine?"

"Very well, Your Grace," she said with a curtsy. "Did you get here in time to see the juggler?"

"I missed him. Was he good?"

"He was exceptional. What's in the basket?"

He held up the wicker hamper. "I'm not sure, but I was told it's refreshments for us to enjoy. After the puppet show is finished, we'll find a place to spread the blanket and see what's inside."

"Excuse me, Your Grace, I don't want to interrupt your afternoon on this fine day, but I didn't want to pass by without stopping to speak either."

Esmeralda looked around to see a tall, slender young man walking up to them. Like the duke, he was dashing in a black cloak secured around his shoulders and his hat held under his arm.

"No, Mr. Lambert," the duke said with a nod and a gaze of scrutiny. "You're not. I'll introduce you."

Esmeralda had heard of Mr. Peter Lambert, nephew to the Lord Mayor. He was a handsome fellow with straight, neatly trimmed dark brown hair. His brown eyes weren't remarkable in any way, but she noted that, when he smiled, it showed in his whole face, making him appear friendly and cajoling. He wasn't quite as tall or broad-shouldered as the duke, but a fine-looking man just the same. Most important of all, he wasn't on Lady Evelyn's list of possible suitors for the twins. No doubt she didn't consider his social standing high enough for the twins.

After introductions were made, Mr. Lambert and the duke started chatting about how lovely the day was, about Napoleon's name, and about the rise in footpads accosting people on the streets. Esmeralda watched the twins' reaction to the man. Lady Vera seemed to dismiss him outright without a second glance. He wasn't Lord Henry, so she was completely uninterested in him. Lady Sara was taking a different approach. She made eye contact with Mr. Lambert when she spoke to him, and his gaze kept straying back to her.

Instinct told Esmeralda that though she'd had a difficult time telling the twins apart, Mr. Lambert was having no problem seeing a distinct difference in the two sisters. It was quite clear that he'd seen something in Lady Sara that he hadn't seen in her twin.

"There's been a lot of talk about your sisters making their debut this Season," Mr. Lambert said to the duke.

Even before the duke frowned suspiciously and his eyes narrowed and twitched, Esmeralda knew Mr. Lambert realized he'd brought up a subject that should not have been mentioned.

He quickly added, "Not bad talk, of course, Your Grace. No, nothing unflattering about them at all or anything of the sort. Because they are twins. I mean, that is to say, we don't often see twins. That is what everyone, well, some, are talking about. So that's what I was referring to, you see. Twins." He glanced at Lady Sara. "To see if they really look very much alike. It's the rarity of it that has people talking, er—about how rare it is to have twins debut the same Season. Nothing else."

The confident young man was suddenly stumbling over his long-winded explanation so badly Esmeralda might have laughed at how horribly he managed his attempt to explain what he was trying to convey if she hadn't felt sorry for him. Too late he realized that saying people were talking about the twins would make the duke automatically assume he was referring to the gossip swirling about possible mischief concerning them.

Luckily for the gentleman, Lady Vera spoke before the duke had a chance and said, "We are used to people staring at us because we're twins and are quite prepared for it. It doesn't bother us at all and, sometimes, it's actually quite nice to be the center of attention."

"Yes, that's exactly what I was meaning, Lady Vera," Mr. Lambert hastened to say. "Everyone has been eager to see if you and Lady Sara are identical. And it's really quite astonishing how much you do look like each other."

"We'll say good day to you now, Mr. Lambert," the duke said tightly.

"Of course," Mr. Lambert replied nervously. "I didn't mean to keep you from your outing."

By the time he said good-bye and walked away, the puppet show had ended, so they headed over to a nearby tree together. The twins talked quietly to each other. Josephine had stopped to study something she saw lying on the ground while Napoleon sniffed around the closed picnic basket.

"Keep an eye on that man," the duke said in a soft voice to Esmeralda as he shook out the blanket.

She picked up the ends and helped him spread the thick

woolen covering on the cold, hard-packed ground. "I will, but Mr. Lambert appeared to be a nice man."

"Any man can be nice when he wants to."

"I know." Esmeralda glanced over at the twins. They weren't paying any attention to what she and the duke were saying to each other, so she added, "He made it clear he wasn't talking about the gossip that immediately came to your mind and his. Surely you saw how horrified he was when he realized what he said could be misconstrued by you?"

The duke's mouth narrowed with a grimace. "And it was."

"I think he's harmless. He wouldn't be a very good mischief-maker if brought up the mischief to the brother of the young ladies he intended to harm, now would he?"

"All the same, I don't know him well, so watch him."

She smiled at the duke. "I shall watch everyone. Including you."

His brows rose and he tensed. "Me?"

"Yes. To make sure you don't go around accosting innocent young gentleman."

A smile relaxed his face. "I want you watching me," he said. He reached for her hand, which she quickly drew back.

"I only want to help you sit down, Miss Swift."

"Oh, of course." Esmeralda hesitated for a moment longer and then placed her hand in his. At his touch, she felt a shock of sensuous awareness shoot throughout her body and settle low and longingly in her abdomen. His strong fingers took hold of hers in a gentle, possessive way that made her feel warm all over. She couldn't help but wonder if he would seek her out after she was no longer in his employ or if the attraction that sizzled between them now would have faded by then.

While the duke helped Lady Sara and Lady Vera to sit

down opposite Esmeralda, she called for Josephine to come join them.

"Just a minute," her sister replied and continued her inspection of the ground.

Not wanting to make the others wait, Esmeralda said, "Let's start without her. She's obviously discovered something interesting to look at. I'm sure she'll be along in a minute."

"All right." Griffin took off his hat and made himself comfortable beside Esmeralda. "Let's see what we have in here." He opened the basket to a stack of napkins on top. He handed them to Lady Vera and said, "I'll let you pass these around." He reached into the basket again and brought out a silver container with a stopper in it. He opened it and smelled. "Looks like we have warm chocolate in this." He handed it to Esmeralda along with several china cups and said, "You pour this, and I'll see what else we have in here."

"It's probably cheese and bread," Lady Sara offered.

"No," Griffin said, carefully unwrapping a napkin. "It looks like we have tarts."

"Fig or apricot?" Lady Vera asked.

He broke one open. "Fig." Napoleon walked over to the duke, sat on his haunches, and licked his chops. "All right, Emperor. You can have the first one." Griffin took the pastry and held it in the palm of his hand. Napoleon gobbled it down in two chomps.

Esmeralda's gaze kept straying to Griffin while she poured the chocolate. The wind had ruffled his hair. She liked the way it had feathered away from his forehead. It gave him an approachable appeal that didn't show when he stood so tall, strong, and masculine.

She handed a cup to Lady Vera and then to Lady Sara. There was something about sitting with Griffin and his sisters, and enjoying light conversation, that felt good and right. It was a foolish feeling, she knew, but it was as if she belonged—that she was a real part of their lives and equally acceptable socially.

She smiled to herself when she realized she'd been thinking of the duke as "Griffin" rather than "Your Grace" since they sat down to have the refreshments. Perhaps it was because he'd decided to call her Esmeralda when they were alone. She felt comfortable thinking of him as Griffin and in her thoughts would continue to do so.

When Esmeralda handed a cup to Griffin, his fingers closed over hers and held for a moment before releasing her so she could let go of the cup. Surely if he knew how topsy-turvy her stomach felt when he touched her, he wouldn't do it. Or maybe he knew, and that was why he did it. It could be that he had a wicked desire to torture her, for it was sweet torture to be filled with such delicious sensations.

Esmeralda called to Josephine again as she poured chocolate for herself. "There may not be anything left for you to eat or drink if you don't hurry."

"Griffin," Lady Sara asked, "is Lord Henry more handsome than Mr. Lambert?"

The duke's gaze darted to Esmeralda's. She shrugged slightly. She couldn't help him because she'd never seen Lord Henry.

"I'm not one to ask how handsome a man is, Sara. You best ask your aunt about that."

"There's no point in asking her, Sara," Lady Vera said. "Aunt Evelyn wouldn't have told us Lord Henry was the most handsome eligible bachelor if it wasn't true."

"Perhaps, but I'm going to tell her we met Mr. Lambert in the park today and ask her more about him when we return. And I noticed he had very nice hands too."

"Essie, look what I found!" Josephine ran up between the twins. She held a large frog, its plump body squeezed between her small hands. Long skinny legs and webbed feet dangled right at the twins' eye level when she thrust it toward Esmeralda.

Lady Sara and Lady Vera screamed.

Suddenly arms and hands were flung wide, cups, tarts, and parasols were thrown into the air as the squealing continued. Lady Vera jumped up and stumbled over the duke's legs, trying to get away. He caught her before she hit the ground. Lady Sara bolted to her feet, immediately tripped over her skirt, toppled over the chocolate container and the basket, and fell on top of Esmeralda while screeching like a banshee.

In a blur of dresses and flying limbs, Esmeralda's dress flew up past her knees as the force of Lady Sara's fall knocked both of them to the ground with a swoosh and a grunt. Napoleon gave a playful growl and woof before jumping into the fray.

Lady Sara screamed again before the duke could shoo Napoleon away and catch his sister's flailing arms and help her to stand. Esmeralda scrambled to lower her skirts to her ankles and right herself. With the twins screeching and hanging on his arms, Griffin reached down to help her to stand too. She gladly accepted his assistance.

"Are you hurt?" he asked.

Esmeralda appreciated the concern she saw in his eyes. "No, no, of course not. I'm fine," she whispered, straightening her bonnet on her head. "Please take care of your sisters."

"They're fine too."

"What is that thing?" Lady Sara asked, using the duke's body as a shield to keep her away from the frog.

"It doesn't matter what it is," her twin hissed. "Get it out of here."

Esmeralda was horrified. The last thing she needed was another calamity involving Josephine. Esmeralda wouldn't be surprised if the next thing they said was that they wanted Josephine and Napoleon out of their house immediately.

"Josephine, for the love of heaven!" Esmeralda said in an exasperated voice, brushing at the dark stain of chocolate on her new skirt. "Put that thing down right now and let it hop away. Can't you see you're scaring the twins with it?"

"It's just a frog," Josephine said, holding it up for the twins to see again, obviously oblivious to the true state of the duke's sisters' state of mind. "It won't hurt you."

That explanation didn't satisfy Lady Vera, and she screeched again. "Throw it away. I don't like it."

"What's wrong?" Mr. Lambert asked, rushing up to see if he could help. "What happened?"

He wasn't the only person who'd heard the commotion and screaming. Three other men were coming up right behind him to give aid to the ladies if need be.

The duke ran a hand through his hair in frustration. "Nothing is wrong, Mr. Lambert, gentlemen," he said with a nod of greeting to all. "As you can see, it's just a frog that has frightened my sisters. No harm has been done to anyone."

Mr. Lambert looked down at Josephine's defiant expression and the firm hold she had on the middle section of her large amphibian captive. "That's a mammoth frog you have there, young lady."

"I know," she said proudly. "I don't think I've ever seen one this big. It took me a while to sneak up on it and catch it. It kept hopping away."

She held the beast up to her face and looked at it. It made a noise that sounded like a deep manly burp, and Josephine started laughing. "See, it's not scary."

Esmeralda, Mr. Lambert, and the duke all chuckled too. So did the other people who had gathered around. Lady

Sara and Lady Vera didn't find anything about the frog amusing.

"It's horrid," Lady Vera said again, making sure she made eye contact with her brother, Esmeralda, and Mr. Lambert. "And it's certainly not comical. Make her take it away, Griffin."

After a forced cough to clear his laugh, the duke said, "You're right, Vera. A frog can look frightening when you're not used to seeing one up close."

Seizing the moment to impress Lady Sara, Mr. Lambert stepped closer and said, "I'd be happy to take care of it for you, Your Grace. That is, if you don't mind and the miss will hand over the frog."

"Yes, give it to him," Lady Sara said.

"Thank you, Mr. Lambert," Griffin said. "But I have everything handled. No need to trouble yourself." Griffin looked at the other people who'd wandered over to see what the screaming was about. "It was kind of you to look in on us, but as you see, all is fine. Please go back to your picnics and enjoy your afternoon."

"Of course, Your Grace," Mr. Lambert said with a smile. He gave Lady Vera a passing glance, then let his gaze linger on Lady Sara. "My ladies, I'll see you at the ball tomorrow night. I'd be pleased if you'd both save me a dance."

"Of course, we shall," Lady Sara answered quickly for herself and her sister. "Thank you for coming over to make sure nothing was wrong. That was very kind of you."

"It was my pleasure," Mr. Lambert said with a nod, letting his eyes linger on Lady Sara again before turning away. The others followed behind him.

"Now that I look at it from a distance, I guess it's not that scary-looking," Lady Sara said, "but I don't want to touch it."

Lady Vera was not as forgiving, "I don't know how you

can allow Josephine to touch something like that, Miss Swift. I've heard it said that those things cause warts, bumps, and all sorts of horrible things to appear on your skin."

"If they did, Josephine would have warts all over her hands by now. She has been touching frogs for years. I admit I have no desire to hold a frog, but Josephine has never been afraid of anything, be it bugs, beetles, or butterflies." Esmeralda looked at her cheeky sister and, though she saw the humor in the incident, felt compelled to say, "Josephine, that wasn't a nice thing for you to do."

Josephine's expression remained impish and unrepentant. "What did I do wrong? How was I to know they were scared? It's just a frog. They don't bite."

Esmeralda had no idea what Griffin was going to say to her. In truth, he had reason once again to dismiss her from his employ. That thought made her stomach quake. But no, she insisted to herself, lifting her shoulders straighter. She had resolved not to live in constant fear that she or Josephine were going to do something that made Griffin remove her from her position as the twins' chaperone. She must have confidence that she would see this challenge to the end and earn her payment—and the promised bonus if possible.

"But they don't look or sound very nice," Esmeralda said calmly, wanting to smooth over the incident quickly. "Now apologize to Lady Sara and Lady Vera for scaring them."

Griffin put his hands on Josephine's shoulders and looked at Esmeralda with a soft expression. "No apology is necessary."

Her gaze flew to Griffin's. He wasn't angry.

"She didn't intend to frighten Sara and Vera. Come on, Josephine, I'll go with you to take the frog back where you got him."

"You want to hold him?" Josephine asked as she lifted the frog up to Griffin.

"Why not?" he said with a grin, taking hold of it with one hand as he and Josephine walked away.

Esmeralda's heart softened. The duke always surprised her. He didn't have to be so understanding. She never expected him to be, yet he always was. Maybe all peers weren't as coldhearted as her uncle had been to her mother.

She looked down at the skirt of her new dress. Once cleaned, the chocolate stain wouldn't look so bad on her dark gray dress, but it had completely ruined the twins' pastel dresses. Lady Evelyn would probably have something to say about that.

Esmeralda's gaze swept down to the blanket. It was a mess of stomped-on tarts—Napoleon was happily scarfing up the last of the crumbs—spilled chocolate, an upended basket, and scattered cups, saucers, and napkins.

She remembered the shrieks and expressions of horror on the twins' faces when they saw the fat frog with bulging eyes and dangling legs hanging from Josephine's hands. Lady Vera had stumbled, Lady Sara then tripped and fell on top of her, and Esmeralda's skirt went flying up to her knees. What an embarrassing catastrophe that had been.

Suddenly Esmeralda turned her back to the twins and started laughing. Silently. Her shoulders shook but she remained quiet except for an occasional sniff that errantly escaped. Kneeling on the blanket, she started cleaning up the debris from the incident.

Josephine was right. Why was anyone afraid of a frog?

Chapter 17

Do take a man at his word no matter how
muddled that word may be.

~·~

Griffin stepped into the warmth of White's, and peeled off his leather gloves. Frustration had become an all too familiar feeling. Not only was he constantly thinking about who might want to upset the twins' Season, the very tempting Esmeralda was consuming his thoughts as well. She claimed to know nothing about men or kissing, yet for all her proclaimed innocence in the ways of seduction, she had somehow managed to beguile him. She also challenged him, intrigued him, and made him desire her all the more each time he saw her.

There were many beautiful ladies in London that Griffin could long for. Perhaps *should* long for. Some young, beautiful, and innocent—like the young gels looking to make a match. Others older, but well trained in the art of pleasing a man. And there were lovely widows seeking nothing more binding from him than a night in their bed.

He didn't want any of them.

Yet Esmeralda, the one forbidden, the one he had to keep at a distance, was the one who heated his blood like no other, leaving him thirsty for a taste. She was the one he wanted with a yearning he'd never experienced before. It was maddening and challenging at the same time.

He had seldom denied himself anything he wanted, and there was no denying he wanted her. And more than that. Her enjoyed being with her. He liked her banter, her boldness, and her sensitivity. He even liked her sister and their dog. And every day he had to remind himself he couldn't touch her. Not yet. But there would come a time when he could. When he would.

Griffin handed off his hat, gloves, and cloak to the attendant and forced Esmeralda from his thoughts. He strode toward the taproom, nodding at a gentleman he passed along the way and stopping to speak to another. All Griffin's efforts to find out who might have designs to ruin his sisters had failed. He had some suspicions, but that's all he had. They were flimsy at best and a poor substitute for facts.

That's why on this early evening he was back to the source: Sir Welby.

Griffin had been spending more time at White's in recent days. In the taproom, the billiards room, the reading room, all in hopes of hearing a comment, a word, something that might help him figure out who had been talking about him and his sisters that night. He usually had a keen sense and could pick up on the slightest inkling when something felt suspicious. But no one was talking. According to his aunt, even the gossip sheets had fallen silent on the subject.

Rounding the doorway, Griffin saw the old man with long, thinning gray hair sitting at his usual table right by the entrance. His shoulders and back were as straight as men half his age, though much thinner. His eyesight might only be a hazy blur of images, but there was nothing wrong with his hearing. Above the chatter of the patrons, the thud of tankards, and the clink of glasses being placed on wooden tables, Sir Welby had heard Griffin's approach and turned around. He always smiled, knowing whoever was walking in would speak to him as they passed.

Griffin stopped by his chair and said, "Evening, Sir Welby. Do you mind if I join you?"

"Your Grace," he said and immediately grabbed hold to the edge of the table to help him stand. "I'd be honored."

"Keep your seat," Griffin said, placing a hand on his shoulder to keep him from rising. "Your glass is almost empty. I'll order another for you." He glanced over at the bar and saw Holsey.

The man bowed.

Griffin nodded.

"No, no," Sir Welby said. "No more for me. I have enough trouble finding my out of here and out to my carriage in the evenings. I don't want to be blind and staggering too."

Griffin laughed as did Sir Welby. One of the servers approached, but Griffin waved the man away.

"I wanted to ask if you'd remembered anything more about what you'd heard about my sisters," he said, sitting down opposite the man.

Sir Welby's brown eyes squinted. His bushy gray eyebrows twitched. It looked as if he were trying to focus on Griffin's face but couldn't quite manage. "No, no, I can't say that I have. Not a thing more."

"You sit here most every evening. Have you since heard any of the voices from that night?"

He stared at Griffin blankly. "No, no. I'm sure I haven't.

I-I would have sent word to you immediately just like you asked if I had."

"That's puzzling. Everyone stops to speak to you when they come into the taproom."

"No, no. Not everyone speaks, but I'd say most of them do. Some are in too much of a hurry to be polite," he grumbled. "I told you, Your Grace, I'm not sure I'd recognize them again if they did. I don't know everyone who comes in here like I used to. There were too many voices that night. They all blended together just like I said."

"All right," Griffin said. "Has anyone mentioned this to you and questioned you about it?"

"Yes, yes," he answered, suddenly looking excited. "Most everyone who stops by to speak asks me if I've heard anymore from the blades. I tell them the same thing I'm telling you. It was only the two of them. I haven't heard another word, and don't think I will. I don't think they want to say anything else around me for fear I'll tell everyone that too."

That was odd. Griffin rolled his shoulders. "Earlier you said it might have been as many as three, four, or more."

"Yes, yes, that's right. Two to four. It was dark. I'm not sure."

The man seemed to be certain the last time he spoke with him. Griffin glanced around the taproom. The lamps had been lit. It was dim but not dark.

"Have you not found out any indications as to who the young blades might be?" the old gentleman asked.

The last thing Griffin wanted was Sir Welby telling everyone he had narrowed his suspicions down to Sir Charles Redding and Mr. Albert Trent. It would be fine if Trent and Sir Charles suspected he might be watching them, but he didn't want them to know for sure. What still baffled the hell out of him was that no one was talking. London Society wasn't known for keeping secrets.

Griffin shook his head. When he realized that Sir Welby probably couldn't see the gesture, he said, "Not yet."

"I'll ask around for you," he said eagerly. "And see what I can find out."

"It's good of you to offer, but I'd rather you didn't say anything more about this to anyone."

Sir Welby gave him a questioning look, then said, "That's probably for the best. It could be that whoever was doing the bold talk that night has decided against putting their words into action since it's been written about in every scandal sheet in London. Not to mention they'd be downright foolish to try anything with a duke's sister."

"That's what I'm hoping, but we both know there are some men willing try anything."

Chapter 18

Do make the best of any unpleasant situation
put before you.

❧

MISS MAMIE FORTESCUE'S DO'S AND DON'TS FOR
CHAPERONES, GOVERNESSES, TUTORS, AND NURSES

The old and magnificent Grand Hall had been favored with the first ball of the Season since it was built over half a century ago. This year was no exception for the famed building, which had been honored with the presence of kings, queens, emperors, and nobility from countries all over the world. When Esmeralda stepped inside, she'd gasped at the opulence of the décor. It far exceeded anything she'd ever seen.

Keeping in the grand style of elegance, the vestibule had gilt-covered chairs with plush, rose-colored velvet cushions lining the walls and filling the beautifully appointed, scalloped alcoves. It was the perfect area for patrons wanting a reprieve from the music, chatter, and laughter of the guests. Couples could steal away for intimate conversations or gentlemen could conduct business discussions in privacy while the festivities continued in the main room.

The ballroom glimmered with flickering candles that threw pale yellow light from corner to corner, windows to doors, and back again. A wide archway leading into the gathering place, where guests stopped briefly to be announced, had been decorated with greenery and pale blue, yellow, and violet flowers. Twelve Corinthian columns trussed with flowing ribbons hanging from their gilt-topped capitals were evenly dispersed around the spacious hall and appeared to be holding up the massive ceiling, which had been painted blue with floating white clouds to resemble a sky.

Throughout the room, tall urns, short vessels, and small vases overflowed with spring's most gorgeous blooms. Someone had somehow managed to produce a spectacular stone waterfall in the center of the room about the height of a man. It had also been adorned with flowers. On one side of the spacious area, the musicians were clustered closely together playing a lively tune. The dance floor was crowded with beautifully gowned ladies and splendidly dressed gents swinging, twirling, and clapping in time with the music.

Along the back wall stood four white linen–draped tables. One was filled with sparkling glasses and what looked to be endless bottles of champagne and wine. The other three were laden with food. Gleaming, tiered silver trays were filled with such delicacies as stuffed mushrooms, smoked oysters, quail eggs, and small slices of ham and lamb. A variety of cooked vegetables, fruits, and breads topped another table. The fourth and largest overflowed with pastries, pies, tarts, and other mouthwatering treats for those wanting a taste of something sweet.

The aromas of food and candle wax, sounds of the loud music, the drone of humming chatter and laughter, and the breeze whistling through the open doorways made everything about the room a feast for all the senses. Esmeralda found it impossible to take in the spectacle of it all at once.

"There must be at least two hundred people here," Lady Sara said as they stood in the archway and looked down into the ballroom. "Griffin, you can't possibly know them all, can you?"

"Most, and we might as well get started with the introductions. It looks as if the Earl of Daundelyon and his ladyship are standing closest to us, so we will begin there."

"I want to meet Lord Henry first," Vera said.

"Yes, *we* want to meet him first," Sara corrected, giving her sister a stern look.

"That would be fine," Griffin said. "But I don't see him. There's no reason to pass by others just to go looking for him." He turned to Esmeralda. "Are you ready, Miss Swift?"

"Yes, Your Grace," she assured him.

The earl and his wife were delighted the duke chose them to be the first introduced to his sisters. While they chatted with Lord and Lady Daundelyon, Esmeralda stepped back and scanned the ballroom, looking at each male face to see if she could identify any of them as her cousin, Viscount Mayeforth. If he was present, she didn't recognize him.

After hearing some time ago the viscount was in ill health, she didn't expect to see him at the ball, but there was no way of knowing for sure. It had been almost fifteen years since she'd seen him, but she didn't think he could have changed all that much. Though it was his father who'd banished her mother from the family, she didn't expect her cousin to acknowledge her if they should come face-to-face. Still, she felt a sense of relief that she hadn't spotted him in the crowd.

Immediately after Lord and Lady Daundelyon said their

good-byes and moved away, the Earl of Hatterston walked up and bowed. "Good evening, Your Grace."

Griffin returned the bow and said, "My lord."

And so began the formal and tedious introductions all over again.

The widowed earl was a pleasant-looking fellow with dark brown eyes and a square chin. He had a full head of slightly graying hair and a robust build, but he was at least twenty years older than Lady Sara and Lady Vera. His wife had died more than a year ago. He'd already made it known in Society his mourning had passed and he was looking for a new bride.

Esmeralda didn't know if the earl could sense it, but she certainly could see the twins had no interest in the older gentleman no matter that he carried a title and great wealth along with his name. That made no difference to the sisters. As far as they were concerned, there was only one prize in the room, Lord Henry, and it looked as if they were prepared to fight over him.

Once securing the promise of a dance from Lady Sara and Lady Vera later in the evening, the earl excused himself. That started an avalanche of people standing in line to be introduced to the twins. Twins were such an oddity to begin with, and these two encouraged attention by wearing their hair in the same style and similar gowns of ivory lace over a pale melon underdress.

But that wasn't their only draw. There was the added attraction of the recent gossip concerning them, not to mention the fact they were the daughters and sisters of a duke. Not many young ladies could boast having that many reasons for someone to seek them out at the first ball of their first Season.

After each time Esmeralda was introduced as the chaperone, she would step back on the conversations so as not intrude, and let the others talk pleasantries. Not only was it the right thing to do, but she wanted to make herself as uninteresting as possible so no one would question her too closely about her position or about herself. It wasn't difficult. Everyone's interest seemed to be solely on Lady Sara and Lady Vera.

Esmeralda took special notice when the beautiful, blue-eyed Miss Irene Froste approached with her father. The young lady couldn't keep her eyes off the duke, and Esmeralda couldn't keep her gaze off Miss Froste. Like the twins, it was her first ball, and Esmeralda quickly surmised that the young lady had made up her mind that Griffin was the one she wanted, much like Lady Sara and Lady Vera had set their sights on Lord Henry.

Miss Froste had been schooled well in how to be charming. The duke was her main focus of interest, but she took time to talk with both twins and promised to pay a visit in the next few days, which thrilled Lady Sara. Griffin didn't appear to have a problem listening to every word she said either.

Esmeralda tried not to let the young lady's overinterest in him invade her thoughts and fill her with envy, but she failed miserably. Miss Froste glowed with charisma, confidence, and a smile that invited the duke to call on her. Regrettably, Esmeralda couldn't find one thing to dislike about the young lady—except that she wasn't wearing gray!

At last Miss Froste and her father moved on and the onslaught of other attendees wanting introductions continued. Only a few sets of eyebrows were raised when Griffin introduced Esmeralda as the twins' chaperone, but none higher than when she was presented to the Dowager Countess Norwood. That concerned Esmeralda a little. The elderly countess could very well remember the scandal of Esmeralda's mother eloping with the poet almost fifteen years ago. In all her years of being a governess, Esmeralda had never heard a whisper of gossip about her mother, but that didn't mean it hadn't occurred. Thankfully, the lady excused herself without asking any probing questions.

Esmeralda made mental notes on all the bachelors who stood in line to meet the twins, including Lord Henry when he approached. Lady Evelyn hadn't been wrong about the man. He was divinely handsome. Esmeralda, who had no designs on him whatsoever, felt an uptick in her pulse at the sight of him. He reminded her of Griffin in that he wore his handsomeness as comfortably as most gentlemen wore their everyday coat. He stood tall, like Griffin, but maybe not so wide in the shoulders. His dark blond hair was thick and full of waves that fell attractively to the top of his neckcloth. To add to his handsome looks, his light brown eyes were full of merriment and his smile could have charmed a wild boar. It was no wonder he set all the young ladies' hearts to swooning.

She thought Lady Vera might faint when she was introduced to him, and Lady Sara was positively besotted by him too. But what must have been a huge disappointment to both girls was that Lord Henry didn't ask either sister to save him a dance before he left. It niggled at Esmeralda's mind as to why he didn't. All the other young bachelors, and the older ones too, had asked for a dance. Perhaps reticence was the way Lord Henry kept the young ladies interested in him. Maybe he liked to lead them on a merry chase.

The evening wore on and the crowd thinned. Mr. Albert Trent and Sir Charles Redding finally made their way over to meet the twins. Esmeralda and Griffin had made eye contact when the two approached. If they had gotten wind that Griffin had narrowed his search for the mischief-makers to them, they showed no signs of it. Esmeralda looked both over carefully as they smiled and bowed to the duke and his sisters. She'd expected to see something sinister or devilish in their manner, but they appeared as friendly and interested in Lady Sara and Lady Vera as had all the other bachelors.

After over an hour of formal introductions of the twins, Esmeralda was happy when Lady Sara strolled off to the dance floor with Mr. Lambert and Lady Vera walked away to dance with the Earl of Hatterston.

Griffin turned to Esmeralda and said, "It's time for a glass of champagne." He stopped a passing waiter, took two glasses from a tray, and handed one to her. He clinked his glass against hers and said, "May the Season progress quickly."

She'd never tasted champagne, though she'd always wanted to. She lifted her glass and took a very small sip. *Hmm,* she thought. It was really quite tasty. She took a larger sip.

"I noticed you wore my least-favorite color tonight," Griffin said.

Esmeralda saw a twinkle in his eyes and suddenly felt warm all over. It amazed her that just a look from him could do that to her. She lowered her glass.

"Did you?" she asked innocently.

"You know I did." His lips crooked into a captivating grim. "It's the only color I've seen you wear."

"It's the only color I have," she said. "It's serviceable."

She looked down at her gown. A delicate pink lace lined the scooped neckline, which fell a respectable three inches below the hollow of her throat. A drawstring of pink satin ribbon cinched the high waist and the cuffs of the sleeves.

"And it's a light shade of gray," she argued. "Silver really."

"It's gray."

"If I had known you had such an aversion to the color, I would have chosen another. Perhaps mulberry would have suited you better."

A wrinkle formed in his brow. "The thought of you in

such a dark and dull shade of red is no better than the col-orless gray you are wearing now," he murmured and took a drink from his glass.

Esmeralda smiled. "Then there will be no pleasing you with my wardrobe choices, so I'll change the subject. Tell me, what did you think of Sir Charles and Mr. Trent tonight? Did either of them appear pensive, ill at ease, or untrustworthy to you?"

"Not in the least. I kept my eyes on them the entire time. I didn't sense any mischief. I really shouldn't have expected to. If anything will be done, it won't be when I'm present."

"I agree with your assessment," she answered. "If they are some of the ones who were spouting off that night, they could have very well changed their minds once it was made known you were aware of their dangerous talk. Dukes can be very powerful when they choose to be."

One corner of his mouth lifted slightly with amusement, and her heart tripped ridiculously fast. Her feelings for him were so foolish. Griffin belonged with someone such as Miss Froste, not with a chaperone.

"So you think I might have scared them off when they heard I'd cut their hearts out if anyone dared to touch one of my sisters?"

Esmeralda mouthed a silent O. "You didn't say that, did you?"

"No." He grunted a short laugh. "But I thought about it, and more than once. What did you observe about the other gentlemen the twins met tonight? Any appear suspicious to you?"

"No, but then I've had little experience with men, Your Grace, so I could be wrong about that. I still think Mr. Lambert is harmless and seems to be quite smitten with Lady Sara."

"I noticed that he looked more at her too."

"Lord Henry didn't give either of the twins any lingering glances. Not because they aren't beautiful, of course. It must be that he has so many young ladies to choose from, he has no reason to flatter or favor any young lady in particular."

She stopped talking. Griffin was looking at her in the way that always made her think about being held in his arms and kissed. And that was the last thing she needed to be thinking tonight, so she took another sip of her champagne.

"I believe you have Lord Henry pegged exactly right."

"No doubt you know how he feels about having his choice of all the young ladies."

His lips formed an attractive half grin. "Let's just say I know that he isn't lacking any female companionship he wants."

"I thought as much. And though I have no knowledge of him, and very little of men in general, I feel comfortable saying I doubt he will have any interest in matrimony for the foreseeable future."

Griffin chuckled softly. "For someone who has little knowledge, you seem to be right about most things. Now tell me, what else did you make note of?" he asked, changing the conversation back to where it started.

She let her gaze drift over the ballroom. "I see at least five or six gentlemen who didn't come over for introductions."

"I noticed that too," he said. "What do you make of it?"

Esmeralda knew Griffin didn't need her input on the men. Apparently he was trying to make her feel useful. "Probably the same thing you do. They know you are on the lookout for trouble. It could be they are either guilty or perhaps decided to stay away rather than have the possibility you might think they are up to no good concerning your sisters."

"That's exactly what I'm thinking."

"All the ones we met tonight looked to be genuinely interested in your sisters. And why shouldn't they be? Lady Sara and Lady Vera are intelligent, lively, and beautiful. All the things a man could want in a dance partner or when thinking of making a match. I hope that means that your worry over their being compromised in some way is all for naught."

"That is my hope."

His eyes met hers and she found herself wanting to smile at him, to engage him with clever banter. The duke was divinely handsome, standing beside her in his crisp white shirt, elegantly tied neckcloth, white quilted waistcoat, and black evening jacket. An intense longing filled her. She wished she were free to let him know she wanted him to pursue her the way Miss Froste had let him know. Esmeralda would have liked to be dressed in a stunningly beautiful gown made of silk and organdy, trimmed with the most delicate of laces and tiniest of bows.

But she wasn't, so she finished off her drink.

"Would you like another?"

She looked into the empty glass. "No. That was very nice, but I won't have more. I'm afraid I drank it much too fast."

"It's easy to do with champagne. It can go to your head quite quickly."

"Thank you for the late warning," she said absently. *Miss Froste would have been told that and taught the proper way to drink champagne,* she thought grudgingly. "I'll be more careful next time."

"Was it your first taste of champagne?"

"Yes," she offered quietly while continuing to stare into the bottom of the glass. "I've not spent a lot of time in social settings where champagne is offered."

"I keep forgetting that because you handle yourself so well in every situation."

Her livelihood depended on it. Esmeralda had been

taught many things a young lady should know before her mother absconded with Myles Graham, but not everything she needed to know.

"What are you thinking about?"

Seeing no reason not be honest, she raised her head and said, "I was wondering why you didn't ask Miss Froste to dance."

"What do you think my reason was?"

"I asked because I don't know," she answered. "She's lovely, friendly, and she—and her father I might add—made it quite clear they wanted you to ask her. Lady Agatha wanted to dance with you as well."

"Hmm," was all he said.

Suddenly exasperated she said, "Oh, for the love of heaven. You cannot make me believe you didn't notice they both practically asked *you* for a dance."

One corner of his mouth lifted in humor. "You forgot Miss Waldegrave. I believe she expected me to ask her for a set around the dance floor too."

Esmeralda laughed. "It's impossible to get the best of you, Griffin."

He laughed softly too. "All right, I noticed. And I noticed that you just called me Griffin."

Esmeralda gasped. "I didn't." Oh, she should have never started thinking about him as "Griffin." She should have known she would slip up and land herself in trouble. "Please tell me I didn't."

"You did, and I don't mind. I'm glad you realize that when no one else is around, you are Esmeralda and I am Griffin," he finished in a low tone as Lady Vera and Lady Sara were delivered back to their brother's side by their dancing partners, laughing and out of breath from the fast quadrille.

As soon as the earl and Mr. Lambert left, two more dapper gents approached the twins, and they were quickly off to the dance floor again. Having seen a woman who once worked for Miss Fortescue, Esmeralda excused herself from the duke and walked over to speak to her. They chatted for a while and then walked around the ballroom eyeing the beautifully prepared food on the buffet tables, the flowing fountain in the center of the room, and all the flowers. But Esmeralda was careful to keep glancing toward the twins as well.

The duke talked with various people throughout the evening, but he and Esmeralda would always meet up together again when Lady Sara and Lady Vera returned from their dances.

It was much later when Lord Henry finally approached and said, "Excuse me for interrupting, Your Grace."

"You're not interrupting."

"Good. I wanted to ask Lady Vera or Lady Sara to join me in the next dance." He took the time to bestow a smile on each twin. "They are both so lovely, I'm not sure which one to ask first."

Stepping forward, Lady Vera said, "I'll help you with that, Lord Henry. Of course you should dance with my sister, Lady Sara, first. She's the oldest, we've been told, but only by a few minutes." Lady Vera turned and smiled sweetly at her sister. Lady Sara was clearly astonished by her sister showering her with such a favor. "I wouldn't dream of putting myself before Sara. Would you mind if she danced with you first?"

"Not at all, Lady Vera. I shall return for you another set."

"Yes, do."

Esmeralda was amazed by Lady Vera's generosity too, and knew there had to be a reason behind it. A reason that would only benefit Lady Vera.

After the two walked away, Griffin said, "That was kind of you, Vera."

"It wasn't kind at all. It was strategy, dear brother. Lord

Henry will not remember he danced with Sara first, but he has made note of my willingness to so eagerly let my sister go first. Now, he has to wonder whether or not I want to dance with him. That means he will be thinking about me and not her."

"Perhaps you are more clever than I gave you credit for."

"Oh no," Lady Vera said under her breath. "Maybe not. Here comes Mr. Trent, and I can tell by his determined smile he's coming straight over here to ask me to dance."

Griffin glanced at Esmeralda before asking, "What do you find objectionable about him?"

"Nothing I'm sure, except for the fact that he's not Lord Henry."

A few moments later, Esmeralda smiled as she watched Lady Vera dancing with Mr. Trent. *Serves her right,* Esmeralda thought. Vera had been nice to her sister but only because she wanted to gain from it.

When she turned back to Griffin she saw two tall, handsome gentlemen walking up to greet him. One had an instant, exotic appeal, with wide dark eyes and black hair that almost touched his shoulders. Most Englishmen were much fairer. He had a lean stride to his step and a slight swagger to his shoulders. The other man was no less attractive, and maybe more so. His hair fell just below his collar. He'd been blessed with intriguing green eyes and more of the classic handsomeness of Griffin and Lord Henry.

Everything about the two projected power, privilege, and wealth. By the confidence in their expressions and the tilt of their heads, Esmeralda knew they had to be the other two-thirds of the "Rakes of St. James." The three of them standing together made for a powerful, commanding trio of males.

"At last, my friends have decided to arrive at the ball," Griffin said.

"We've been here," the rake with the longer, darker hair

said, trying not to be obvious that he was looking Esmeralda over.

"You couldn't see us for the flock of people waiting to meet your sisters," the other one added.

"You should have plowed your way through and joined me in my misery at having to do my brotherly duties."

"It was more enjoyable just to watch you stand in one place for so long, hating every boring moment of it," the light-haired gentleman said with a friendly smirk.

"Remember, it will be your turn next year, my friend, and you may need my help."

"Don't remind me," he said on a hushed breath. "Let me enjoy this Season without thinking about the responsibility of seeing my sister wed in the next."

"Rath, Hawk, may I introduce Miss Esmeralda Swift, the twins' chaperone. Miss Swift, the Duke of Rathburne and the Duke of Hawksthorn."

Esmeralda curtsied. "Your Graces."

Her gaze strayed from one duke to the other, and subtle though it was, they were both looking her over carefully too. She had assumed she would meet the other two rakes tonight, and they had unquestionably measured up to her expectations.

"I was just talking with Miss Swift about the gentlemen the twins have met tonight. She had some insights that will be helpful. Have either of you heard anything?"

"Nothing helpful from me," the Duke of Hawksthorn offered. "If anyone is planning anything dastardly, you are going to have a difficult time finding out who. Everyone's quiet on the subject. But there's plenty of time left in the Season."

"I haven't heard any talk worth mentioning either," the Duke of Rathburne added, "However, just before coming here I heard that the first wager concerning the rumor has shown up on the books at White's."

Griffin grimaced. "I was hoping that wouldn't happen."

"We all were, but it's not as bad as it could be," he answered and glanced at Esmeralda again.

"Just tell me what it is."

"What we expected. Whether or not either of the twins will be touched by scandal this Season."

"And if so," the other duke added, "will it only be one of them or both."

Griffin looked at Esmeralda. Assuming that was her permission to speak she said, "I agree this doesn't sound disastrous, Your Grace. The twins will probably get wind of this from one of the young ladies they've met tonight, but it will be easy enough to explain. Daughters of a duke can be set upon by envious people who feel justified in their meanness. Scandalous things like this are to be expected during the Season and can be upsetting, but aren't usually lastingly harmful."

"Well said, Miss Swift," the Duke of Hawksthorn said. "I believe that too."

The Duke of Rathburne turned to Esmeralda. "The musicians will be starting a new dance soon. Are you two dancing this set?"

"No, of course not," Esmeralda said with a smile. It was an outlandish thing for him to ask. She took it as amusing that he would suggest Griffin do such a thing as dance with his sisters' chaperone.

"Then I would like to dance with you, Miss Swift."

There was a casual charm about the duke's slight smile that was infectious. She returned his friendly manner and said, "Thank you, Your Grace, but I must decline. I'm not here to dance with anyone. Only to be available to Lady Sara and Lady Vera."

"Nonsense." His gaze held steady on hers. "A ball is for dancing. Being here as a chaperone doesn't mean you can't enjoy yourself too."

Esmeralda would have liked to glance at Griffin, but decided against it. She was afraid he might think she would be silently asking for his permission to join the daring duke. She didn't want him to think that. "You're quite right. I'm enjoying myself very much."

"Good. Then it should continue. The twins are dancing right now. There's no better place to keep an eye on them than from the dance floor."

The Duke of Rathburne knew how to pour on the charm. While she appreciated his interest and could enjoy his exotic allure, she had no desire to dance with him.

"I prefer to take care of my responsibilities from the position where I am now, Your Grace. However"—she deliberately paused and glanced around the room—"I see many young ladies who are looking at you right now, and I'd be willing to wager all are hoping you'll go over and ask one of them to be your partner for this dance."

The Duke of Rathburne chuckled softly. "I don't believe I've ever had anyone turn me down for a dance, Miss Swift."

"I'd wager on that too," she said, knowing peers didn't like to be denied anything they wanted, and they never expected to be told no. "I do regret that I had to be the first to break your perfect record, Your Grace, but I must. I can't dance with you."

His gaze sparkled at her. He reached down and picked up her hand and started pulling her away. "I insist."

More than a little shocked by his touching her, she resisted his efforts, refusing to move her feet and trying to pull her hand out of his grasp. "No, Your Grace, I insist you accept my refusal and let go of me."

Griffin's hand clamped around the Duke of Rathburne's cuffed wrist. Looking pointedly into his friend's eyes, he said, "She declined."

Chapter 19

Don't let anything take you by surprise.

~❧~

MISS MAMIE FORTESCUE'S DO'S AND DON'TS FOR
CHAPERONES, GOVERNESSES, TUTORS, AND NURSES

Griffin's hand tightened. He knew exactly what his friend was doing and he didn't like it. Rath had always pushed the boundaries. With strangers, his relatives, his friends—everyone was fair game to him. The blackguard had always been too damned perceptive too. Rath must have seen the way Griffin looked at Esmeralda, as if she were a sweet confection he couldn't wait to eat with a spoon. Or perhaps he just sensed that Griffin was aching to make her his.

In either case, the strength in Griffin's grip let Rath know the answer. Esmeralda wasn't fair game between the three of them. Grasping the hand of a lady was a ploy the three had sometimes used when they'd first entered Society. After a brawl between the three of them early on, they'd learned it wasn't in their best interest to pursue the same female be she tavern wench, paid mistress, or proper young lady. Griffin's hold on Rath's wrist answered him concerning Esmeralda's availability.

"She declined," Griffin said again.

"So she did." Rath gave Griffin a knowing smile. He let go of Esmeralda and bowed. Griffin let go of Rath. "My apologies, Miss Swift. Maybe some other time."

"Yes, of course," she said politely and took a step away from the forward duke. "Another time."

Esmeralda glanced at Griffin. He knew she sensed something was going on between the two men that she didn't understand, but he had no intentions of telling her his friend was making sure that she was not someone to be pursued.

Griffin gave Rath a nod. "We'll continue this later."

"As expected. Let's meet at White's after you see the twins home."

Griffin heard a familiar squeal. He looked around to see his sisters leaving their dance partners behind and rushing toward him.

"Your Graces," Sara said, stopping next to Rath. "We haven't seen you in months."

"Why haven't you two been to visit us?" Vera asked with her practiced pout. "We've been in London more than a week."

"I just returned to London a few days ago myself," Hawk offered.

Vera looked at Rath. He gave her a noncommittal shrug. "I have no excuse."

"I'm not surprised." Smiling, she added, "Thank you. Griffin told us you would be here tonight and that both of you would ask us to dance. Now, which of you wants to dance with me first?"

Griffin noticed Esmeralda was shocked at how freely and familiar Vera and Sara talked to the dukes. It was uncommon. She didn't know that Rath and Hawk had always treated them like sisters when they were younger, playing hide-and-seek or blindman's bluff with them whenever they visited the Griffin estate.

To Griffin's surprise, Esmeralda spoke up and said, "It's providential the two of you arrived just now. The Duke of Rathburne was looking for someone to dance with."

"Then look no further, Your Grace," Vera said to the duke.

Rath glanced at Griffin. "I know when I have lost the war." He turned to Vera and bowed. "Will you accept this dance with me?"

"Happily."

"Lady Sara, would you enjoy this set with me?" Hawk asked.

"Delighted," she answered with a smile.

"And this will be the last dance of the evening," Griffin said. "We'll meet you at the entrance with your wraps in hand."

"Griffin, surely not."

"Yes, Vera. There will be more dances tomorrow night and the night after."

After the two couples walked away, Griffin said, "That was a clever way for you to retaliate against the duke for his insistence you dance with him."

"It was no such thing," Esmeralda prevaricated. "I wasn't retaliating for his poor judgment in asking me to dance."

Griffin chuckled. "I find it utterly enchanting when you so earnestly deny what I know to be truth."

"Perhaps his insistence did get the better of my good nature," she offered innocently.

"You know, he's the one who first called us the 'Rakes of St. James.'"

"No, I didn't know that, but I can now understand why it's an apt title."

"I never thought it fit us."

"That's surprising."

"We always had a rule. We don't touch innocents."

Esmeralda gave him a doubtful look, and he knew further explanation was needed. He didn't mind telling her.

"Don't look at me like that, Esmeralda." His expression turned rueful. "Not because of some high and lofty honor. It was much more selfish than that. We were all afraid of being caught in a parson's mousetrap and leg-shackled. None of us wanted that, so we stayed to our mistresses—as most gentlemen do."

Her face softened. "I believe you. Thank you for telling me that. Hearing it does make all of you seem less of a rake." She hesitated. "Well, perhaps except for the Duke of Rathburne."

Griffin laughed.

"Your Grace, Miss Swift, excuse me for interrupting."

Griffin turned to see the dowager countess he'd spoken to earlier in the evening. "Yes, of course, Lady Norwood."

"I forgot to inquire as to the health of Lady Evelyn and whether she's accepting visits."

"Not at this time."

"Such a pity. We were all sorry to hear she's missing your sisters' debut after she's looked forward to it for so long."

Griffin listened to the countess with a skeptical ear. She said all the right words, but he didn't hear a hint of concern for his aunt in the woman's tone. No doubt she was only after gossip to spread to the other widows sitting around the hall in hopes an older bachelor would ask them for a set.

"Yes, she has looked forward to the twins' Season. She gains strength every day. Just this week she was up and sitting by the window in her room, looking to see how many of the flowers had bloomed in the garden."

"And such a lovely garden it is you have in Mayfair." Lady Norwood sniffed into her lace handkerchief. "Glad to hear it. Do tell Lady Evelyn I asked concerning her welfare."

"I'll be sure to."

She turned to Esmeralda. "I was hoping I might have a word with you, Miss Swift, about something that's been puzzling me greatly since we met."

Griffin was about to excuse himself so the ladies could talk in private, but hesitated when he glanced at Esmeralda. There was an unusual, wary expression on her face. That stopped him. Something was wrong. For some reason, she felt threatened by the countess. A primal need to protect her rose up in him.

Instinctively, he moved closer to her side.

"How can I help you, Countess?" Esmeralda asked quietly.

"I remember the former Viscount Mayeforth had a daughter who was married to a Swift. While I don't recall her name, I do recollect she had a daughter named Esmeralda, because that's my daughter's name."

The dowager paused as if waiting for Esmeralda to say something, but Esmeralda remained silent.

Lady Norwood continued. "The viscount's daughter's first husband died, and if my memory serves me well, she later defied her family's wishes and eloped with . . . a poet, I believe. Do you know anything about her or about that? On occasion, I've wondered what happened to her since our girls had the same name."

That fleeting fragile expression that Griffin had seen on Esmeralda's face the first day he saw her had returned. Once again, it caught him off guard. He remembered thinking that day that she was hiding hurts, regrets, demons, something from her past that had wounded and troubled her deeply. He'd considered questioning her about it at the time to find out what haunted her, but he'd denied his first instincts and hadn't inquired. Now he wished he'd pried into her personal past.

"Yes," Esmeralda said, an innocent vulnerability visible in her face and in her voice.

"Are you by chance that Esmeralda, and the grand-daughter of the third Viscount of Mayeforth?"

Esmeralda the granddaughter of a viscount?

The roar of the chatter around them and the tune of the music in the distance all faded from his hearing. Listening for Esmeralda's answer was the only thing that interested Griffin. What was her answer? He should already know, but he didn't.

Esmeralda's back remained unbowed. Her chin and shoulders lifted just enough to make her appear strong, composed, and slightly disinterested. Her expression slowly changed to the professional expression that had first attracted him to her.

"Yes, Lady Norwood, I am."

Griffin felt as if a fist was pressing on his throat. He digested what Esmeralda's words meant. She was the grand-daughter of a viscount. Not a poor or distant relation of Sir Timothy Swift who had to earn her living, but a lady of quality by her own birthright. Why hadn't she made this known? No, she hadn't just failed to tell him. She had hidden it from him.

"I was thinking that must be so," the old dowager continued in her inquisitive manner with no thought for how quietly Esmeralda had answered. "And I believe I heard long ago that that your mother had a child with her second husband. Is that correct?"

"Yes." Esmeralda shifted her contemplative gaze to Griffin. "Josephine is my sister, and she is doing well."

All Griffin could think was that Esmeralda was a lady, and she was working in his house as a paid chaperone. No wonder she had always appeared so refined, so circum-spect, and so well above her station in life.

She was!

How in damnation had that happened?

He intended to find out.

"And thank you for asking about Miss Josephine, Lady Norwood," Griffin stepped in to say.

The dowager sniffed. "Have you met her?"

"Yes. She lives in Mayfair with Miss Swift, Lady Sara, Lady Vera, and Lady Evelyn."

"Well, if Lady Evelyn—"

"If you'll excuse us, Countess," Griffin interrupted. "The dance has ended. I told my sisters we would meet them at the entrance as we'd already planned to leave after this set."

"Yes, I must get their wraps. Excuse me, my lady." Esmeralda turned away without a glance to him.

Not five steps past the countess, Griffin fell in step beside Esmeralda and said emphatically, "That was a quite an enlightening conversation we had with Lady Norwood."

"Is that how you would describe it?"

She didn't bother to look at him when she answered. That irritated him greatly. The least she could do was face him.

"Finding out you're the granddaughter of a viscount? Yes, I'd say that qualifies as enlightening—and damned surprising too. You have some explaining to do when we get home tonight, Miss Swift."

"I know," she said and kept on walking.

Chapter 20

Don't give in to guilty pleasures.
There's a reason they're called "guilty."

❧

MISS MAMIE FORTESCUE'S DO'S AND DON'TS FOR
CHAPERONES, GOVERNESSES, TUTORS, AND NURSES

When we get home.
Esmeralda could no longer count the times
that Griffin had strung together words that touched her
deeply and renewed her spirit. *You're the one I want. I
will come to you. When we get home. You are a part of my
household.* And all the other innocent words spoken by
him, and sounding so incredibly heartwarming to her.

But alas, this night, Esmeralda had a feeling that she
might have done what Josephine's and Napoleon's antics
hadn't been able to do—given the duke a reason to dismiss
her from his household.

A heavy downpour rushed the four of them into the
house from the carriage. Esmeralda and Griffin remained
quiet. The sisters didn't seem to notice. While Lady Sara
and Lady Vera took off their gloves and wraps, they kept
the conversation going with talks of all the gentlemen

they'd met and danced with, the young ladies they'd enjoyed and the ones they hadn't, as well as an annoying amount of oohs and ahhs over the jewelry, headpiece, and gown of each female in attendance.

Esmeralda was happy their first ball had been a rousing success with not a hint of mischief in the air. But her glee for them was tempered. The duke now knew her secret.

Ever since Esmeralda had walked away from Lady Norwood at the ball, she'd been tamping down the unwelcome feeling of trepidation that kept wanting to rise inside her. If she let it, she knew it would defeat and devour her. That couldn't happen. There was no reason for the feelings of apprehension simmering inside her. She'd done nothing wrong. Yes, she'd withheld information that the duke would have probably wanted to know, but she hadn't deceived him. She hadn't been under any obligation to tell him about her mother's past as it had no bearing on her ability to do what was expected of her.

It had been easy to avoid his penetrating gaze in the dark carriage, but now, while she was busy removing her outer clothing, she couldn't stop glancing at him. He was looking at her too. That the duke was also shedding his damp cloak dashed her faint hope that he might leave without questioning her.

She wondered what was going through his mind as he peeled his gloves from his hands. Did he know she was troubled? Was he unsure about what to say or do? Would he think she was tainted by her mother's refusal to obey her brother? And what would he think of Josephine once he knew who her father was?

No! Esmeralda silently reprimanded herself once again. She would not allow thoughts of despair to weigh her down.

"Are you going to sit with us for a while before you go, Griffin?" Lady Sara asked.

"Yes, do," Lady Vera added, taking hold of his hand.

"It would be lovely to continue our discussion about the evening with you."

Pensive, he said, "Not tonight."

"Then why have you taken off your cloak?" Lady Sara asked with an amused smile. "Was it just so you could put it on again, or are you getting forgetful in your old age?"

"Neither is the case, so stop being impish." He patted her cheek affectionately. "You two go on up. I have a few things to discuss with Miss Swift and then I'll be on my way."

"I'm not sleepy and don't want to go to bed. Perhaps we can join your discussions."

Griffin pulled his hand out of his sister's grasp. "You can't join me, but I see no reason why you and Sara can't talk in one of your rooms for the rest of the night if you want to."

Lady Vera reached up and kissed his cheek. "Thank you, dear brother. That's exactly what I wanted to hear you say anyway."

Lady Sara bussed his other cheek. "Let's go to your room, Vera, since it's the farthest from Aunt Evelyn's. That way we won't wake her with our laughter."

Lifting their skirts, the twins headed up the stairs.

The time had come. No more delays were afforded her. She had to face Griffin. Inhaling a deep breath, she met his steady blue gaze. There was no anger or disappointment in his expression. He didn't even look perplexed. He looked determined.

Very determined.

Quietly, almost softly, he said, "Would you join me in the book room, Esmeralda?"

Staring up into his gorgeous blue eyes, Esmeralda felt an unwavering strength come over her and settle in her bones. She was going to be all right. No matter how he chose to deal with this information, he would not cower her.

"Very well," she said as she heard the door to Lady Vera's room close.

Depending on her inner strength, she walked past him and headed down the corridor. If the duke decided to turn her off, she would manage. She had always managed.

There was no lamp burning, no fire on the grate when she walked into the chilled room. The only light was a faint yellow glow that spilled down from the vestibule, brightening only a few feet into the room. Welcoming the darkness, Esmeralda went farther into the shadows near the window before turning around.

Griffin stood in the doorway. Their gazes met across the room. In that instant she almost wilted. Backlit by the lamplight cast down the corridor he looked magnificent, powerful, and commanding. All those things and so much more. This unattainable man had captured her heart, and she had no idea how she was going to free it. There was no will inside her to do so.

Without a word said and with long, purposeful strides, Griffin strode over to her and in a single fluid motion slid his arms around her waist, caught her up in his arms, and quickly claimed her lips for his own. His startling and unexpected actions took her breath away, frightening and thrilling her all at the same time. His lips were warm, smooth, and moist, moving slowly, surely, deftly over hers. A pleasure she'd never known spiraled through her body, like fireworks shooting into the sky, and she surrendered into the bounty of his embrace.

The kiss was no brief, light brushing of his lips against hers, as she'd imagined many times in her dreams. It was seeking, demanding, and savoring, continuing second after glorious second, making sure she knew he wanted to kiss her as much as she'd wanted him to.

Instinctively she parted her lips. His strong, firm arms pulled her more solidly to his wide chest and wrapped tighter around her back as if in fear someone would rip her from his grasp. His lips moved over hers in a hungry, greedy way that caused a tightening in her breasts, a quickening in the depths of her abdomen and between her legs. Somehow she knew he wanted her to open her mouth and, when she did, his tongue slipped inside. She heard him swallow small gasps of pleasure as he explored the depths of her mouth.

Their kisses ebbed and flowed. At times they kissed long, hard, and generous. Some kisses were soft and quick. Their breaths, moans, and sighs mingled quietly and eagerly together, becoming one passionate sound.

Esmeralda lifted her arms and circled his neck, allowing him to press her closer to his hard, muscular body. Her hands cupped the back of his head and her fingers tangled in the rich thickness of his hair before exploring the width of his shoulders.

Griffin's lips left hers and he kissed her cheek, her chin, and down to the crook of her neck before searching out her lips once again. With an urgent touch, his hand raked across her breast to her waist, her hip, and around to her buttocks, lifting her tightly against him before finding her breast again.

"You are a beautifully shaped woman, Esmeralda," he whispered against her lips. "You should never be hidden behind gray cloth."

"It is best for me," she answered quickly before her breaths were once again claimed by his kisses.

His caresses were eager yet tender and sure. She gasped from the onslaught of all the different sensations mounting inside her as he breathed deeper, faster.

Griffin raised his head long enough to look into her eyes and whisper, "Not nearly enough," before claiming her lips once more.

Her body trembled, but so did his.

His kisses moved from her lips to her cheeks, her chin, and her eyelids, leaving no place on her face or neck untouched. Holding her close, his caresses were confident, commanding as he molded her breast in his palm with one hand and pressed her backside against him with the other. Esmeralda felt a hard bulge beneath his trousers. Her breaths quickened again. She had never felt anything like the sensations exploding inside her and, without really knowing why or how, she met his ardor with a surprising fervency of her own, pressing near him, clinging to him, and encouraging his touch.

With a long, desperate-sounding breath, Griffin suddenly turned her loose. He expelled a short, humorless laugh and stepped away from her.

Dismayed by the abrupt end to their passion and slightly dizzy from her still-reeling senses, Esmeralda moistened her lips and swallowed. She had no idea that kissing would feel so amazingly wonderful and so satisfying, and yet leave her wanting so much more. Surely Griffin couldn't deny that he'd been enjoying her kisses as much as she'd relished his. She'd clearly felt his desire for her through their clothing.

What would happen now? He'd said he couldn't kiss her as long as she was in his employ. But now he had. Fear started mounting inside her.

"I swear to you I didn't expect to kiss you when I asked you to come in here."

"I know. It was an afterthought."

"That doesn't do justice to what I was feeling, Esmeralda." He grunted. "I wanted to be angry with you, but . . ." He paused.

Her eyes had adjusted to the darkness. Frustration etched his handsome features. "But?"

"When I saw you standing in here in the shadows, all I could think was, dear God, I want to kiss her right now.

To hell with my honor, to hell with what was right and proper. To hell with what was best for you. I just wanted to kiss you and I could no longer deny myself the taste of you. I have wanted you in my arms almost from the moment I saw you."

That admission sent her heartbeat spinning again. She'd wanted that too, but she was too vulnerable at the moment to confess it out loud as he had.

If not for Griffin, how could she have ever known that such stirring sensations existed inside the body, waiting to be brought so vividly to life? She'd dreamed about being gathered gently in his arms, about sharing a soft kiss or two, but her thoughts hadn't prepared her for the consuming desire that had seeped into her soul, satisfying her so intimately she ached for the wonderful feelings to never end. And even now she couldn't wait to experience them again.

"Is what you told Lady Norwood true?" he asked, his breath sounding calmer. "The current Viscount Mayeforth is your cousin?"

Esmeralda hadn't talked about her past since she'd applied for a position with the agency. Miss Fortescue had listened to her story about her mother and deemed Esmeralda acceptable, so there was never a reason to talk about it again.

"Yes. I suppose you think it was wrong of me not to tell you."

"I would have rather heard it from you, yes."

"You're upset with me."

"No, but I want you to explain why you kept this information a secret from me."

From a habit she'd developed when challenged, she lifted her chin. "I didn't tell you about my mother's family because they have no merit concerning my life."

"That puzzles me." He sighed heavily as he raked a hand through his hair. "Maybe I am upset with you. You and Josephine are granddaughters of a viscount. And yet, you earn a living by working at an employment agency. You led me to believe you were a—"

"Commoner," Esmeralda said, suddenly defensive. "Not worthy."

His eyes and forehead narrowed into a frown. "That's not what I was going to say. Nor is it fair of you to suggest it was."

Peers always thought they were fair. Hiding her hurt in anger, she glared at him. "My mother's brother said those words to her about Myles Graham, the man she was in love with and wanted to marry."

"I was going to say you led me to believe you were a poor, distant relative of Sir Timothy Swift's, and there was no one to offer you protection or help," he said tightly. "There has never been anything common about you, Esmeralda, and now I know why. You aren't."

His words hit in the heart of her heart and her legs went weak. He'd never know how desperately she needed to hear that from him right now. She wanted to be worthy. To be worthy of him. Suddenly she felt close to that dreaded feminine weakness called crying.

Instead, she reached deep into her reserve of strength and said, "It's also true that I am a poor relative of Sir Timothy. My father never accrued wealth of his own."

"What I don't know is why you aren't under the care and protection of the current Lord Mayeforth. I know he's ill, but that doesn't absolve him from his duty to you and Josephine."

"He has no duty. My mother was disowned by her brother," Esmeralda said, suddenly feeling on the verge of tears again for all her mother had lost and for the loss of her mother. "Banished from her brother's house, his wealth, and his life. From all her family."

Griffin gave her an incredulous stare. "She might have

been, but you shouldn't have been. You and Josephine are granddaughters of a viscount and should be treated as such. You shouldn't be a chaperone for my sisters' Season, you should be under Lord Mayeforth's household and having your own Season."

Esmeralda huffed. "I have no reason to believe my cousin is any different from his father. I have no desire to be under his roof or his guardianship."

"You deserve it by right of your birth."

"So did my mother, but she was denied it simply because she disobeyed her brother," she offered earnestly. "He told her if she married Myles Graham she was never to show her face at his house again. She didn't. Neither shall I. I have proven I don't need his assistance to take care of Josephine."

Griffin searched her eyes. "It's his responsibility. If you wouldn't go to him for yourself, why not for Josephine?"

"Because she is my sister."

A quizzical expression settled on his face. "There's more that you aren't telling me, isn't there?"

"No," she expelled on choppy breath. Tears threatened again, but she held them at bay. "We may have different fathers, but it matters not to me. I will do everything I need to do to protect her."

"That has never been in doubt." His voice had softened. His questioning glance was replaced with concern. "I see how well you care for her, but you didn't answer my question."

Holding tightly to her emotions, refusing to let her voice waver, she said, "Josephine knows little about our mother and nothing about her past with the Mayeforth family. I intend to keep it that way."

"Why?"

Oh, those unwanted tears continued to threaten her. How could she explain to him and not cry? She knew how

Griffin persisted when he wanted something. He would be relentless until he had the answers he sought. She had to tell him before his intuitiveness and gentleness made her fall into his arms and weep.

"She loved her father. He was loving to her, wrote poetry for her, read it to her. She wrote poetry until her father's death. Now, she swears she hates it, and I know it's just her way of coping with his death. It was difficult for her. I refuse to let Josephine know her mother's family didn't approve of him. That, in fact, they called him a wandering Irish poet who would never take care of her. They said she would die penniless and unhappy." Her voice broke on a sob, which she sucked back quickly. "And the horrible, horrible truth of it is that they were right. My mother was wrong about him." Her voice broke on the last word.

"Esmeralda."

"No."

Griffin reached for her, but she spun away and wiped quickly at the wetness on her cheeks. "No," she said again, brushing off his concern. If he held her in his arms and pressed her head to his chest, she would start weeping and only heaven knew when she would stop. She cleared her throat, wiped her eyes again, and turned back to face him. "Do not feel sorry for me, or Josephine, or even for my mother. I don't want Josephine in Society. I don't want her looked down upon because of who her father was. I don't have to tell you how unforgiving Society can be."

"No, you don't."

"Do not dismiss me from this post." Her voice broke again, but she sniffed, shored up her courage, and added, "Not after you begged me to come here."

Griffin gave her an incredulous stare and moved to stand toe-to-toe with her again. "Begged you?" He lowered his head, bringing his face to where it nearly touched hers. "I beg no one, Esmeralda."

She leaned away from him. "I could have chosen another word."

"How about 'insisted.' "

"You hounded me."

"I outmanipulated you."

"You gave into my demands without really putting up much of a fight."

"I did so willingly, not begrudgingly, and only because it suited me to do so, Esmeralda."

Why did he always have to have an answer for everything she said? "Nonetheless, we have an arrangement, Your Grace. One that you insisted upon, and I am determined to hold you to it."

"Those are brave words."

She had to be. If she lacked the courage to speak now, she was doomed. "I'm sure Lady Norwood has already started spreading the news of who my mother is, but because I am Viscount Mayeforth's first cousin, I see no reason it will reflect badly on Lady Sara and Lady Vera for me to continue as long as you allow it."

"That is not the point about this, Esmeralda. You are a lady and shouldn't be working at all."

He brushed his hand through his rich, thick hair again.

She had exasperated him, but she couldn't back down. "I play the cards life dealt me," she answered, sounding stronger than she felt. "Now, do I have my position here in your household or do I return to the agency tomorrow morning?"

His gaze locked on hers. "I can't have you in my employ, and it has nothing to do with my sisters."

"That's rubbish," she argued. "You don't live here. What else could it be? If you find me so objectionable, I can have a separate carriage take me to the evenings' events."

"You don't understand yet, do you?" He leaned his body in close to hers. With his lips just inches from hers, he reached up to pull a pin from her hair and dropped it to the floor.

"What are you doing?"

A low, attractive chuckle whispered past his lips. "Taking down your hair so I can see it."

Another pin followed the first. Esmeralda wished she had the willpower to jerk away from his touch, but it was as if his hands in her hair had mesmerized her and she couldn't move. The third pin hit the floor, and several tendrils of hair fell down past her shoulders.

"Don't you know that the only things I find objectionable about you are that you hide your golden-brown hair in that tight knot at the back of your head and you wear no color other than gray."

"They are appropriate for me and my station in life."

"Not anymore. You know I couldn't kiss you as long as you were part of my household."

"Only ogres take advantage of their staff in that way."

Another pin slipped from her chignon, and the length of glass beads she wore in her hair plopped onto the rug at their feet. The duke threaded his fingers through her long tresses as they fell around her shoulders.

The smile on his face was gentle, and earnest. "Much better."

Esmeralda's heart felt as if it were melting in her chest.

"Now that I know you are an innocent, properly brought up young lady, and we are equals, I'm not supposed to kiss you either."

"Equals?" She harrumphed, her distaste for the power of peers rising inside her again. "You jest. Dukes are equal to no one but other dukes. Sisters are not equal to their viscount brothers, and I am certainly not equal to you."

He placed a finger on her lips to silence her and, rather than move away as she should have, she accepted his touch without a flinch.

His gaze swept up and down her face as if searching for something. "We are social equals, Esmeralda. If you stay here, when I come over, I will want to kiss you again." With the back of his palm he slowly, softly caressed her cheeks. First one and then the other.

"Not even a duke should always get what he wants," she countered.

He smiled. "I will explain by showing you what I am nobly trying to save you from. I desire you, Esmeralda. With the intensity of a desperate drowning man swimming for dry land."

His expression was so tender it caused her breath to catch in her throat.

He ran his thumb across her lips once, twice, three times. "I want to kiss you here on your beautiful lips."

She wanted that too.

With the delicate touch, and without letting his fingers leave her heated skin, they skimmed down the column of her throat to the hollow at its base where they rested. "I want to kiss you here where your blood pulsates against my touch."

Yes.

His hand slipped farther down and caught her breast up in his palm. Keeping his gaze settled on hers, he gently massaged her. Seconds ticked by before he said, "I want to kiss you here where I can feel your heart beating so fast beneath my hand it excites me."

With his gaze still penetrating hers, his hand moved down to her waist and cupped it briefly before moving around to let his open palm and splayed fingers rest firmly on her abdomen.

A soft moan escaped her lips. She heard his breathing increase.

He waited.

Slowly his hand slid down her gown and cupped the apex of her legs.

She gasped in surprise but didn't move. She was still too engrossed by his seduction.

"Your allure is great. I want to lie with you and make you mine. Now do you understand why you can't stay here where you are so easily within my reach?"

Esmeralda's body tingled with the discovery of yet another new sensation. The duke's hand was warm, firm, and strangely comforting, though it should be outrageously horrifying that he would touch her in such an intimate and inappropriate way and place. Yet she had no desire to ask him to move it.

"If you're trying to frighten me, it's not working."

"It frightens *me,* Esmeralda." His voice was low, husky, inviting. "You tempt me like no other lady ever has. Don't you know that now that I have held you and kissed you, it will be even harder to stay away from you?" He lowered his hand, stepped away from her, and asked, "So what am I going to do with you?"

"Leave me be. Don't relieve me of my duty here. Let me stay here and continue watching over Lady Sara and Lady Vera." She pressed harder, heedless of the fact she had no right to do so. "If you are a true man of honor, you will not go back on your word to me."

"Honor?" He smiled ruefully. "There are two honorable reasons I should have never touched you the first time. You are in my employ, and you are an innocent lady of noble birth. I have never pursued either with thought of seducing."

"I believe you."

"I'm not sure you do. I am a strong man, but still just a man. Your charm is almost impossible to resist."

"I understand the risks you have outlined so intimately, and I accept those risks."

"I can't," Griffin whispered and turned away.

From somewhere deep inside her the courage to continue challenging him rose up. Perhaps it was because she'd poured her heart out to him and felt she was deserving of more from him in return, or maybe it was just that she had nothing to lose and so much to gain.

Esmeralda quickly grabbed his arm and forced him to face her again. "You are a fair man. You must realize that if you dismiss me because of who you are and who I am it will be very difficult for me to find another post anywhere in London. I may even lose my position with Mr. Fortescue. If that happens, Josephine and I would have no place to live. "

"You ask a lot of me, Esmeralda."

"I must. You relentlessly pursued me for this position, and now I must keep it."

His gaze raked across her face, and she shivered with a need she couldn't explain.

"All right, for now, you can stay and continue your duties. I can't make any promises for the weeks to come."

"Fair enough," she whispered.

My Dearest Readers:

The long-awaited debut of the Duke of Griffin's twin sisters, Lady Sara and Lady Vera, came to an end last evening. And, yes, they are remarkably alike in appearance, manner, and temperament. However, whether or not the duke was aware of it, much attention was on him last night as well to see how ably he carried out his duties as guardian for his sisters. Conscientiously I'd say, much to the chagrin of all the young ladies who were hoping he'd forsake his post of watching over the twins for a dance with a lovely maiden. But perhaps the most scintillating gossip from the first ball of the Season wasn't about the duke or his sisters. It centered on their intriguing chaperone, Miss Esmeralda Swift.

MISS HONORA TRUTH'S WEEKLY SCANDAL SHEET

Chapter 21

Do listen to your friends. There's a reason
they aren't your enemies.

◆◆◆

MISS MAMIE FORTESCUE'S DO'S AND DON'TS FOR
CHAPERONES, GOVERNESSES, TUTORS, AND NURSES

A noise disturbed Esmeralda's slumber. She retreated
from it, but it came again.

She moaned contentedly and snuggled deeper into her
covers. If she had to get up, she might as well be thinking
about last night with the duke and remember his strong
embrace, commanding caresses, and devouring kisses that
touched deep into her soul.

The annoying sound came again.

Her eyes opened to bright sunshine streaming through
the open draperies. Startled, she rose up in bed, brushing
her long hair from her eyes. There was a strange woman
tying back the drapery panels. Esmeralda didn't recognize
her as one of the servants. And no one had ever come in
to wake her anyway.

The robust woman wore an expensive-looking light
blue dress and a dark blue hat with an outlandish amount

of dyed leaves and feathers on it and colorful ribbons poking out of the crown.

"Excuse me," Esmeralda said, pulling the sheet up past her shoulders. "I think you are in the wrong room."

The small, sturdy, black-haired woman turned to face her. Her eyebrows were thick, wide, and very black. She smiled broadly. "Ah, Mademoiselle, you are awake."

How could I not be with so much light streaming into the room?

"Good, I asked that some tea be brought up for you. We must begin at once. There can be no delay."

Two more ladies, just as beautifully dressed as the Frenchwoman, walked into her open bedchamber door, their arms laden with stacks of fabrics, pelts of lace, and reams of ribbons.

"What is this?" Esmeralda asked. "And who are you?"

The woman smiled again. "Of course, I am Madame Donceaux. I'm here to dress you for the duke."

Dress me?

For Griffin!

As if last night with the Duke hadn't been emotional enough with his kisses and caresses that she'd never forget. There was also the baring of her soul about Josephine's father, and her arguing and demanding of Griffin that she retain her position in his household. Now, he was making demands of his own. If she had more gowns made, she'd never be able to pay him back.

"The Duke was banging on my door so early this morning. Eager he was that I should come to you at once." Madame Donceaux motioned for the women to put their wares on the foot of the bed while she continued to talk to Esmeralda. "He told me you must have a new gown ready tonight. That will be difficult, but we can do. We must hurry. No time to waste. Up, up."

"He should have asked me if I wanted a new gown," she said more to herself than to the dressmaker.

"Why should a gentleman like the duke have to ask to gift you such beautiful gowns. It is his right, no? It will make you happy."

No, it didn't make her happy that he'd decided to take it upon himself to have more gowns made for her.

"Wait a minute, I will not have this."

"Fine, fine," the woman said and drew back the covers away from Esmeralda. "Keep talking, but stand so I can get measurements. We have no time."

Perturbed, and not knowing exactly what to do first, Esmeralda scooted off the bed and stood up, ready to do battle.

"It would be better for you to remove your, your night rail. Better to measure."

"I am not taking off my shift," she said indignantly, knowing she didn't have a stitch on beneath the white long-sleeved sleeping gown.

"Good. I will measure anyway." The woman immediately lifted Esmeralda's arms in the air, whipped a strip of white cloth from a sash around her waist, and circled Esmeralda's waist before she knew what had happened. "Don't look at me," she said to Esmeralda, pointing to the end of the bed. "I measure. You look at fabrics. Which you like?"

"But wait. I told you I don't want to do this. I have gowns. Beautiful, well-made gowns."

"Oh, I am sure. But they are gray." She called out a measurement in French to one of the ladies, who marked it on a card with a pencil. "The duke say, no gray. No gray. I tell him I understand, no gray." She measured around Esmeralda's breasts and gave the measurement again.

"No, no, Mademoiselle. Do not look what I do," she said

again. "Look at the exceptional fabrics. How luxurious they are. The pale yellow. You like it?"

"It's lovely, but—"

"Good. I thought so. It will make your eyes so beautiful. The duke will be happy. And the gold trim, right?" She measured from under Esmeralda's breasts to the top of her foot, and called out more measurements to her helper. "At the waist and perhaps the hem too? No. I think that the hem too much. Right? Cap sleeves, I think. We'll put it on the sleeve."

Madame Donceaux was answering her own questions as she moved her piece of measuring cloth from one part of Esmeralda's body to another almost as fast as a whirlwind.

"What about the lavender fabric? The blue? No, no, with your eyes, the green is better for you. I will make green. And the dark ivory? That one too? You will be stunning."

Esmeralda spun away from the modiste. "Now, wait a minute. Just how many gowns do you think you are going to make?"

Madame Donceaux looked confused. "As many as you want."

"Fine. I want one. The yellow one."

The dressmaker laughed a deep throaty laugh. "No, no, Mademoiselle. The duke—"

"I don't care what the duke said. Now, you have your measurements, it's time for you to go."

"Good." She smiled as if Esmeralda's irritable temperament hadn't bothered her at all. "I will go. I will choose fabrics for you that show your beauty. Not gray." She motioned for her helpers to gather up the fabrics and trimmings. And then, instead of leaving the room, she walked over to Esmeralda's wardrobe and started pulling out her dresses and gowns and throwing them over her arm.

This woman was unbelievable. "What are you doing?"

"Taking the gray with me. The Duke say, take the gray."

Did he! "You can't do that. Those are my clothes."

She smiled. "I will bring you more, Mademoiselle. Blues, greens, corals. Before the day has ended, I will be back."

Esmeralda tried to grab hold of her clothing, but the modiste swung away from her and made a run for the door. Esmeralda dashed in front of her and blocked the entrance. "You are not taking my clothing. I need those."

A worried expression etched its way across Madame Donceaux's face. "I do what the duke tells me. He says take the gray."

"Oh, yes. The duke loves to tell people what to do, but I say no."

"Good," she said again. "These go with me."

"No."

"I have left you enough for today."

Esmeralda grabbed hold of the clothing, but the modiste gathered them up tightly to her chest in a fierce grip. Madame Donceaux's helpers stood to one side looking horrified at the tug of war between Esmeralda and the French dressmaker.

"What are you two doing?"

Esmeralda turned to see Lady Sara and Lady Vera, also in their nightclothes, watching her and Madame Donceaux fight over the clothing.

"You two sound like us when we are fighting over something," Lady Vera said.

Esmeralda silently groaned when she suddenly realized how ridiculous she must look. The dressmakers grip didn't loosen, so Esmeralda's did.

"Let her have them, Miss Swift," Lady Vera said. "It will be pleasant to see you in another color. Isn't that right, Sara?"

Sara walked over to one of the ladies holding the fabrics and pulled a frothy parchment-colored material from her hands. "This will match your coloring perfectly, Miss Swift."

Knowing she'd lost the battle, Esmeralda relented and slowly let go of the gowns and dresses and stepped away from the modiste. "What will you do with them?" she asked the woman.

"Charitable hospital is always in need of clothing. Will that please Mademoiselle?"

Esmeralda inhaled deeply and lifted her shoulders. "Yes. That will please me greatly."

Chapter 22

Don't speak for anyone other than yourself.

❧

MISS MAMIE FORTESCUE'S DO'S AND DON'TS FOR
CHAPERONES, GOVERNESSES, TUTORS, AND NURSES

The afternoon tea party was elite, lavish, and noisy. True
to her word, Miss Irene Froste had befriended Lady
Sara and Lady Vera by first having just the two of them
over for afternoon tea a week ago and today by inviting
them to a garden soirée at her home. More than two dozen
beautifully dressed young ladies and handsomely dapper
gentlemen sat at white linen–covered tables that held a
small bouquet of roses in the center of each one. A trio of
musicians had been set up at the far end of the small lawn,
but the soft, mellow sounds coming from the harp, violin,
and viola were no match for the cheerful chatter and laughter, or the teacups and spoons clinking against saucers.

The sky had been threatening rain all afternoon. Moist
air held a chill. The gloomy day hadn't dampened the en-
thusiasm of the small group. Esmeralda stood off to the
side talking with other chaperones and some of the mothers

who had accompanied their daughters to the gathering. She occasionally added to the conversations about gowns, parties, and what gentlemen were interested in which young ladies, and what the fathers had to say about the match. However, more often than not, Esmeralda remained quiet and let her thoughts drift in other directions.

Over the past two weeks of the Season, there had been relatively few questions and little mention of the fact she was cousin to the ailing Viscount Mayeforth. She had expected more gossip about that revelation. One lady had asked how she managed to obtain the prized position of chaperone for the Duke of Griffin's sisters while another had suggested she must have known someone in the family. Still another had said that the duke wouldn't have allowed anyone with a lesser social standing than the cousin of a viscount to get anywhere near his sisters.

Esmeralda accepted all their comments with a smile and was thankful they left Josephine out of their observations. Not one of them seemed to know she was found through the highly trusted Miss Mamie Fortescue's Employment Agency. She had no desire to enlighten them.

They were into the third week of the Season and all was well. There had been no further mishaps with Josephine or Napoleon, for which she was grateful. Both had settled into a regular routine quite nicely.

For all of Lady Vera's bluster insisting Lord Henry was the man she wanted, she had the strangest way of showing it. She'd rebuffed him earlier in the week when he asked if he could take her for a ride in the park, citing it was much too early in the Season for such a forward outing. Which of course wasn't true at all.

Mr. Lambert was clearly besotted with Lady Sara, and Esmeralda felt Lady Sara had given up on Lord Henry and was smitten with Mr. Lambert too.

The Duke of Rathburne and the Duke of Hawksthorn

had both sought Esmeralda out at times to greet her, to ask about the twins, and to offer to get her a glass of champagne. Despite the fact they were dukes, rakes of the highest order and terribly spoiled by always getting what they wanted, she'd enjoyed and even welcomed their repartee with her each evening. Neither had asked her to dance again.

So far there had been no further talk from Griffin about dismissing her from his household, for which she was grateful. He arrived in the evenings, handsomely dressed, to escort her and his sisters to the parties, then left without coming inside after delivering them back home. During the course of each evening, they would discuss the twins, the gentlemen pursuing them, and little else.

At times, she'd catch him looking at her, and then at other times, he'd caught her watching him. There was an undercurrent of tension between them that hadn't surfaced. They'd both done quite well in keeping their personal feelings and thoughts to themselves.

The only thing that had bothered her was the fact the duke hadn't made one comment concerning her new gowns. She felt certain she'd seen glowing appreciation for her in his eyes the first time he'd seen her wearing a color other than gray, but he said nothing.

Several times she'd watched him dance with Miss Froste and Miss Waldegrave too. And at least twice he'd invited Lady Agatha to join him for a quadrille. All the young ladies were beautiful, poised, and more than acceptable as brides, if he was looking. She could only hope that the envy that bubbled up inside her chest every time she saw him with one of the young ladies didn't show on her face.

Then there were other young ladies the duke danced with whose names she didn't know. And probably still more dances, quiet conversations, and interested glances she hadn't seen because she and the duke spent little time together once they entered the ballroom, party, or whatever event they were attending that night. Esmeralda would find other people to talk with and so would Griffin.

She couldn't count the times she'd thought about Griffin's kisses or how she'd felt the few heavenly moments she'd been wrapped in his strong embrace. She remembered his touch, his sighs, and his deep excited breaths. Recalling that night with the duke was especially lovely when she went to bed and let thoughts of him ease her into sleep. That one night in the duke's arms sustained her.

The afternoon passed, the sky grew darker and the air heavy with moisture. Esmeralda looked around the garden and saw that Lady Sara was sitting at a table with Miss Waldegrave and Miss Froste, and Lady Vera was talking to Mr. Lambert. Knowing the twins, that situation could have a bad ending. Esmeralda decided to suggest to the sisters they leave before a downpour started.

She excused herself from the group of ladies she was with and walked over to the table where Lady Sara sat and was about to lean down and speak to her when she heard Miss Waldegrave say, "Lady Sara, are you at all concerned about your Season being ruined?"

Esmeralda's first impulse was to step in quickly and stop this conversation before it went further, but she heard Lady Sara say "Worried?" in such a carefree tone that she wanted to wait and see how Griffin's sister handled herself.

"Why should I be worried about such a ridiculous thing?" Lady Sara asked. "The Season has been enchanting."

"That's good to hear," Miss Waldegrave said, fingering the pink bow under her chin. "There was that horrid gossip about you and your sister. I thought perhaps it might have upset you."

"Horrid? I've heard there's been talk about us since coming to London. We are twins after all. That makes for a roomful of idle talk. And then our aunt fell ill and we are now being chaperoned by the young and lovely Miss Swift. I've heard there is much discussion recently about who she is and why she has taken on a paid position in our home. There are so many things that people find to talk about concerning us that I'm simply not sure which gossip you're referring to."

"None of that," Miss Waldegrave exclaimed, as if she couldn't believe Lady Sara was not comprehending what she was alluding to. "Surely, you've heard the tittle-tattle I'm referring to. It has nothing to do with you being a twin, your aunt, or the chaperone."

Staying calm, Lady Sara said, "Then I'm afraid I don't know what's in your mind. You'll have to tell me if you want me to know."

"I know what you are talking about," Miss Froste said, coming to Lady Sara's defense while giving a harsh look toward Miss Waldegrave. "I really don't think this is a subject you should be bringing up. Let's talk about something else."

"No, it's quite all right," Lady Sara told Miss Froste, patting her hand. "Let her tell me. I want to know what she's heard. It might be something new that I don't know yet."

"Of course, I'll tell you if I must. Everyone knows that you and your sister are being pursued by an unknown and unscrupulous man or men out to ruin your Season or possibly even your reputation. All because of your brother's misdeeds a few years ago."

Esmeralda listened intently and remained poised to step in at any moment if she felt needed, but so far her charge was handling herself with perfect aplomb.

Lady Sara gently pushed her teacup aside. "What nonsense. Where did you hear such ridiculous blather?"

"It's not blather. I actually read it in one of the scandal sheets myself. More than one of them I might add, so it must be true."

"Oh my, I find it quite surprising that your mother allows you to read those things, Miss Waldegrave. We're forbidden to look at them."

"She doesn't know, of course," Miss Waldegrave said, leaning forward. "I do it in secret," she whispered.

"Then you shouldn't have told us," Lady Sara offered. "She'll probably find out about it now. I mean you just told two of us at this table. How can you expect it to be kept a secret if others know about it?"

Esmeralda relaxed and smiled. She was impressed with how Lady Sara had turned the conversation from herself to Miss Waldegrave. She would have expected it of the outspoken Lady Vera but she really had no idea that Lady Sara was that clever or capable.

"Well, I do insist on silence about this from both of you," Miss Waldegrave said firmly. "And if my secret leaves this table I'll never speak to either of you again."

This seemed a good time for Esmeralda to step in.

"Lady Sara, pardon me for interrupting your lovely afternoon, but I'm afraid we must be going."

Lady Sara looked up at her and smiled. "I was just thinking the same thing, Miss Swift. It looks as if a storm is on the way and I do hate to get my feet wet." She rose and turned to Miss Froste. "So lovely of you to invite us over. We'll return the favor soon."

Miss Froste stood too. "I'll look forward to another invitation at your home. Perhaps I can visit at a time when the duke will be there."

A stab of envy struck Esmeralda and she stiffened. That

was rather brash of the young lady to be so bold about her intentions.

"I don't know if that can be arranged," Lady Sara said innocently. "My brother doesn't make us privy to his schedule, and he doesn't visit often during the day."

"Oh, well, yes, of course," Miss Froste answered, clearly not knowing what to say to Lady Sara's simple decline to arrange a rendezvous between her brother and Miss Froste. "He would be very busy, I'm sure."

"I'll see you tonight at Grand Hall," Lady Sara said to her hostess. Turning to Miss Waldegrave, she said, "I do hope no one finds out that you read the gossip sheets. That would be dreadful. If you couldn't read them, then you couldn't tell we who are less fortunate than you what's in them."

After saying their good-byes to everyone, Esmeralda and the twins walked the short distance to their carriage and climbed inside. As soon as they were seated, Lady Sara turned to Lady Vera and asked, "What were you and Mr. Lambert talking about?"

"Don't be a silly goose. I'm not going to tell you about my conversations with him. I don't ask you about discussions with him."

Lady Sara's face turned red. "You don't have to ask because I always tell you."

"Since I won't tell you what was said," Lady Vera said, smiling, "you don't have to tell me anymore."

"You are a horrible sister," Lady Sara said and threw her reticule at Lady Vera.

She caught the velvet purse and laughed. "I was only teasing you, Sara. Don't be such a ninny. He only wanted to talk about you. And I was really quite bored telling him what a wonderful sister you are."

"Oh, you are horrible."

"Only sometimes." She handed the reticule back to

Lady Sara. "I was excruciatingly miserable after Lord Henry left the party and couldn't wait for Miss Swift to tell us it was time to leave."

"I don't understand that," Esmeralda said. "You declined when he asked you to go for a ride in the park with him."

"I had to. If I seem too interested in him, he'll treat me like he treats all the other ladies—I want to be different."

"You certainly know how to do that," her sister said.

Lady Vera sighed. "But I don't know if it will work and I don't want to talk about him anymore. I do hope you heard some luscious gossip at the party, dear sister."

"Not much," Lady Sara answered. "There was that old news about someone wanting to disrupt our Season because of Griffin's secret admirer letter a few years ago."

Esmeralda's heart jumped. "You know about that?"

"Of course," Lady Vera said. "We know all the gossip about our brother and most of it about us."

"Then I am going to ask Lady Sara what Miss Waldegrave was trying to ask her but couldn't get the question out: How do you know this?"

"How could we not know? It's been in all the gossip and scandal sheets," Lady Sara said.

Astonished, Esmeralda was speechless for a moment. "I was told you're not allowed to read them."

"We're not."

"But you just indicated to Miss Waldegrave that you didn't read them and yet . . ." Esmeralda's voice trailed off as Lady Sara smiled.

"It was shameful of me to do it, I suppose, but I wasn't going to confess to such outrageous behavior just because she was foolish enough to do so. I mean, I shouldn't have, right?"

"Of course, you were right, Sara," Lady Vera said.

"We've been reading them for years, Miss Swift. Our maid hides them for us in our wardrobe so we can read them when we're alone."

"Vera, you shouldn't have told her how we get them."

"Don't be silly. Miss Swift will not tell Auntie Eve, Griffin, or anyone else. We've never been caught with them." Lady Vera's gaze looked pointedly at Esmeralda. "You won't tell, right?"

"It is not my place to get involved in what you read, my ladies. However, I am pleased that you are aware there is such disturbing talk concerning you out there." She paused. "And I'm even more pleased that you're not upset about it. I have to admit I thought you would be."

"We have been the topic of discussion as long as we can remember."

"Don't you think you should tell your brother you know about this? He thought knowing someone might want to ruin your Season would upset you."

"You can tell him we know, if you like. He might take it easier coming from you. He still thinks we're children."

Because you sometimes quarrel like children, she wanted to say out loud, but knew better.

"But you mustn't tell him how we know or we'll be in trouble from Auntie Eve as well," Lady Sara added.

"You heard about it at the tea party this afternoon," Esmeralda said, "and that's the truth, is it not?"

"Yes, thank you, it is," Lady Sara said with a satisfied smile.

"Tell me truthfully," Esmeralda continued, "has any of the gossip ever bothered you at all?"

The twins smiled at each other, and then Lady Vera said, "Not at all. We rather like being the center of attention."

That was easy to believe.

"It's been that way all our lives."

Esmeralda could understand why. It was rare that both

twins lived to be adults. "Tell me, have either of you had any misgivings from any of the gentlemen who have shown you attention? Have you sensed any of them being disingenuous?"

"Not in the least. We've never thought they would."

"I know Griffin doesn't like Mr. Lambert," Lady Sara said wistfully, "but he's such a dear man."

"And handsome and kind," Lady Vera added.

"You are only saying that because you want me more interested in him than in Lord Henry because you know Lord Henry favors me."

"I know no such thing because it isn't true," Lady Vera exclaimed

"Wait, my ladies," Esmeralda said, holding up her hand to silence them. "May we please get back to what we were talking about in the first place?"

They looked at her and then each other before nodding.

"Good. So neither of you have felt any kind of threat from any of the gentlemen who have shown interest in you?"

"No, and we never expected any," Lady Vera said. "We've always thought the gossip was started to ruin Griffin's Season, not ours. In fact, I think one of the scandal sheets said it would be a good punishment for the duke to have to worry about his sisters. So we think this was to worry him, not to harm us."

Lady Vera's words whirled through Esmeralda's mind. "Yes, I do remember something about that."

Esmeralda leaned heavily into the back of the cushion. She needed to talk to Griffin.

Tonight.

Chapter 23

Don't start something you don't intend to finish.

❧

MISS MAMIE FORTESCUE'S DO'S AND DON'TS FOR
CHAPERONES, GOVERNESSES, TUTORS, AND NURSES

Esmeralda's hurried footfalls were silent as she came down the stairs. The hour was growing late. She wanted to be below stairs and in the book room waiting when Griffin arrived. After she and the twins had returned from the garden party, she'd sent a note to Griffin asking that he come over early to pick them up for the evening so she could discuss a matter with him.

Josephine wasn't happy to be hurried into her night-clothes and put to bed with a book, but Esmeralda wanted to get her sister settled before she dressed for the evening. And then as Esmeralda started out the door, Josephine surprised her by asking for a book of poetry. Her sister hadn't wanted to read or write poems since her father died. Seeing this as a good sign, a sign of healing, Esmeralda couldn't deny her the request. But it put Esmeralda even further behind because she had to make a dash to the book room to pick out an appropriate poetry book for a twelve-year-old girl. Thankfully, the duke's library was in perfect order and all the books of poems were lined up together.

At last, when Esmeralda made it to her room to dress, she saw that Madame Donceaux had delivered yet another new gown. It was breathtaking. Esmeralda couldn't resist the temptation to wear the alabaster-colored shift with a sheer biscuit-colored gown flowing over it. It was simple but beautifully elegant. The scooped neckline plunged low as was the fashion and, having no jewelry, Esmeralda tied an inch-wide band of gold velvet ribbon around the base of her neck to draw attention away from the expanse of her chest.

For once, she was happy that it took the twins a ridiculously long amount of time to dress, have their hair swept up and entwined with ribbons, pearls or combs, and don their jewelry in the evenings. After all that, they would make a stop by Lady Evelyn's room so that she could give a final inspection and approval.

When Esmeralda finally entered the book room she stopped suddenly. Her heart felt as if it swelled in her chest. Griffin stood in front of the window, looking magnificent in his black evening wear. All her senses were instantly on alert to everything about him. She wanted to run and throw herself into his arms and shower him with kisses.

Instead, she said, "You're already here."

His gaze swept her up and down. Oh, she was so smitten with him. For a moment she would have sworn to anyone that he was looking at her as if she was the most beautiful woman on earth.

"When I get word you need to see me, Esmeralda, I will come to you."

I will come to you. The words were a soothing balm to her soul, beautiful music to her ears. She gloried in them and savored how they made her feel that she was special to him whether or not he intended them that way.

She walked farther into the room. "An idea came to me today, and I thought it might be worth discussing."

He met her in the center of the room and stopped close to her. Close enough she caught the clean, enticing scent of shaving soap. Close enough she felt warmth from his body. Close enough that if she were bold enough and had the courage, she could raise up on her toes and press her lips to his without having to take a step.

"What were you thinking about?" he asked so softly it almost sounded like an endearment.

She willed her heart to stop beating so fast and forced herself to stop thinking about kisses. This was the first time they'd been alone since their passionate embrace. She was finding out quickly that it was much easier to control her desire for the duke when others were around.

"I don't know anything about Sir Welby, of course, but do you think it's possible he made up the entire story about some gentlemen's reckless talk because he wanted to cause you undue worry about your sisters?"

His eyes searched hers. "I recently had reason to consider that. I've talked with him twice and I have no evidence to back up that line of thinking."

"Is it possible he's in some way related to any of the young ladies who were wronged in your prank?"

Griffin grimaced. "Wronged?"

"It may seem harsh for me to put it that way, but you must accept they were. You made them all think they had a secret admirer when they didn't. That was wrong."

He studied her intently. "I thought I'd already admitted that."

She gave him a skeptical look. "Did you?"

"Maybe not in those exact words but yes, I think I did admit it."

How could she have forgotten? He was a peer. That was the best she was going to get out of him.

"What happened today that brought you to this conclusion about Sir Welby?"

"I am only trying to look at this objectively," she said. "I have now met most, if not all, of the young bachelors attending the Season. I'm not sensing that any of them want to do harm to the twins. I wondered if you had considered that Sir Welby or whomever it was he heard make these unscrupulous claims simply wanted to see *you* disturbed and fretting over the twins' Season and never had any intentions of harming them at all."

A wry grin lifted one corner of his masculine mouth. He reached up and cupped her cheek. An intake of breath caught in her lungs. His hand was warm, gentle, and it too had the scent of shaving soap. Why did he have to touch her? Surely he knew she had longed for his touch and had no willpower to resist him.

"I don't fret, Esmeralda."

She knew. He was much too strong for that. It just happened to be the first word that came to her mind. "I suppose I could have chosen a better word."

His blue gaze stayed on hers. "How about 'concerned'?"

"Yes, concerned," she agreed, fighting with herself. Part of her wanted to step away from his caress but her stronger side wanted to remain still and enjoy the comfort his touch brought. "But what if you were the target all along and not the twins at all?"

"That is a possibility. I had a conversation with Sir Welby not too long ago. He remained firm on his story. Perhaps I should have another. I'm finding it peculiar that the Season is half over and no one has made any attempt to harm the twins."

His hand slid down to the velvet around her neck. His fingers and thumb raked back and forth across the soft ribbon, sending trills of thrills coursing through her.

She was spellbound by his touch and steady, searching gaze on her face, but managed to keep from falling into his arms by saying, "My thoughts exactly. I was talking to your sisters today. They, too, also seemed to think the rumor had more to do with you than with them."

His hand stilled on her throat. His features hardened. "You told them about this?"

"No, of course not," she hurried to say. "I forgot to mention that one of the young ladies at the garden party today mentioned the gossip to them."

"Which one?"

She had to be careful. "I promised not to tell you all that was said today. Young ladies must have some privacy." That wasn't exactly accurate but it wasn't quite a prevarication either. She added, "How they know isn't important anyway, is it?"

An easy, attractive smile formed on his lips, and her stomach tightened. His hand slid over to her ear. He caressed the lobe between his thumb and forefinger, occasionally letting his other three fingers caress the soft, sensitive skin behind her ear.

"So now you are keeping secrets from me for my sisters."

"No." She frowned and shook her head. It was difficult to think straight with him touching her so gently, so intimately. "I mean yes. I suppose I am but it's—they aren't bad secrets. It's just that they must trust me. And you must trust me that they aren't worried or dismayed about this whatsoever."

Griffin lifted her chin with the pads of his fingers and looked deeply into her eyes. Esmeralda felt as if she could melt away to nothing. "I trust you."

"So you won't force me to tell you, will you?"

They both knew he could. He had that power over her. She was his employee. He was a duke. If he demanded it, she would have to reveal all that was said. Her breaths became dangerously shallow while she waited for him to answer.

With his middle finger he lightly drew a path from her ear over to her chin, down her chest to her cleavage, where he let his finger nestle. A light fluttering sensation attacked her chest. Lace from the cuff of his sleeve tickled and tingled her heated skin. She wondered if he knew just how heavenly it was to be so near him. Did he know that right now, she was very close to reaching up and kissing him?

"I would never force you to do anything, Esmeralda."

His voice was husky. His expression was caring as he started drawing a pattern across the swell of her breasts with his finger, moving from one side to the other and back again. He wouldn't force her, but he was definitely trying to seduce her.

And it was working.

"Thank you," she said on a loud intake of excited breath as his finger dipped beneath her gown and raked across her nipple. The movement was shocking and arousing. Esmeralda gasped at his boldness even while her lower body squeezed deliciously.

"The color you are wearing tonight shows just how beautiful you are, Esmeralda."

At last, he decided to make mention of the new gowns. And just in time too. She didn't have the willpower to step away from the sensual plunder of her breasts, but she desperately needed something to distract her from his seduction.

"Does it?" she challenged with a slight lift of her chin.

He nodded while his fingers continued to make her body grow tighter and tighter.

"It's about time you said something about my new clothing. I've worn a new gown every other night for over two weeks and you haven't once said a word. After all your complaints about my wearing gray, I'd say it's past time you said something about them."

A low, attractive chuckle passed his lips as his arm went around her waist and caught her up against his chest.

Yes, that is what she wanted.

"You're miffed at me for waiting so long to tell you how stunningly beautiful you are."

Yes I am.

"No, I'm not." Her words were a whisper because his embrace was so divine she could hardly breathe let alone speak. "I'm just surprised you've never once noticed after you railed at me for wearing gray."

He laughed softly again. "I don't fret. I don't rail, Esmeralda. But I do notice. I notice everything about you. Somehow, I've managed to keep my hands off you until now, but surely you know I haven't be able to keep my eyes off you." He bent his face close to hers. "Do you want to know what else I've noticed?"

"What?"

"It's been two weeks, four days, and approximately eighteen hours since I last kissed you."

You missed a day.

He touched his nose to hers. "I want to kiss you again, but contrary to what you think of me, I'm not a man without honor. I'm not going to kiss you unless you ask me to." With that, he turned her loose and took a step back. "You are free to walk away from me. Free to go right now."

"No, Griffin, I can't," she whispered on an impatient sigh as she jumped into his embrace. Strong arms caught her. Her lips claimed his for her own.

Desire flamed hot and urgent between them. He hugged

her tightly. Tremendous joy filled her. Her arms circled his neck as she melted against him.

Their kiss was moist, warm, deep, and long. Esmeralda parted her lips. His tongue slid inside, tasting the depths of her mouth. Immense pleasure washed over her, filled her to overflowing, and settled into her soul.

"I like the way you say my name," he murmured. His lips left hers and he kissed his way over the bridge of her nose and up to her eyelids.

"You prefer it to Your Grace?" she asked while her hands explored the width of his back and shoulders.

"I am Your Grace for others. I am Griffin for you."

Griffin's mouth and tongue ravaged hers in slow savoring kisses, time and time again. She loved the way they made her feel, the way they made her want more.

He placed soft raindrop kisses on her forehead and along the edge of her hairline before kissing his way across first one cheek and then the other, teasing her skin with his tongue as he went. His lips slid over her jaw, along the column of her neck to her chest. He lingered over the swell of her breasts that billowed from beneath the neckline of her gown.

"You're so soft," he whispered. "I must have a taste of you. I have waited past my endurance."

Quickly, his hand slid around her midriff to cup and massage her breast. He lifted the plump flesh from her gown and quickly covered it with his mouth. Esmeralda moaned a gasp of pleasure. It was such a glorious feeling. His lips on her breast sent chills of pleasure skipping along her spine.

She closed her eyes, and leaned her head back to enjoy the delicious sensations. Wave after wave of desire crashed and tumbled in her stomach.

A longing ache started between her legs and rose up to

spread throughout her abdomen and skimmed along breasts. Her hands roamed down his shoulders to his slim hips. And then farther, to his buttocks. She grasped the firm mounds in her hands and pressed his hardness against her as he continued to caress her softly, deftly.

"Yes," he whispered as his breathing grew faster.

Esmeralda smiled against his lips. There was no place she didn't want him to touch her. No place she didn't want to touch him.

Yet, through the fog of desire, Esmeralda remembered they were not alone in the house. She fought the desire not to stop what was happening between them, but her sensible self kept urging her to show caution.

"I mustn't get caught in your arms," she whispered. "Sparks or the twins could walk in and see us behaving like this."

He chuckled against her skin. "How are we behaving, Esmeralda?"

"Like two people who are so desperate to taste every inch of each other they are being reckless."

He bent his head and captured her lips in a fierce kiss of passion before whispering, "Oh, yes, you do know exactly what I'm feeling."

"Yes," she murmured in return. "But we must deny what is happening between us."

"Being reckless doesn't frighten me. What I am feeling right now does, but it's worth the risk."

"It would devastate Lady Sara and Lady Vera to see us like this."

"They won't. I'm listening for footsteps and voices in the hallway," he answered as his mouth found hers again.

Griffin's mouth and tongue ravaged hers in a slow savoring kiss, time and time again. His hands caressed her breasts, and then moved down to her waist, over the flare of her hip and around to her buttocks, lifting her against his hardness again.

Esmeralda's couldn't fight the sensations her body was craving. She raised her hips up to meet his demand. She felt him shudder. A soft moan of pleasure passed his lips. He dipped his tongue in her mouth, deeper, farther. They kissed again and again. Harder and then softer. Slower and then faster. Each kiss was building to something, but Esmeralda didn't know what.

She gasped with each new place he caressed.

Quickly Griffin lifted his head and stepped away from her. His breathing was fast and erratic. "I hear the twins coming down the stairs."

"For the love of heaven!" she whispered, whirling away from him. "What madness came over me to allow this?"

Griffin combed through his hair with his fingers and straightened his coat. "Passion, Esmeralda. The raw passion that we have been fighting since the first day we met. And it was as powerful between us as I knew it would be."

"We could have been caught," she stressed while straightening the neckline of her gown.

"But we weren't. I'll go out and meet them while you catch your breath. I'll tell them you are checking on something for Lady Evelyn."

His gaze caressed her face and he smiled so sweetly her fears melted away.

"No hurry," he said. "Join us whenever you're ready."

Chapter 24

Don't ever think life is easy.

~ъле~

MISS MAMIE FORTESCUE'S DO'S AND DON'TS FOR
CHAPERONES, GOVERNESSES, TUTORS, AND NURSES

Esmeralda sat in a chair near the doorway that led into the drawing room, looking at her book. There was no way she could read it. Even though it had been over a week since their last kiss, the Duke of Griffin was the only thing she could concentrate on.

It was a blissfully quiet afternoon—except for Napoleon barking in the back garden as he and Josephine frolicked. He must have sensed a cat nearby or another dog because he was being unusually noisy. If he didn't quiet soon, she'd have to talk with Josephine about him when they came inside.

Lady Sara and Mr. Lambert were on the settee, a respectable distance apart, having a quiet conversation. If she'd tried, she probably could have understood most of what they were saying, but she had no desire to intrude and listen in on their intimate conversation. Though Griffin continued to have his misgivings about the young gentleman's intentions toward Lady Sara, Esmeralda didn't. From all she could tell, Mr. Lambert was smitten with Lady Sara and had been since he first saw her. And it was easy to see she'd grown quite fond of him in the few weeks they'd been seeing each other.

Lady Vera and Lord Henry were off for a ride in Hyde Park in his fancy curricle. They'd left shortly before Mr. Lambert had arrived. Lady Vera's rejection of Lord Henry's first invitation for a ride in the park didn't deter him from asking again. That it had taken Lady Vera until the fourth week of the Season to get Lord Henry to this point in her objective hadn't bothered her in the least. She insisted she knew what she was doing and what it would take to get the very handsome but equally elusive earl's son ready to propose to her by the end of the Season.

It had certainly made Esmeralda's job easier since she hadn't had to worry about the twins competing to win the affections of the same beau. Esmeralda still had her doubts that Lord Henry would be ready to take Lady Vera to the altar by the time the last dance was held, but Mr. Lambert just might be ready to make a match with her sister.

Life was moving along more quickly than Esmeralda wanted but there was no way to slow it down. Once again, after their last kisses, Griffin had fallen into the routine of not coming inside when he picked up Esmeralda and the twins nor when he delivered them home. She knew what he was doing. If they weren't alone, there would be no chance of passionate kisses, earth-shattering caresses, and desires she had that were too intimate to contemplate. She didn't know whether he was simply trying to be an honorable man and not touch her again while she was in his employ or whether he simply did not want to kiss her again. That was a disheartening thought, but one she had to consider. Maybe because she had allowed him to touch her so freely, he no longer had the desire to do it.

In less than two weeks, she and Josephine would pack up and return to live at the agency. What she didn't know was if the duke would forget about her or would she have to forget the duke. A heaviness settled on her chest. Not seeing him again would be heart wrenching. Esmeralda sighed, uncrossed her legs, and then immediately crossed them in the other direction. She would make herself go mad if she thought about how her life at the duke's house would end, in the not too distant future.

Esmeralda folded her book in her lap and let her thoughts drift. Even if he never came to see her when she returned home, how could she ever forget him? How could she ever forget his soft touch, his whispered words of passion, or his heart-stopping kisses? The taste of his mouth, the scent of his soap. Not that she wanted to, but it would be impossible even if she did. She smiled to herself. Why would she want to forget all the wonderful feelings she'd experienced with him? Those sensations were meant to be enjoyed, and she would enjoy them every time she thought about the duke.

The back door opened and quickly slammed shut, making Esmeralda jump. Lady Sara and Mr. Lambert jumped too and looked around at Esmeralda. Rising from her chair, Esmeralda looked down the corridor. Josephine leaned against the door. Her eyes were unusually wide and her cheeks looked red and blustery. Napoleon stood at her feet and barked up at her.

"Josephine, what are you doing? You know that's not the proper way to close a door."

"I know," she said breathlessly. "I didn't mean to close it so hard."

"All right. You and Napoleon have been playing too

hard. Go to the kitchen and get water for both of you. And find a way to keep him quiet for a while."

The two of them disappeared around the corner. Esmeralda turned back to tell Lady Sara and Mr. Lambert all was fine, but they were already back into their quiet conversation and, Esmeralda noticed, sitting a little closer together than they were before the distraction. She smiled to herself. The book was a good ruse, so she settled back into her chair and opened it.

A short time later, she heard a loud knock from the front of the house, and soon after male voices. She didn't let it disturb her thoughts of the duke. It wasn't unusual for people to drop by throughout the day and leave their calling cards for Lady Evelyn, the twins, or sometimes the duke because some people weren't aware that he didn't actually live at his Mayfair home when his sisters were in London.

It wasn't long before Esmeralda heard someone coming down the corridor. She looked up to see Sparks lumbering her way. His expression was grim. She rose when he stopped in front of her.

"There's a gentlemen here you need to speak with, Miss Swift. A Mr. Verney Chambers. He lives a few streets over."

"I can't speak to him now, Sparks." Esmeralda quickly glanced over at Lady Sara and Mr. Lambert, who were paying no attention to what was happening in the doorway. "I can't leave Lady Sara. He'll have to come back at a later time."

Sparks dire expression didn't change. "I'm afraid he says it's urgent, and I believe it is."

"Oh." Suddenly fearing this might have something to do with the employment agency, she said, "I can't leave Lady Sara unattended. Would you mind staying here while I go speak to the man?"

Sparks' eyebrows rose considerably, clearly signaling that what she was suggesting was outside the boundaries of his duties in the household.

"Oh, for heaven's sakes," she whispered under her breath. "Ask the man to come here. I'll speak to him from the doorway."

He nodded, and a few moments later the butler returned with a short, rotund man with graying hair and an overly long mustache, stomping down the corridor behind him.

"Miss Swift?" the man asked before he even reached her.

"Yes," she answered.

"I'm Mr. Verney Chambers," he proclaimed loudly. "I'm here for the dog. The butler tells me I'll need to speak to you."

A shiver of something akin to foreboding skittered up Esmeralda's spine. Her breath hitched with apprehension. "What are you talking about?"

From the kitchen Napoleon started barking. Josephine yelled, "No!" as the Sky Terrier came running down the corridor as if hellhounds were nipping at his back paws. Josephine was right behind him, screaming his name. The man bent down, and Napoleon jumped into his arms and started licking his face.

A cold chill shook Esmeralda as Josephine skidded to a stop beside her.

Josephine's face was set with a stern expression. Her angry eyes were fixed on Mr. Chambers. Her small hands lay clutched into tight fists at her side. "You can put him down, now," she said. "He's my dog."

The man rose and looked at Esmeralda with a beaming smile. "No. Spook is my granddaughter's dog."

"No, he's mine!" Josephine yelled loudly at him. "And his name is Napoleon."

The man's back bowed. "I won't be spoken to like that by a child," he said indignantly.

Instinctively, Esmeralda moved to stand behind Josephine, placed both her hands on her sister's shoulders, and held firmly. "I'll take care of this, Josephine."

"There's nothing to take care of, Miss Swift." Mr. Chambers grunted in disdain. "The dog was lost, but now I've found him."

From the corner of her eye, Esmeralda saw Lady Sara and Mr. Lambert approach them. "I'm going to need more of an explanation, sir."

Mr. Chambers patted Napoleon's head and the dog licked him again. "I told you. He belongs to my granddaughter, Gracie. She and her family were here visiting with me from Manchester about a year ago when Spook ran off chasing a cat. He never returned."

Another cold shiver shook Esmeralda. She and Josephine had found Napoleon wet and shivering by their door just about a year ago.

"We searched the area from morning until evening for several days and couldn't find him. Now I know why. He was locked behind your garden walls."

"That's not true!" Josephine said defiantly, crossing her arms over her chest with jerking motions.

Rigid with fear, still trying to process what was happening, Esmeralda's fingers dug into the top of her sister's bony shoulders. "Quiet and let me handle this."

"I had no idea he was only a few streets away until mere moments ago," the man continued, ignoring Josephine's outburst.

"We don't live here, Mr. Chambers. We are only visiting."

He harrumphed. "Then it was fate that had me walking to the mews at the right time. I saw this girl walking with Spook outside your yew hedge. When I called to her,

Spook recognized me and started barking straightaway. He wanted to greet me." He looked down at Josephine sneeringly while running a thick short hand down Napoleon's long coat. "But she grabbed him and ran inside. And then locked the gate against me!"

"You probably scared her to death," Lady Sara said, speaking up for the first time. "A big man like you running after such a little girl. Have you no shame?"

The man huffed at Lady Sara as she looked at him contemptuously.

"Josephine?" Esmeralda whispered her name. "You disobeyed me and went outside the garden?"

She looked up at Esmeralda. Tears had collected in her big, scared green eyes. "I had to," she sniffed. "I threw the stick over the fence, and Napoleon wanted to go get it."

"And it's a good thing she did," Mr. Chambers added. "Otherwise, I might never have known that you'd taken Spook as your own."

"His name is Napoleon," Josephine demanded fiercely, not giving up an inch of ground. "Your granddaughter lost him. She didn't take good care of him. I found him. That makes him mine."

"You can say that as often as you want but I'm afraid this has no bearing on the fact that the dog is rightfully my Gracie's. As you can see, the dog knows who I am."

Yes, Esmeralda could see that Napoleon knew the man, but how could she let him take Napoleon from Josephine? She had to think, and that meant first things first.

She turned to Mr. Lambert and Lady Sara. "I'm sorry for interrupting your afternoon together, but I'm going to have to ask Mr. Lambert to leave. I have to take care of this matter right now and can't be available to the two of you."

"I understand, Miss Swift," Mr. Lambert said softly.

"But perhaps I should stay. I'm willing to help in any way that you ask."

The young man's sweet words made Esmeralda feel like crying. "That's very kind of you, Mr. Lambert. Thank you for offering, but I'll manage fine. Sparks and Lady Sara will see you out. I hope you'll be able to come another afternoon."

"I will, Miss Swift."

Mr. Lambert, Lady Sara, and Sparks walked away. Esmeralda turned back to Mr. Chambers. "I must ask that you reconsider your position on this. I would assume your granddaughter has already adjusted to the loss of Napol—Spook—and while she would—"

"Say, no more, Miss Swift," he said, holding his hand up to stop her. "Gracie loved this dog. She was heartbroken when we couldn't find him. I shall return him to her."

"It's heartbreaking, I know, for two girls to love the same dog, but I can't let you take Napoleon from my sister."

"There's nothing you can do to stop me. He is my granddaughter's property. I'm taking him back to her."

"He's been mine for over a year now." Josephine's voice was shrill, harsh, and loud. "You can't take him."

"I refuse to respond to a child," Mr. Chambers said.

Napoleon woofed a couple of times and struggled to get down, but the man held him firmly. He had been happy to see the man, but now it was as if he sensed exactly what was being said and he wanted to get down and go back to Josephine.

"I'm sure we can come to terms about this. I will be willing to pay you whatever—"

Mr. Chambers snorted derisively. "That is insulting, Miss Swift."

She gave him a hard stare. "Be that as it may, I'm not going to let you take Napoleon away from my sister."

"You have no choice. You know the law will be on my side concerning this. I hope you don't let it come to that."

He whirled on his heels and started stomping down the corridor. Josephine jerked away from Esmeralda and ran after Mr. Chambers. Catching up with him in the vestibule, she started hitting him in the back with her small fists and kicking the backs of his legs with her feet while screaming, "No! You can't have him! He's mine! Give him back!"

Napoleon yelped again and scratched to get down.

Esmeralda grabbed for Josephine's thrashing arms and fists while Lady Sara tried to pull the man's coat from Josephine's grasp. As soon as she did Mr. Chambers rushed past Sparks, flung open the door, and disappeared.

"He's my dog!" Josephine cried. "Bring him back! Bring Napoleon back to me!"

Shaking from anger, Esmeralda wrapped her arms tightly around Josephine and held her. "Shh, don't cry, my darling."

Josephine cried even harder. "He's mine! I want him back. He's mine!"

"I know, I know," Esmeralda answered as soothingly as she could, but her heart was breaking too. She rocked back and forth trying to calm her sister. If only Griffin were there to help her know what to do. Surely, he could have kept Mr. Chambers from taking Napoleon.

Josephine's slim body shook and trembled with rage and brokenheartedness. Esmeralda felt helpless to lessen her pain. Her sister had been just as upset when she'd lost her father. It took days for her to calm down and stop crying. Esmeralda looked from Sparks to Lady Sara, but knew they couldn't help either. Their faces showed they were upset by what happened too.

Her throat and chest ached with unshed tears.

"It will be all right, my sweet," she whispered again,

brushing Josephine's damp hair away from her face. "We'll find a way to get Napoleon."

Lady Sara laid a comforting hand on Josephine's shoulder. "I do hate to see you so upset. Maybe the duke can help us get Napoleon back for you."

Esmeralda gave Lady Sara an appreciative smile. "We can ask him and see what he thinks. He might be able to."

When Josephine's screams and crying finally quieted, Esmeralda loosened her hold.

"I'm going to get him back now!" Josephine said and tore away from Esmeralda's arms. Sparks reached for Josephine but missed as she swung open the door and went flying out.

"Josephine! Come back!"

Esmeralda hurried after her sister but Josephine was already down the steps and out to the street. The man was nowhere to be seen but that didn't stop Josephine. She simply started running down the road.

Esmeralda picked up her skirts and rushed after her.

Chapter 25

Don't let sudden anger rule your actions.
Do be sedate in all reactions.

❧

MISS MAMIE FORTESCUE'S DO'S AND DON'TS FOR
CHAPERONES, GOVERNESSES, TUTORS, AND NURSES

Griffin hopped up onto the seat of his curricle and picked up the ribbons. He clicked the strips of leather on the rumps of the horses a couple of times and they took off with a rattle of harness and rumble of wheels.

The visit with Sir Welby hadn't yielded anything new, except maybe that he'd been more guarded with Griffin. He really couldn't blame the man. It was the third time Griffin had been to see him about what he'd overheard that night at White's. And for the third time Sir Welby had remained firm that he'd heard the young bucks suggest that someone needed to teach Griffin a lesson and ruining his sisters seemed a good way to do it. Griffin was doubting the truth of Sir Welby's tale because there'd been no trouble, and the gossip about it had almost dried up. It wasn't that Griffin wasn't grateful that nothing had happened. He was, but he didn't like the thought of being the center of a hoax either.

The Season would be over in a couple of weeks and Griffin couldn't wait. Whether or not either sister would be off the marriage mart was anyone's guess. Vera certainly had her hankie set for Lord Henry, and Mr. Lambert could hardly leave Sara alone in the evenings. Neither sister seemed to be making much progress in that area, but several engagements had already been announced from the new flock of debutantes.

There was no one ahead of him on the street, so he flipped the ribbons again, forcing the horses to pick up their pace. He wanted to see Esmeralda. No, he wanted more than just to see her. He wanted to hold her, feel her soft body in his arms again. Tightly. He wanted to kiss her thoroughly. He desired her. No question about that. He desired her to the point it distracted him from all the things he needed to be doing. All he could think about was being with her. Often. No question about that either.

And, he'd finally come up with a plan on how to make that happen.

Vera had finally accepted a ride in Hyde Park with Lord Henry so he didn't have to worry about her being at Mayfair. Lambert was visiting with Sara at Mayfair, but what young blade could resist the opportunity to be seen in a brand-new curricle? Griffin was going to suggest Lambert take the curricle for a jaunt around the neighborhood and have Lady Sara accompany him. That would give him a few minutes alone with Esmeralda.

A young buck on an older curricle went racing by Griffin. The horses kicked up a cloud from a road that hadn't seen rain in several days. Griffin smiled and muttered an oath. He slowed his horses so he wouldn't have to breathe in the dusty air as it settled on his hat and shoulders. It amused him to think he used to be just as careless and reckless. Now, instead of thinking about how fast his horse could run or if he'd win the next wager, he was thinking about Miss Esmeralda Swift.

Somehow, for the past few days, he managed not to seek out Esmeralda when she was alone. It'd been damn hard, though, and he'd finally reached his limit of endurance. He was counting the days until she was no longer in his employ. At the parties, he continued to engage with Miss Froste, Miss Waldegrave, and other young ladies by dancing and talking with them. They were all lovely, acceptable, and available, but not a one of them interested him.

Esmeralda was the only one who consumed his thoughts, and left him aching to see her again. Every evening he'd watch other men looking at her. Some, like Rath, had even tried to get her to dance with them. She always declined. Was she doing that because she was as intent on Griffin as he was her, or was she merely saying no because of her position in his house?

Griffin stopped the curricle in front of his Mayfair house and jumped down. After tethering the horses and securing the ribbons, he reached back onto the floor of the small carriage and picked up a bouquet of flowers for his aunt. He would see her before he left.

Griffin opened the door of his home and stepped inside. The day had been warm enough he hadn't needed his cloak, but he left his hat, gloves, and the flowers on the vestibule table. Usually Sparks could hear the front door open and come running, but all was quiet in the house.

He walked down the corridor, rounded the entranceway to the drawing room, and stopped dead still. Sara was wrapped in the arms of Mr. Lambert and they were kissing madly. Her dress was off one shoulder. Griffin glanced around the room. Esmeralda was nowhere in sight.

"What the devil is going on here?" he asked striding into the room.

The two separated like a rock shot from a sling.

"Griffin?" Sara gasped, pulling her dress back onto her shoulder.

Anger rose up in Griffin. It was Lambert all along. He was trying to ruin Sara's reputation. Where was Esmeralda? He'd hired her just so this wouldn't happen.

"Your Grace," Lambert said. "We—we're glad you're here."

If Griffin hadn't been so angry at the moment, he would have laughed. That was about the stupidest remark the man could've made. "You're glad I'm here. Well, that's good because I'm glad I'm here too." He glanced at Sara. "And it looks like I got here just in time."

"Don't be upset, Griffin," Sara said, nervously working the neckline of her dress. "It was just a little kiss."

"Little?" He inhaled deeply, thinking he wasn't nearly as upset with Sara as he was with her chaperone. "Where's Esmeralda?"

"She went to find Josephine," Sara answered with tears pooling in her big blue eyes.

Josephine?

Esmeralda left *his sister* alone in the house with a man to go to *her* sister.

Griffin's anger grew. It wasn't that he was so angry about the kiss between Lambert and Sara. Hell, he'd kissed more than his share of innocent young ladies. It was that Esmeralda had left them alone. He'd trusted her to watch after his sisters. Esmeralda betrayed him. Betrayed his faith in her.

"The kiss just happened, Your Grace," Lambert said, taking a nervous step toward Griffin. "We didn't—I mean I didn't plan to kiss her. I swear it. Don't be angry with Lady Sara, Your Grace."

Griffin advanced on the man. "Don't tell me what to do, Lambert."

"Yes, Your Grace—I mean no, Your Grace. I won't tell you what to do. But I don't want you angry with Lady Sara either. If you are going to be angry with anyone it should be me. It was my fault."

"All right, I'll be angry with you." Griffin grabbed the man by the bow of his neckcloth. "You're damned right it was your fault."

"Griffin, no!" Sara exclaimed. "It was mine! Don't hurt him. It was all my fault."

The blame lay squarely at Esmeralda's feet.

"I'd like to explain what happened," Lambert said. "There was this—"

Griffin let go of him with a shove and said, "I don't want to hear what you have to say. Get out of my house before I do something we'll both regret. And don't let me see you near either of my sisters again."

Sara grabbed Griffin's arm. "You can't tell him that."

He didn't take his gaze of Lambert. "I just did. Now get out."

"Your Grace, if you'd let me or Lady Sara explain."

Griffin didn't want to hear from anyone but Esmeralda. "Leave Lambert. Now," he said quietly.

"Yes, Your Grace." He looked at Sara and hurried from the room.

"You are a horrible brother, Griffin. If I can't speak to Mr. Lambert ever again, then I will never speak to you again either."

"You'll change your mind about that once you realize all that he really wanted was to ruin you for marriage to any other man."

"That's not true," she declared. "I don't want any other man. I want to marry him."

"Has he asked you to marry him, Sara?"

Her eyes blinked rapidly. She didn't answer.

"Has he asked you to marry him?"

"No," she said, her anger at him suddenly changing to sorrow. "But he will. I know he will."

"But he hasn't."

Sara's bottom lip trembled.

Griffin hated seeing her upset, hated treating her so coldly, but she needed to face a few facts about men. They don't get as emotional about a few kisses and it doesn't mean they want to marry whomever they were kissing.

That might happen only if Griffin decided to force Lambert into it.

Esmeralda came rushing into the drawing room. "Your Grace, Lady Sara, I saw Mr. Lambert leaving."

"Griffin is an ogre," Lady Sara cried. "He's the worst brother a sister could ever have. I'm never going to speak to him again."

Griffin was aware of Sara running from the room, but his gaze never left Esmeralda's face. She was flushed and out of breath, as if she'd run a long distance. Tendrils of her hair had fallen from her chignon and framed her face. Even though she'd let him down, she was still the most beautiful woman he'd ever seen.

"What is going on?" Esmeralda asked.

She looked worried. No, more than worried—panicked. But then she had good reason to panic. She'd been caught neglecting his sisters. "If you'd been here, you would know."

She blinked rapidly. "I had to go to Josephine."

"So I heard. You had to go to your sister while you are being paid to watch mine."

He heard her suck in a deep breath. "That's not fair."

"Is it true?"

"Yes. I left Lady Sara to go after Josephine, but Sara was fine when I left her."

At least she wasn't denying her guilt.

"When I came in she was wrapped in Lambert's arms with her dress off her shoulder. Thankfully I arrived before things went too far."

Her eyes widened as she took a step toward him. "But how did that happen?"

"Do you really want to ask that, Esmeralda? We know how quickly things can go too far, don't we?"

Her gaze dropped to the floor. "Yes, we do. Was she harmed?"

He knew his harsh words had stung her, but she'd left Sara vulnerable to something far worse.

"It doesn't appear so, but obviously he was out to harm her. I guess you were wrong about Lambert's intentions."

"Yes, I must have been. I'm sorry. I should have been here."

She looked up at him with those gorgeous golden-brown eyes, full of remorse, pain, and tears. Something moved inside him that he'd never felt before. He didn't know what it was but he knew this woman was the last person on earth he wanted to hurt. He almost reached for her, but his anger was too raw.

Instead, he said, "Your one job was to watch after my sisters to keep this very thing from happening. You let them down and you let me down."

She sucked in another deep breath, but it was so deep no sound came out. "I know," she whispered.

"You felt Josephine needed you more than Lady Sara?"

Her chin lifted. "At that moment, yes."

"Your services are no longer needed."

A soft moan passed her lips. Once again, Griffin almost reached for her, but Sparks walked into the room.

"You're Grace, I'm glad you're home."

"So am I, Sparks. Make arrangements to see to it that

Miss Swift and her sister are taken back to their home this afternoon. You can have their things delivered to them tomorrow."

Sparks looked at Esmeralda and seemed about to speak when Esmeralda said, "Thank you for doing that for us, Sparks." Without looking at Griffin she turned and walked out of the room.

"Your Grace, I—"

"Damnation, Sparks, just do what I said!"

Griffin swore again the second Sparks left the room. Already he wanted to go after Esmeralda and tell her he didn't want her to go. But he couldn't. She was wrong to leave Sara and Lambert alone together in the house no matter the reason. He walked over to the side table and poured himself a generous portion of brandy. The first drink burned all the way down.

Griffin heard a door close. He looked toward the entranceway. Was Esmeralda leaving already? He felt his stomach wrench. Still, he took another drink.

A few moments later Vera walked into the drawing room. "Thank goodness you're home."

She looked almost as wary as Esmeralda had.

"What's wrong?"

"Oh, Griffin, it was Lord Henry," she cried and flung herself against his chest. The brandy sloshed over the glass.

"What are you talking about?" He put down the glass and wrapped his arms around her. Good lord, he'd never had a day where three women were crying in front of him. "What happened?"

"It was Lord Henry all along." She sniffed. "He's the one who was up to mischief."

The Earl of Berkwoods' son?

Griffin took her by the arms and forced her to look at him. "Tell me what happened."

Vera sniffed and suddenly looked defiant. "After we left Hyde Park where Lord Henry was a perfect gentleman, he took me to a secret alleyway."

"He didn't!"

Her tears dry, she nodded. "That wretched man said he knew I loved him and that with the looks I'd been sending him I'd been begging for his kisses since the moment we met. He said he aimed to kiss me, so I slapped him first on one cheek and then the other. That made him angry with me. He said someone needed to make good on the gossip about ruining our reputations, and since the cowards who'd said they'd do it hadn't, he might as well do it himself."

"I'll kill him," Griffin muttered under his breath.

"I think I may have already done that."

His hands tightened on her arms. "What do you mean?"

"I didn't like what he said so I started hitting him on the head and shoulders with my parasol and he started bleeding. Blood ran down his face and onto his collar. It was horrible."

"Never mind about him. What I want to know is did he hurt you?"

"Only my pride," she admitted with another sniff. "He wanted to bring me home but I told him I'd rather have my reputation ruined by walking home alone than ever being seen with him again. He's a bore and an oaf."

"And if you didn't kill him, I still may."

Her lips twitched with a little smile. "I don't want you to do that, Griffin. I'm not hurt. Just tired from walking. You are such a good brother, Griffin."

He wasn't feeling much like one. "Go upstairs and ask your sister if she feels I'm a good brother."

"I don't want her to know what Lord Henry did."

"Why?"

"I don't want her to know she was right about him. She

didn't like him after she met him, and she told me I should set my hat for someone else. I don't want her to know she was right and I was wrong."

"Just go talk to your sister. I think she would like that and it will make you feel better, too."

"You won't actually kill Lord Henry will you, Griffin?"

He smiled and patted her cheek affectionately. "No, but I'll do my best to make him wish I had."

Chapter 26

Don't be afraid to admit when you are wrong.

MISS MAMIE FORTESCUE'S DO'S AND DON'TS FOR
CHAPERONES, GOVERNESSES, TUTORS, AND NURSES

Griffin sat at the table with the newsprint in front of his face. The draperies were pulled wide from the window, but the day was so gray it did little to brighten the room or lift his temperament. For the third time he tried to focus on the article about why there was a delay in getting gas lights on more of London's streets, and for the third time his thoughts turned to yesterday. And Esmeralda.

His gaze strayed over to the letter that had been delivered that morning from Lambert. With an overabundance of words, the man had apologized for his ungentlemanly treatment of Lady Sara and then professed his love for her and hopes that he could offer for her hand in marriage.

Frustrated, Griffin wadded the newsprint he held and threw it across the floor. He didn't know if Lambert was serious about his marital intentions toward Sara or if he was just trying to keep Griffin from enacting some form of revenge on him for ravishing her.

Placed on the white linen in front of Griffin was a plate of food he hadn't touched: scrambled eggs, a slice of ham, boiled potatoes. On a saucer beside it lay a slice of bread and a serving of cooked figs. In the center of the table sat a three-pronged candlestick, affording the only bright light in the room. It was an oval table with six chairs. All empty save his. He looked at the chair beside him and imagined Esmeralda sitting there, her golden-brown hair hanging down her back. Her expression serene, and her beautiful lips smiling at him.

He hadn't stopped thinking about her. Why had he put so much faith in what Esmeralda had believed about Lambert, Lord Henry, or all the other gentlemen? She'd told him she knew nothing about the ways of a man, so why had he trusted what she'd thought? Because he'd been drawn to everything about her, including all she said. That hadn't changed. That empty feeling that had formed in his gut when he'd told her to leave hadn't changed either.

Griffin hadn't stopped wanting her simply because he was upset with her. His desire for her hadn't changed. If anything it had increased since he'd held her warm, supple body in his arms and tasted her tender lips. No, the way she made him feel had become more than desire. It was a hunger. He wanted her morning and night. Midday and afternoon. Twilight and midnight. He wanted her with him. In this house. In this room. Right now, sitting at this table with him enjoying a cup of chocolate, or tea, or whatever her heart desired. He didn't care as long as she was there.

Somehow, deep inside he'd known all along that she wasn't just a poor relation to a well-respected baron. And finding out she was a lady of quality had complicated his craving, but it hadn't stopped it. And now, rejecting her, sending her out of his life, hadn't made it stop either.

Maybe he wouldn't have acted so coldly to her if he understood his feelings for her. If he understood why he couldn't get her out of his thoughts or why he couldn't stop wanting her. He had no doubt she wanted him—not his title, not his wealth or his influence, but him—as much as he wanted her.

Esmeralda had thought Lambert had a genuine interest in Sara. Maybe he did. Griffin would meet with the man and hear what he had to say for himself. He wouldn't be opposed to Sara marrying Lambert, but was it his intention to offer for her or simply continue to dally with her? And he had certainly acted differently than Lord Henry had.

He looked down at his scuffed knuckles and winced as he opened and closed his hand. Lord Henry would not only be nursing the crack on his head from Vera's parasol, he'd be sporting the swollen eye and busted lip that Griffin had left with him last night. It would be a few days before he'd want to be seen in public again.

A noise from the front of the house caught his attention. Someone was at the door. Female voices. His sisters? They never came to St. James. He rose as his butler stopped in the doorway, and said, "Your sisters and Lady Evelyn would like to see you."

Lady Evelyn?

"I've asked them to wait in the drawing room for you."

His aunt? Out of the house? His heart started beating a little harder. Something had to be wrong.

"Prepare chocolate for them." Griffin lay aside his napkin and strode down the corridor and into the drawing room. Sara and Vera were on the settee and Lady Evelyn, wearing a plum-colored hat with a sheer black veil covering her face, was perched on a straight back chair near them. All three stood when he walked in. He put his hand out for them to sit.

"What's wrong?" he asked, though he was feeling better now that he saw no one was harmed, or crying. In fact, they all looked rather perturbed.

"You tell us," his aunt said, almost sharply.

"All right. I'm thinking it's wrong for you to be out of the bed. If you wanted to see me, you could have sent for me."

"I may look like a beast," she answered, "but I'm still quite capable of walking. When you do drastic things that are harmful to this family, I don't have time to wait around until you decide you have the time to come see me."

Had she received word that he paid a visit to Lord Berkwoods' son? Griffin opened and closed his injured hand again, thinking his aunt was sounding a bit like Esmeralda did the first day he met her.

"What are you talking about?" he asked.

"I had a letter from Miss Swift this morning telling me that she was sorry she had neglected her duties to Sara, and she completely understood why she could no longer chaperone them, and to please forgive her."

"We had similar notes from her," Vera added curtly.

"And we don't know why," Sara continued. "Bring her back, Griffin. No matter what you think of me or Mr. Lambert for kissing me, it wasn't Miss Swift's fault."

"I know everything that happened yesterday with Sara and Vera, Your Grace," Lady Evelyn said. "They both confided in me this morning and have sought my help. I agree with them. Bring Miss Swift back."

He frowned. "She left Sara alone in the house with Lambert," he said without mercy.

"No," Sara said. "I was so upset with you yesterday I didn't think to tell you everything that happened."

"You can spare me the details, Sara. I have a pretty

good idea about what happened between you and Lambert."

"That's not what she's talking about, Griffin," Vera interjected. "He'd left the house, but came back after Miss Swift went chasing after Josephine. He saw Sara standing in the doorway crying."

Esmeralda chasing after Josephine. There was nothing uncommon about that. There was no telling what Josephine had gotten into. "Why were you crying? What happened?"

"We all were," Lady Sara said. "Even Sparks had to wipe his eyes."

"What the devil are you talking about?"

"So, as I thought, you don't know the whole story of what happened yesterday." Lady Evelyn said.

His stomach clenched. "Apparently not, but someone tell me right now."

"I'll tell it since I was there," Sara said. "We were sitting in the drawing room talking, when Josephine and Napoleon came in from the back garden. A few minutes later Sparks came to Miss Swift and said there was a man who wanted to see her."

"Oh, botheration, Sara," Vera complained. "Let me tell it. You will take forever, and I simply don't have the patience for it today."

"You can't tell it because you weren't there. You were still out with Lord Henry."

"Both of you stop bickering, and one of you tell me what happened."

"I'll tell it," Lady Evelyn said, rising from her chair to stand before Griffin. "Sparks was there and I spoke with him this morning to make sure I had all the facts straight from the twins. A Mr. Chambers from several streets over saw Miss Josephine playing with Napoleon outside the back gate. He called to her but she ran back into the garden with Napoleon. Of course, he came right over and demanded the dog be turned over to him because he said it belonged to his granddaughter. He then forcibly took Napoleon away with him."

Both Griffin's hands made tight fists despite his injury. "He took Napoleon from Josephine?"

"With her crying, screaming, and beating him on the back," Sara added.

I will strangle that man with my bare hands!

"Sometime during all this," his aunt continued, "while Miss Swift was still trying to reason with Mr. Chambers, she asked Mr. Lambert to leave so she could handle the situation properly. According to Sparks, Mr. Lambert did leave the house. However, he watched from his carriage across the street as Josephine rushed out of the house to chase Mr. Chambers, and Esmeralda and Sparks ran after her. Mr. Lambert saw Sara standing in the doorway visibly upset, and he came back to comfort her. That is what led to the kiss you witnessed."

"So you see, Miss Swift didn't leave me unattended with Mr. Lambert. I should have made that clear to you yesterday that she thought Mr. Lambert had left."

"I don't care about Mr. Lambert or his leaving right now, Sara. Did they get Napoleon back?"

"But it's important for you to know Miss Swift didn't do anything wrong."

"Sara," he said impatiently, "we'll settle that later. Did Esmeralda get Napoleon back?"

"No," Vera said.

"Mr. Chambers said that Napoleon's real name is Spook and he belongs to his granddaughter, Gracie. Spook wandered off when she was visiting him last year and they couldn't find him. Now that he's found Spook he was taking him back to his granddaughter."

No, hell, he isn't.

"Napoleon definitely knew the man," Sara continued, but Griffin was no longer listening.

His fists grew tighter.

"Did Mr. Chambers say where he lives?"

"I don't think so."

"Doesn't matter. I'll find him." Griffin looked from his aunt to Vera to Sara. "I'm going to bring Napoleon and Miss Swift back."

Chapter 27

Don't think that you will never be wrong.
You will be.

⟿⟾

Miss Mamie Fortescue's Do's and Don'ts for
Chaperones, Governesses, Tutors, and Nurses

The door of Miss Mamie Fortescue's Employment Agency was locked. Griffin looked around. The sun had set but the street lamps hadn't been lit along the storefronts. He hadn't noticed before, but even though it was still twilight most of the shops were closed.

He knocked on the door and waited. Impatiently. There was no answer. He knocked again. Louder. Finally, he heard the soft patter of footsteps. They stopped but there was no click of a key turning in the lock.

"It's Griffin, Esmeralda. Open the door."

Nothing but silence greeted him from the other side. He knew she was angry with him and had every right to be, but he would see Josephine.

"I'm not going away. Do I keep knocking and disturb your neighbors or will you let me inside?"

The door opened. He didn't ask if he could come in and

she didn't try to stop him as he walked past her into the office. She looked tired. Sad. She clutched the brown woolen shawl she'd been wearing the first day he saw her around her slim shoulders.

She avoided his eyes when she said, "We have nothing to say to each other."

"We do, but I want to talk to Josephine first."

"That's not possible. I'm sure she doesn't wants to see anyone. She's been quite upset."

Griffin grunted softly at her rejection. She'd spoken with that authoritative tone she'd used with Miss Pennywaite. It had scared the governess right down to her unmentionables, but it wasn't going to work with him.

"I will see her, Esmeralda," he said calmly.

Again she didn't look at him. He watched her spine stiffen, and he almost smiled. She hadn't lost her spunk. Good. That was the Esmeralda he wanted to confront.

"Only if she agrees to see you. I won't force her. I'll ask but if she says no, you'll have to respect her wishes."

Griffin had to think about that. He wasn't good at just accepting something he didn't want to accept, but should he force Josephine to see him if she didn't want to?

Finally he said, "I agree."

"Wait here. I'll go ask her."

"I'll just follow you."

For a second, he thought she was going to argue. Instead, she turned and led him out into a narrow, unlit corridor where they climbed a set of steep stairs to the top of a landing that dead-ended into a door. She opened it and they entered.

It wasn't a large or fancy area but it was orderly. The draperies had already been drawn. A single lamp burned on a side table and a bed of hot coals added warmth to the room. There was a floral printed settee in the center of the room; an armchair was placed in front of it with a small tea table between them. Two unlit sconces and a painting of an Irish hillside dotted with sheep were the only things hanging on the walls.

Griffin's admiration for Esmeralda grew. She had made a relatively nice and safe home for herself and Josephine. He didn't know any other young lady who had accomplished so much, and to have done it without the help from her family was commendable.

"Josephine has been in her bed since we arrived home yesterday afternoon," Esmeralda said, leaving all warmth out of her voice again and still refusing to look into his eyes. "She didn't sleep at all last night. Or today. She's very tired."

"I won't keep her long but I must see her."

Esmeralda nodded and then disappeared into a room.

He waited only a few moments, and Josephine walked out in a gray quilted dressing gown. Her red hair hung limp and tangled about her shoulders. Her eyes were swollen and her nose and cheeks were red. At that moment, Griffin knew he loved her as much as he loved Sara and Vera. Josephine was his sister too. He wanted to take care of her so that she never had a reason to cry again. And, as he had with Esmeralda, he'd see to it that she never wore the unattractive color gray again either.

She curtsied. "Good evening, Your Grace."

He bowed. "Josephine. I've come to see you how are you doing."

"All right, I guess."

"I'll put a kettle on the fire and heat some chocolate," Esmeralda said and then glanced at him for the first time that evening. "I'm sorry I don't have anything stronger to offer you."

Her gaze was weary and wary. A stab of self-inflicted pain tightened his chest, and he knew he never wanted Esmeralda to be wary of him again.

"Chocolate's fine," he said softly and when she turned away, he looked at Josephine and said, "Will you come sit with me on the settee?"

She nodded, and he waited until she made herself comfortable with her hands folded in her lap before he settled himself beside her.

"It's been a sad couple of days for you, hasn't it?"

She nodded again but didn't speak.

"I didn't know what had happened to Napoleon until earlier today. I would have come yesterday if I'd known."

"It's all right," she said in a very grown-up voice. "I didn't want to see anyone yesterday."

"Still, it's my own fault I didn't know sooner." His gaze traveled over to where Esmeralda stood with her back to him. He knew she heard him, though she gave no indication. Hopefully she knew he was admitting he'd been wrong yesterday to dismiss her before he'd heard a full explanation of what had happened.

Giving his attention back to Josephine, he said, "I found out where Mr. Chambers lives and I went to see him today. I wanted to get Napoleon back for you, but I couldn't." Damn, he hated telling her that. "Mr. Chambers had already left to take Napoleon to Manchester. I'm going there to find him as soon as I leave here, but I had to come check on you first and make sure you're all right. I want you to know I'm not coming back until I have Napoleon with me."

"No." She sniffed, looking up at him with her big green eyes. "I can't let you take him away from another girl. That would make you as mean as Mr. Chambers."

Griffin tried to swallow, but a lump had formed in his throat. "I don't mind."

Josephine's lashes became moist. "But I don't want you that mean, Your Grace," she said softly. "I like you the way you are."

The lump grew. "I will get him for you," Griffin promised passionately.

"No," she said again and shook her head. "She had him first."

Griffin glanced down at Josephine's hands resting in her lap. They were small. Clasped. Steady. She had thought through her feelings and knew what she was saying.

"He wasn't mine anyway," she continued, her eyes brimming with unshed tears. "I always knew he belonged to someone else. I was just keeping him safe until we found his owner. Besides, I don't want her feeling the way I do right now. She'd probably feel worse than I do right now if she lost him again, because she'd be losing him twice."

Griffin was never at a loss for words, but Josephine had him mute for a few seconds. She was being more rational and thoughtful than a lot of adults he'd known.

He praised her by saying, "That's a very brave way to think about this."

"It's my fault anyway. I disobeyed you and Essie by going out of the back gate when you told me not to. Mr. Chambers would have never seen Napoleon if I hadn't gone out."

"We all do things we're not supposed to do sometimes. I know I've been guilty of it more times than I can count."

"But it hurts really bad."

"I know," he said softly.

She threw his arms around his neck and started sobbing. He pulled her slight body into his embrace and pressed her cheek against the soft velvet of his waistcoat. Her shoulders shook with wracking sobs. She poured her heart out with deep, loud crying. Griffin wanted to find Chambers and strangle him for taking Napoleon away from Josephine.

"Cry as long as you want to," he whispered to Josephine, brushing her hair with his hand, kissing the top of her head as he would Vera's or Sara's. "I'm going to be right here holding you."

He felt Esmeralda come up to stand beside them and glanced over his shoulder to her. Her eyes were filled with tears too. The only comfort he could offer her right now was compassion for the little girl he was holding, and he hoped she saw that in his face.

A sudden feeling of peace about life swept over him. The reason was standing right beside him. Esmeralda. Without a stirring of doubt, he knew he loved her with all his heart, his body, his mind, and his soul. There had been many women in his life, too many to count, but none of them had ever touched him like Esmeralda had. His love for her was the reason he couldn't stop thinking about her, couldn't stop wanting her, couldn't stop wanting her to want him. She was a part of him. She was his other half. His soul mate. He would find a way to make her believe that he loved her and that she loved him, too. For now, all he could do was hold her sister and let her cry.

Long after Josephine fell asleep, Griffin continued to hold her tightly in his arms. He finally looked up when he heard Esmeralda bend down to whisper, "Put her to bed, and then I'll show you out."

Chapter 28

Don't hesitate to forgive, and then do forget.

—◆—

It had been a hellish two days.

It was so unfair that some people went through life seeming to always have so many wonderful things happen to them while others were all too often neglected and left on their own by the cruel hand of fate. Josephine had lost her mother and her father way too young. It wasn't right that she'd lost Napoleon too.

Esmeralda had been devastated for her sister but had remained strong for her too, just as she had when Josephine's father had died. When Griffin had arrived half an hour earlier it was easy to weaken, to let go of the tight control she had on her emotions and allow him be the strong one. While Josephine cried in the Duke's arms, Esmeralda had silently cried too. In those minutes, she'd been overcome by his compassion for her sister. His kindheartedness had filled her with so much love for him it swelled in her chest until she ached.

"She'll probably sleep through the night now," Griffin said as they walked back into the main room.

"Probably," Esmeralda answered curtly, refusing to look at him and walking straight to the door that led to the stairway. If she didn't talk to him, if she didn't stare into his blue eyes, she could tell herself she didn't love him. Every time her gaze caught sight of his, it was impossible to lie to herself and deny it. She hadn't wanted to leave her heart with him when she left his employ, but that's exactly what had happened.

Griffin stopped beside her. So close she inhaled his scent, felt his warmth. It made her want to bury her face in his chest so he could console her the way he had Josephine. But suddenly consumed by the unfairness of life, instead of seeking the solace she needed, in a rush of words and emotions too deep to contemplate or understand, she said, "I don't care what Josephine says. I don't care how mature she sounded, or how brave you think she is about doing the right thing, I want you to go and get Napoleon back for her."

A muscle twitched in the side of his mouth. "Esmeralda?" he said softly.

"No, don't say it," she whispered on a winded gasp of despair that pushed from her aching lungs. "You don't understand. Finding Napoleon helped her get over her father's death. He means the world to her. I don't want her to hurt anymore. I want her to have Napoleon back."

"I want that for her too. But I believe she meant it when she said she didn't want the other little girl to lose him again."

"I don't care about the other little girl." Esmeralda swallowed a sob. "I only care about Josephine."

"You don't mean that, Esmeralda."

"I do," she said earnestly, her heartbeat surging inside her chest, her shoulders shaking from holding tears at bay once again. "I do mean it. Josephine's been hurt enough. Too much, and I'm asking you to get him back for her."

His eyes remained soft, his expression concerned. "Josephine is going to be fine. She's thought this through. She's made her decision, and it was her decision to make."

He was making too much sense for her distraught state. She didn't want to hear it. Defying his claim, she argued, "Josephine is twelve. She doesn't know what she wants, and she doesn't know what's best for her. I do."

"I would try to move heaven and earth for her if she wanted me to, but I won't go against her wishes."

"Fine," Esmeralda whispered, brushing away strands of hair that had fallen to the side of her face. "I'll find a way to get Napoleon back for her by myself."

"You don't want to do that, Esmeralda." He spoke softly.

"I will," she insisted.

"I don't know what kind of man Chambers is, but as far as I'm concerned only a monster would take a dog from a crying girl's arms and run away with it. You aren't that kind of person, Esmeralda. You couldn't take Napoleon from another child and leave her with the pain Josephine is enduring."

But she wanted to.

Oh, she hated it when he was right. And he was right again. She had to let go of Napoleon the way Josephine, had but it was so hard to watch her sister suffer again.

"Just go, please," Esmeralda said. "Leave us alone."

"You don't want me to go."

She lifted her chin and sniffed. "You're wrong. I do."

"Then prove it. Open the door."

Her chest heaved with emotion. She looked at the door but didn't make a move.

Why was he making it her choice whether he left? He

must know she didn't really want him to go. For heaven's sake, why didn't he take the decision from her and either leave or sweep her into his arms and carry her into her bedchamber?

Time stretched on. Neither of them moved. She could tell herself all day long, and all night too, that she didn't love him, that she didn't want to be in his arms, but that wouldn't make it true.

"If you want me to go, open the door, and I'll go out it. But know this, Esmeralda, I'll be back tomorrow and the next day and the next."

"Don't do this to me, Griffin. You know I can't resist you."

"Then let me hold you."

His strong, masculine arms went around her, pulling her gently against him. He put his hand to the back of her head, cupping her to his chest and sealing her inside the comfort of his embrace. Esmeralda closed her eyes and leaned against his warmth, his strength, and hid her face in his shirt.

Griffin's clothing was still damp from Josephine's tears. After kissing the top of her head, he laid his cheek against her hair. One hand moved soothingly up and down her back, over her shoulders, and around her neck. She heard the steady beat of his heart, and relaxed.

"You can cry if you want," he murmured. "Or I can just hold you until you fall asleep."

There were no more tears to be shed. All the emotions of despair, anger, and revenge swirling around inside her were impossible to fathom, so she didn't try. She must let all go. All of them. The only emotion she kept was her love for Griffin. It welled up inside her and wouldn't be denied.

Esmeralda moistened her lips and raised her head. "Will you kiss me?"

He looked down into her eyes and, saying nothing, slid

a hand to the back of her neck. Dipping his head, he covered her mouth with his in a long, gentle, and sweet kiss.

"Is that what you wanted?"

She nodded.

"Now, will you kiss me?"

Letting her shawl drop to the floor, she rose up on her toes to palm each side of his face with her hands and kissed his lips, the tip of his nose, each cheek, and his closed eyelids before resting flat on her feet again.

She smiled. "Is that what you wanted?"

"It's a start, but I want more."

Griffin caught her up in his arms and captured her open lips with his. Esmeralda gloried in a passionate, desperate kiss. Their tongues swirled in each other's mouths while their bodies strained to get closer. Griffin's hands moved up her ribcage to fondle her breasts with eager yet soothing, titillating strokes.

She moaned softly. His fingers found her nipples hidden beneath the layers of her clothing. At his touch, ripples of desire flooded her. Pleasure swept down her body and settled into her most womanly part.

Reluctantly, leaning away from him, she looked up into his eyes and said, "Josephine is asleep now, but she could awaken and leave her bed. Will you come with me into my room? I can lock the door."

Surprise glinted in his eyes. "I want nothing more than to go with you, but I'm not asking this from you tonight, my love."

My love. Oh, such endearing words that made her heart soar. From the first day she'd met him, he'd said things to make her feel as if she belonged to only him.

Esmeralda knew there could be life-altering consequences for what she wanted. Griffin could walk out her door and never see her again. Their night together could leave her in the family way. She knew the risks. Perhaps she should, but right now she didn't want to contemplate either of those possibilities. He had made it clear he desired her. He had said he couldn't touch her because she was in his employ. Now, she no longer was. And she wanted to have this night with him.

"I know. I'm asking *you*." Entwining her arms around his neck, she pulled him closer, smiled shyly, and said, "But I won't force you. I will never force you to do anything you don't want to do."

He chuckled softly, attractively. "You have a bad habit of using my own words against me. You will not ever have to force me to do this."

He swooped down and covered her mouth with his in a ravishing kiss that stole her breath. Esmeralda knew no matter the consequences, no matter the future, she'd made the right decision for tonight. Their kissing continued and she started walking backward, toward her room while pulling the tail of his shirt from the waistband of his trousers. It seemed natural to want to feel his skin beneath her hands. When her back hit the door, he reached around her, opened it just enough for them to enter, then closed and locked it behind them.

Light from a shadowed moon shone through a window. "The room is small," she whispered against his lips. "And so is the bed."

"All I need is you."

All I need is you.

Yes, he knew exactly what she wanted to hear.

Griffin shrugged out of his coat while Esmeralda untied his neckcloth, wound it from around his neck, and tossed it away. He yanked the rest of his shirt out of his trousers and pulled it over his head, sending it the way of the neckcloth. Her breaths quickened at the sight of the strong chest and broad shoulders before her. In the dim light, she wished for more to better see his beauty. She would make do with just touching him. It was a glorious feeling to feather her hands up his rippled ribs and across the smooth, firm skin of his chest and shoulders.

Taking her into his arms again, Griffin hissed with pleasure at her caresses and claimed her lips with a searing kiss while his hands worked the laces at the back of her bodice. It fell away from her shoulders, and he helped slip it off her arms and over her head. He reached around her and untied her skirt, letting it drop to the floor. Quickly they made short work of removing her stays, shift, drawers, and the rest of his clothing and boots too.

When they both stood bare before each other, Griffin brushed his fingertips softly down her cheek to her breast before pulling her into his arms. Cool, soft breasts met warm, strong chest. It was the most heavenly feeling Esmeralda could imagine experiencing. His confident hands moved across her shoulders all the way down her back and over her buttocks. Her untutored hands explored down the length of his chest, his midriff, his lean narrow hips, and around to his manhood.

"Yes," he murmured into her mouth, and then hooked his arm under her legs, picked her up, and carried her over to the bed to lay her down.

Griffin stretched his lean body beside her and rose over her to look into her eyes for a long moment before his gaze drifted down her face and lingered over her breasts, her body, before sweeping back up to her eyes again.

"You're beautiful," he said huskily.

She smiled. "It's too dark in here. You can't see me."

He grunted a short laugh. "If it makes you feel better to think that, go ahead. My eyes have adjusted to the light. I can see you."

What he said was true. She saw his desire for her in his eyes.

"Do you know what to expect?" he asked.

"Not entirely, but I've found with you that nature and instinct have a way of taking over.

"And so they shall."

Griffin kissed her tenderly, slowly, while the pads of his fingers traveled over her chin and down to rest in the hollow at the base of her neck. A tremor of expectancy shivered through her. He kissed her soft and long. Sweet and soothing. Without letting his lips leave her skin, he kissed the path his fingers had walked and then moved back up to her lips again and showered her with short, eager kisses.

While they kissed, one hand slipped down her body to her breast. He palmed it, gently squeezed and felt its weight. The thrill of his touch was shattering to her senses. His lips left hers and glided across her cheek, over her chin, and to the soft, sweet skin behind her ear. He kissed his way down her chest and across her shoulders to her breast again, covering her nipple with his mouth, and gently sucked. Delightful shivers of pleasure tingled along her spine, down her abdomen to settle and gather between her legs.

Esmeralda's head fell back, and her chest arched forward. Her breasts tightened with anticipation of more to come. His tongue circled her nipple, bathed it, and then gently drew it fully into his mouth again. A thousand sensations blossomed inside her, and her senses reeled in delight.

While his mouth tugged on her breasts, his hand slipped down her hip between her legs, and he cupped her. The feeling was warm and strangely comforting. His fingers found the intimate place between her legs. She swallowed and moaned with pleasure.

The gentle, gliding movements created even more desires and feelings she couldn't explain and couldn't control. She rose up and wound her arms around Griffin's neck, burying her face into his shoulder and, hugging him to her, she gave herself up to the exquisite feelings spiraling through her as waves of explosive sensations tore through her womanly core, robbing her of breath before fading into pleasant, languid ripples.

"Griffin," she whispered before collapsing back down onto the bed with no breath left in her lungs, no strength in her bones.

"That is what loving is supposed to feel like," he whispered against her ear.

Griffin fitted his body between her legs and nestled his manhood against her as he covered her mouth with his. His kissed ravenously, gently pushing his body against hers, over and over again. He brought his tongue down the long sweep of her neck, tasting her, devouring her with more eager kisses and caresses.

Esmeralda gasped softly from the constant pushing of his body. She trembled and twisted beneath him. Her hands combed over the solid wall of his back, hips, and buttocks. Her lips kissed the heated skin of his shoulders.

"It's all right?" he whispered against her lips.

"Yes," she answered. It was all right.

When at last he'd fully entered her, he whispered her name and kissed her softly.

Griffin made love to her with a tenderness that overwhelmed her. His movements were slow, sensual, and reverent. He kissed her, stroked her body, and moved gently on top of her. That same indescribable pleasure she'd felt before kept mounting and caused her to join the rhythm of his hips meeting hers.

The delicious sensations continued when his movements changed to long, sure strokes that grew stronger, fuller, until with breathless wonder all the sensations in her body exploded once again.

Griffin's breath quickened. His body shuddered as he slid his arms under her back and hugged her to him.

Esmeralda relaxed on a contented sigh. Moments later, his rough breathing slowed and he rolled to his side facing her and pulled up the sheet.

They lay there side by side, not moving. For how long, she had no idea. It was just comforting having him beside her. She was too filled with the wonder of everything she'd experienced to want to move. If anyone had tried to tell her how magical it was to lie with a man, she couldn't have comprehended what they were saying.

"You'll have to tell her," Griffin said into the darkness. "You know that, don't you?"

Esmeralda tensed. *About us? About tonight?* "Tell Josephine what?" she asked.

"The real story about her mother, your family, and her father."

"No," she said unequivocally.

He raised up on his elbow and placed a short kiss on her lips. "Yes. She will have to know everything that you know. Not now. She's still young, but in time you will have to tell her. You can't keep it from her."

"In time," she said and looked past him out the small window. "Maybe."

"She will ask you one day."

Esmeralda knew he was right—again—but that was another one of those things she didn't want to think about tonight.

"I still want to get Napoleon back for her."

"But you won't."

"No."

"Look at me," he said. With the tips of his fingers under her chin, he turned her face toward him. "I should have allowed you to explain everything that happened yesterday."

"Is that an apology?"

He smiled. "I only learned this morning that you'd

asked Mr. Lambert to leave and thought he had. You didn't know he'd returned."

It didn't matter. She was no longer a part of his household.

"I don't want to talk about that, Griffin. It will serve no purpose."

"It will for me."

She looked at his broad shoulders and wanted to touch him again. "You," she mumbled softly. "This is why I don't like peers. It's always about what you want. It never matters what others want. I have enough to deal with concerning Josephine and the agency, and your feelings about what happened aren't high on my list right now."

He gave her a lopsided smile that made her heart start spinning.

"After what just happened between us? After what you felt and I felt, you're still miffed with me?"

Was she?

"Perhaps I am," she admitted honestly.

"Are you going to forgive me for making a human mistake yesterday or are you going to hold it against me the rest of my life?"

Didn't he know he wouldn't be in her bed if she hadn't already forgiven him?

"I don't know," she said as she reached over and kissed the crook of his neck.

His arm went around her shoulders. "It's partly your fault, you know."

"And why is that?"

"You should have interrupted me and told me to stop ranting about Sara and Lambert because someone had come and taken Napoleon away from Josephine."

"You were already too angry."

"I was rash."

"You were being a beast."

"I talked before I had all the facts."

"You didn't want to listen."

He chuckled as his hand traced the line of her shoulder and down her arm to the plane of her hip. "You really have a low opinion of me, don't you?"

"Peers in general," she admitted honestly. "Though, I have to say that when I first went into your employ, you were kinder than I thought you would be."

"But then yesterday I acted just the way you expected me to, didn't I?"

"I knew you would eventually show your true self. And you did. You overreacted."

"I talked before I had all the facts," he repeated.

"You wouldn't have listened anyway."

All of a sudden, he rolled her over onto her back and propped himself on his elbows as he settled his body between her legs. "I'm afraid what I'm going to tell you now will not change your opinion of me, but I'm going to say it anyway because you are right. I do like to get my way. I do intend to get my way. I'm going to marry you, Esmeralda."

A tremor shook her. "What?" She tried to rise, but he remained solidly on top of her.

"Lie back down," he said softly. "You heard me. I'm going to marry you. I'm in love with you, Esmeralda. You're the one I want. And you're going to be my wife."

You're the one I want. You're going to be my wife.

She was breathless. "You don't mean that."

"I would have never made love to you just now if I hadn't already made up my mind that I wanted you for my wife."

Esmeralda felt as if her heart were going to spin out of her chest. "I don't know what to say."

He looked deeply into her eyes and then kissed her so tenderly she felt all her bones turn liquid beneath him.

"You must say yes. Didn't I just tell you that I love you? You are mine and I'm not going to let anyone else have you, so get used to being told what to do."

"I will never stand for that."

"Good." His hand molded over the fullness of her breast. "I will have a pleasurable time trying to bend you to my will. You and Josephine belong with me in my house as my wife and sister. Not as a member of my staff but as my equal. All you have to do is say yes."

"Don't you want to know if I love you?" she asked breathlessly as she slid her hands down his sides.

He smiled. "I already know that you do, but it would be nice to hear you say it."

Esmeralda swallowed past the lump in her throat and whispered, "Griffin, I love you, and yes, I'll marry you."

My Dear Readers:

London may never be the same. One of our favorite bachelors to write about has just been taken off the marriage mart. All in Polite Society expected the Duke of Griffin's sisters, Lady Sara and Lady Vera, to be betrothed by the end of the Season, but no one expected the duke to be posting the banns for himself. He will be the first of the notorious Rakes of St. James to wed. The Duke of Griffin has made his intentions known, and the maiden who made the prized catch is Miss Esmeralda Swift. She and the duke will say nuptials in a private ceremony at his Mayfair home.

MISS HONORA TRUTH'S WEEKLY SCANDAL SHEET

Epilogue

Do remember that all is well when all ends well.

～⚬～

MISS MAMIE FORTESCUE'S DO'S AND DON'TS FOR
CHAPERONES, GOVERNESSES, TUTORS, AND NURSES

Griffin strode into his Mayfair house whipping off his hat. He laid the copy of a book of poetry, *The Quarterly Review,* and *Blackwood's Magazine* on the table, then removed his cloak and gloves.

"Esmeralda," he called. "Josephine?"

"Her Grace and Miss Josephine are in the garden," Sparks said, coming to Griffin with his cloak.

"Thank you, Sparks. So, she's going into the garden again?"

"Yes, Your Grace."

That was a good sign. When Esmeralda and Josephine first moved back to Mayfair, Josephine wouldn't go anywhere near the garden. He knew it reminded her of Napoleon.

He looked out the window and saw Esmeralda sitting on a bench. She wore a soft shade of pink and the single strand of pearls he'd given her for a wedding present. A contentedness he didn't know was possible filled him. Josephine was looking at the flowers. The May Day Flower Fair was tomorrow. Fenton would be displaying his Persian irises, looking to win again. The gardener had asked them to go with him.

Esmeralda turned to look when she heard the back door open. She smiled and so did he. Josephine paid him no mind. He figured she was staring at the flowers, but it might have been another frog.

Holding the book and the magazines behind his back, he strode through the damp grass to Esmeralda and bent down to kiss her.

"That was a pleasant way to be greeted," she said.

"Then I'll make a habit of it."

"I don't think that would make Lady Evelyn happy. She is a stickler for doing everything the proper way."

"I'm glad to see Josephine is out in the garden."

Esmeralda glanced over at her sister and nodded. "She'll let us know when she's ready for another dog."

"In the meantime," Griffin said, "I have something to show you that I want to give her today. From behind his back he pulled his offerings. "This a book of Myles Graham's poetry—it has every poem of his I could find."

Surprise glinted in her eyes as she took it and looked it over. "Where did you get this? He never had anything published in a book."

"I had it published for him. I've heard that books published posthumously usually sell very well."

"This is for sale?"

He smiled. "At every book shop in London, and most of England and Ireland as well."

"I—I don't know what to say."

"You don't have to say anything. I see happiness in your lovely eyes and your face."

"I am. I'm amazed, thrilled. But why?"

"I did it for Josephine. She didn't want me to get Napoleon back for her, and I admit I'm glad she didn't. It would have been difficult to take him away from another girl, but I would have bought her a horse or paid for her and her family to go on a grand tour or whatever she wanted if Josephine had wanted me to."

Esmeralda smiled and covered his hand with hers. "I know that."

"She made a selfless decision. I wanted to do something for her. I asked her if she had copies of her father's poems. That I'd like to read them. She said she had a copy of all of them. I admit I haven't read them yet. I immediately took them to a publishing company and paid to have them published." He picked up the magazines. "Two well-respected journals have reviewed it, and while they aren't glowing, they aren't terrible. Seems his poetry has gotten better with age."

Her eyes sparkled with tears. "Griffin, she will be thrilled. To have all of his poetry in one collection of his works. I don't know what to say, but thank you." She reached up kissed him.

"Esmeralda." Josephine came running up, and they broke apart. She was holding a bouquet of purple Persian irises in her hand.

Griffin stiffened. "Josephine," he asked. "Where did you get those flowers?"

"From right over there in the garden. Essie told me these are her favorites. I've been watching. Mr. Fenton takes very good care of them. And I knew it was the perfect day to pick them."

Fenton was going to faint.

"Josephine, you know you aren't supposed to pick any of the flowers in this garden," Esmeralda admonished.

"Why? His Grace told me this was my home now too.

If it's my home, why can't I pick the flowers? I know you like them." She suddenly beamed with a smile. "They bloomed on your birthday."

Griffin looked at Esmeralda. "I didn't know it was your birthday."

"Sometimes I don't remember it myself."

"Picking those flowers was a lovely way to remember your sister on her birthday," he said to Josephine.

"I'm going to put these in water and bring them back to you," Josephine said as she ran off.

"I'm afraid I don't have a present for you, so I'm glad Josephine got you one."

"You gave me the best present you could have chosen. This book of poetry for Josephine."

"Should we wait until her birthday to show her these?"

"It's not for several months yet. I think we should do it when she gets back. Thank you for being so kind to Josephine."

"She is my sister. I will take care of her." He looked around to the garden where the blooms had been broken off the stalks of the Persian irises. He just hoped Fenton would forgive her. "And I will take care of you, my love." He pulled her into his arms and kissed her again.

"I don't think this is wise. Lady Evelyn or one of your sisters could be watching from a window."

"My aunt is probably napping and the twins are probably in the midst of an argument about Sara's wedding to Lambert."

She laughed. "I love you, Griffin. More and more each day."

"And I love you," he whispered and kissed his wife again.

Don't forget to smile.

✦

✦✦✦✦

Dear Reader,

I hope you have enjoyed the first book in *The Rakes of St. James* trilogy. It was my pleasure to dream up Griffin and Esmeralda's story. I know and appreciate that most Regency authors follow as true to the traditions and history of the time period as possible in their books. Others of us will sometimes bend or reshape what we know to be the truth and the way things really were for the sake of our stories. Such is the case in my trilogy *The Rakes of St. James*.

There is no recorded time during the Regency where there were three young and handsome dukes all eligible for marriage in the same year. But, as I do with all my books when I begin formulating a story, I enjoy starting with the premise *Wouldn't it be wonderful if*... Indeed, wouldn't it have been wonderful if there had been three such handsome and dashing dukes for a bevy of beautiful young ladies to choose from as I have in this book?

Please watch for the next two books in *The Rakes of St. James* trilogy.

I love to hear from readers. Please email me at ameliagrey@comcast.net or follow me on Facebook at AmeliaGreybooks/Facebook.com or on my website at ameliagrey.com.

Happy reading,
Amelia Grey

Coming soon. . .

Look for the next novel in the Rakes of St. James series
from *New York Times* bestselling author

AMELIA GREY

To the Duke, with Love

Available in December 2017 from St. Martin's Paperbacks